v1104	**DATE DUE**		OCT 0 2
9-12-a			
GAYLORD			PRINTED IN U.S.A.

Blue Diary

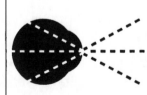
This Large Print Book carries the
Seal of Approval of N.A.V.H.

Alice Hoffman

Blue Diary

Waterville, Maine

JACKSON COUNTY LIBRARY SERVICES
MEDFORD OREGON 97501

Published in Large Print by arrangement with G. P. Putnam's Sons, a member of Penguin Putnam Inc., in the United States and Canada.

The text of this Large Print edition is unabridged.
Other aspects of the book may vary from the original edition.

Set in 16 pt. Plantin.

Printed in the United States on permanent paper.

ISBN 1-56895-1965 (lg. print : sc : alk. paper)

*Heaven belongs to the Lord,
and the earth He has entrusted to mortals.*
PSALM 115

Acknowledgments

With gratitude to my literary angels: Phyllis Grann, Stacy Creamer, Elaine Markson, and Ron Bernstein. Many thanks to Tom Martin, always my first reader, and to the other early readers of this book: Libby Hodges, Bob and Carol DeKnight, Maggie Stern Terris, Pamela Painter, and Sue Standing. Thank you to everyone at Putnam and Berkley Books, especially Dan Harvey, Leslie Gelbman, Susan Allison, Mih-Ho Cha, and Marilyn Ducksworth. Thanks also to Jill McCorkle and Perri Klass for the writing time we spent together. Gratitude always to two who have recently departed: Albert J. Guerard, my great and generous teacher, and Jerome J. Hoffman, who told me my first stories. To my other angels, Sherry Hoffman and Lillie Lulkin, my mother and grandmother: you are with me always.

One

The Hanged Man

IT'S THE LAST MONDAY of the month, a brutally gorgeous morning brimming with blue air and the sweet scent of honeysuckle which grows wild in the woods beyond Front Street, when Ethan Ford fails to show up for work. On this glorious day, the brilliant sky is filled with banks of motionless white clouds, fleecy as sheep, but so obedient and lazy they haven't any need of a shepherd or a fence. June in New England is a peerless month, with long days of glittering sunlight and roses unfolding. This is the season when even the most foolish of men will stop to appreciate all that is set out before him: the creamy blossoms of hollyhocks and English daisies; the heavenly swarms of bees humming like angels in the hedges, hovering over green lawns trimmed so carefully it can seem as though the hand of all that's divine has leaned down to construct a perfect patchwork, green upon green, perfection upon perfection.

On any other day, Ethan Ford would have already been hard at work, for in the town of

Monroe, Massachusetts, there is not a more reliable man to be found. On the chain that he carries, he has the keys to many of the local houses, including the Howards' on Sherwood Street and the Starks' over on Evergreen. For the better part of a month, Ethan has been remodeling both homes, renovating a kitchen for the Howards, installing a second bathroom for the Starks, a family whose three daughters are known for their waist-length hair, which takes half an hour to shampoo, so that there is always a line in the hall as one or another of the Stark girls awaits her turn at the shower.

Everyone knows that if Ethan promises a job will be done on time, it will be, for he's a man of his word, as dependable as he is kind, the sort of individual who never disappears with the last ten percent of a project left undone, tiles left ungrouted, for instance, or closet doors unhung. He's an excellent carpenter, an excellent man all around; a valued member of the volunteer fire department well known for his fearlessness, a respected coach who offers more encouragement to some local children than their own parents do. Most folks who know him would not have thought any less of him had they been aware that on this day Ethan doesn't show up for work because he's in bed with his wife, whom he loves desperately, even after thirteen years of marriage, and whom he still considers to be the most beautiful woman in the Commonwealth.

Jorie had been standing at the sink, washing

up the breakfast dishes and staring out the window with a dreamy expression, when Ethan came to get his keys. He took one look at her and decided not to leave, no matter what a mess his schedule might become and how late he'd have to work for the rest of the week. Even the most dependable of men will stumble every now and then, after all. He'll trip over his own shoes, waylaid by bumps in the road or circumstances he never expected; he'll throw off the bonds of both caution and common sense. Fortunately, Jorie and Ethan's son was on his way to school on this Monday of the last week of sixth grade, for there was nothing that could have kept Ethan away from Jorie on this day, not when he felt the way he did. He came up behind her at the sink, and as he'd circled his arms around her and whispered what he planned to do once he took her back to bed, Jorie laughed, the sort of sweet laughter that summoned the sparrows from the trees, so that one after another perched on the windowsill, just to listen, just to be near.

We shouldn't be doing this, Jorie told him. She began to list the reasons they had to abstain, the many responsibilities facing them on this busy weekday, but even as she spoke, her tone betrayed her. She was already being drawn into the bedroom, diverted by her own desire, and she smiled when her husband locked the door.

People in town would not have been surprised to know that Ethan bent to kiss his wife then, and that she in turn responded as deeply as

5

she had on the night when she met him, when she was twenty-three and convinced she would never fall in love, not really, not the way she was supposed to, head over heels, crazy and rash, all or nothing at all. It was that way for them both even now, though they had a house and a mortgage and a calendar inky with family obligations, those pot-luck dinners and Little League games, the intricacies of married life. Their union was a miracle of sorts: they had fallen in love and stayed there. Thirteen years after they'd met, it seemed as though only an hour or two had passed since Jorie had spied Ethan at the bar of the Safehouse one foggy November night, minutes after she and her best friend, Charlotte Kite, had set up a wager of ten dollars, the prize to be claimed by whoever found herself a sweetheart that night.

And now, on this hot June morning, when the sky is so brilliant and blue and the tree frogs in the gardens trill as though they were calling birds, Jorie wants Ethan just as badly as she had on the night she first saw him. She had left her friend Charlotte behind without even the decency of a proper good-bye, which simply wasn't like her. Jorie was as prudent as she was kindhearted, so much so that when her older sister, Anne, arrived at the Safehouse to see her goody-two-shoes sibling leaving with a stranger, she ran after the truck, signaling for them to slow down; not that they paid Anne the slightest bit of attention or listened to her cries to be careful on the icy roads.

Jorie gave Ethan directions to her apartment over on High Street, where she brought him into her bed before she knew his full name. Certainly, she had never in her life been as reckless. She was the girl who did everything right and, as Anne would readily complain to anyone willing to listen, had always been their mother's favorite daughter. Jorie was the last one anyone would expect to act on impulse, and yet she was driven by what might have appeared to be a fever. Perhaps this explained why she veered from her normal, reliable behavior and unlocked her door for a stranger on that cold November night. Ethan Ford was the handsomest man she had ever seen, but that wasn't the reason she'd fallen so hard. It was the way he stared at her, as if no one else in the world existed, it was how sure he was they were meant to be together that had won her over so completely and effortlessly. She still feels his desire when he looks at her, and every time she does, she's the same lovestruck girl she was when they met. She's no different than she'd been on the night when he first kissed her, when he vowed he'd always been searching for her.

Today, Jorie has once again left her poor friend Charlotte in the lurch, with no explanations or apologies. Instead of meeting Charlotte to discuss the final weeks of her marriage to Jay Smith, blessedly over at last, Jorie is kissing her own husband. Instead of offering comfort and advice, she is here with Ethan, pulling him closer until all the world outside, all of Maple Street, all of Massachusetts, might as well have disappeared, every street lamp and apple tree evaporating into the hot and tranquil air. Some people are fortunate, and Jorie has always been among them, with her luminous smile and all that yellow hair that reminds people of sunlight even on the coldest winter's day when the wind outside is howling and masses of snow are tumbling down from above.

Whenever Jorie and Ethan are hand in hand, people in town turn and stare, that's how good they look when they're together, that's how meant for each other they are. On evenings when Jorie comes to the baseball field at dusk, bringing thermoses of lemonade and cool water, Ethan always walks right up to her and kisses her, not caring if all the world looks on. Along the sidelines, people stop what they're doing—the mothers gossiping by the bleachers, the dads in the parking lot discussing what tactics might win them the county championship—they can't take their eyes off Jorie and Ethan, who, unlike most couples who have entered into the harsh and difficult realm of marriage, are still wrapped up in the vast reaches of their own devotion, even now.

It's therefore no surprise to find them in each other's arms on this June morning, in the season when the first orange lilies bloom along roadsides and lanes. They make love slowly, without bothering to pull down the shades. The sunlight coursing through the open window is lemony and sweet; it leaves a luminous grid on the white sheets and a crisscross of shadow upon their flesh. Next door, Betty Gage, who is nearly eighty and so deaf she can no longer make out the chattering of wrens nesting in her cherry tree or the chirrup of the tree frogs, can all the same hear their lovers' moans. She quickly retreats to her house, doing her best to walk briskly in spite of her bad knees, leaving behind the phlox and daisies she'd begun to gather in a ragged jumble of petals on the lawn. Startled by the strains of so much ardor on an ordinary morning, Mrs. Gage turns her radio to top volume, but even that doesn't drown out those passionate cries, and before long Betty finds herself thinking of her own dear husband, gone for nearly forty years, but still a young man when she dreams of him.

Later, Jorie will wonder if she hadn't asked for sorrow on this heavenly day. She should have been more cautious. She'd been greedy, renouncing restraint, forsaking all others but the man she loved. Who did she think she was to assume that the morning was hers to keep, tender hours to spend however she pleased? She was thoughtless, indeed, but the bees swarming in the garden seemed to be serenading them, the sunlight was a pale and lasting gold. If only such fleeting moments could continue indefinitely. If only they were cunning enough to trap time and ensure that this day would never alter, and that forevermore there'd be only the constant sunlight pouring in and only the two of them, alone in the world.

Jorie is not ordinarily prideful, but how can she help but see herself in her husband's eyes? She imagines ancient prehistoric flowers as he moves his hand along her belly, her spine, her shoulders. The flowers appear behind her eyelids, one by one: red lily, wood lily, tawny lily, trout lily, each incomparable in its beauty. She listens to the bees drifting through the hedges outside. If any of the men in town who thought they knew her, the ones she's been acquainted with since high school, for instance, those she runs into every day at the bakery or the pharmacy or the bank, were able to look through the window and spy upon her, they would have seen a different woman than the one they chat with on street corners or sit next to on the bleachers at Little League games. They would have seen Jorie with the sunlight streaming over her and heat rising up from her skin. They would have witnessed what true love can do to a woman.

You are everything to me, Ethan tells her on this morning, and maybe that sentiment was too arrogant and self-absorbed. Assuredly, they were only thinking of themselves, not of their son on his way to school, or the shades they hadn't bothered to close, or the neighbor at her window, listening to the sounds of their desire. They weren't the least bit concerned about the friends they'd kept waiting, Charlotte Kite, who'd already left the bakery for her doctor's appointment, or Mark Derry, the plumber, one of Ethan's closest friends, stranded outside the Starks' house without a key, unable to work without Ethan present to let him in. The phone rings, long and loud, but Ethan tells Jorie not to answer—it's only Charlotte, and Jorie can talk to her anytime. Or it's her sister, Anne, whom Jorie is more than happy to avoid.

How often do we get to do this? Ethan asks. He kisses Jorie's throat and her shoulders, and she doesn't say no, even though it's close to ten o'clock. How can she deny him, or herself for that matter? Love like this isn't easy to find, after all, and sometimes Jorie wonders why she was the one who'd been lucky enough to meet him that night. November in Massachusetts is a despicable and ruinous month, and Charlotte had needed to talk Jorie into going out for a drink. *You have your whole life to sit around by yourself, if that's what you want to do,* Charlotte had assured her, and so Jorie had grudgingly gone along. She hadn't even bothered to comb her hair or put on lipstick. She'd been there at the bar, already itching to leave, when she felt a wave of energy, the way some people say the air turns crackly before the weather takes a turn, or when a star is about to fall from the sky. She gazed to her left and she happened to see him, and that was when she knew it was destiny that had made her trail along after Charlotte on that damp, foggy night. Fate had led her here.

She closes her eyes on this, their stolen

morning, and as she lets the phone ring unanswered, she thinks again of lilies, shimmering on their green stems. She thinks about the pledges they've made to each other, and about devotion. What she feels for him is so deep, she aches. She supposes this is what people refer to when they say the pangs of love, as if your innermost joy cannot help but cause you anguish as well. It is painful when he leaves her merely to go into the kitchen, where he fixes them iced coffees and bowls of strawberries from the garden. He loads their breakfast onto a silver tray, a wedding present from Charlotte, and brings it back to bed for them to enjoy. Jorie still has never seen a man as handsome as Ethan. He has dark hair and even darker eyes. He isn't a lawyer cooped up in an office like Barney Stark, whose wife complains that he's grown fat, or a beer drinker like Mark Derry, who spends most evenings sprawled out in an easy chair. Ethan uses his body, and the results are evident. When he takes off his shirt at the baseball field, the women stare at him, then look at each other as if to say, *That's what I wanted, but that's not what I got.*

All the same, Ethan is the sort of man who doesn't seem to be aware of his own good looks. His visits to the gym aren't driven by vanity, but are a necessity for the work he does as a member of the Monroe Volunteer Fire Department. He needs strength and stamina, both readily apparent last fall when he climbed onto the roof of the McConnells' house, long before many of his fellow volunteers had gotten out of their trucks. That particular fire had started in a pan of bacon, but by the time the first volunteers arrived, it was burning through the house, one of those sly, scarlet infernos that moves with unexpected speed. There was so much smoke that day, the white chrysanthemums outside Hannah's Coffee Shoppe turned gray and remained that way for the rest of the season; frogs in the shallows of the lake began to dig themselves into the mud, ready to hibernate, misreading the ashes falling from above for an early dusting of snow.

When it became clear that the regulation ladder wouldn't reach the McConnells' little girl's window, Ethan had taken matters into his own hands. From his perch on the roof, he went on; he pulled himself across the shingles and over the peak, then went in through the window. Outside, the crowd watched as though bewitched. Not a word was said after Ethan disappeared through the window, especially not after the flames rose up, a burst of heat circling into the clotted gray sky. Ethan found the child hiding in her closet, and it was a lucky thing he'd been so nimble scaling the roof, for the girl hadn't more than a few minutes left before she would have begun to suffocate. By the time Ethan carried her out of the house, half the town was gathered on the lawn below, holding their breaths, inhaling smoke, blinking the soot from their eyes.

It's no wonder that people in Monroe adore

Ethan Ford. Why, even Jorie's sister, Anne, who on most occasions cannot find a nice word to say about anyone, is surprisingly well behaved in his presence. There's rarely a time when Ethan walks down Front Street and some child he once coached doesn't lean out a car window in order to shout his name and wave. The parents are just as pleased to see him; they honk their horns and switch their headlights on and off in a show of appreciation. Warren Peck, the bartender at the Safehouse and a courageous volunteer fireman himself, refuses to let Ethan pay for his own drinks, and why shouldn't he be grateful? Ethan was the first on the scene when Warren's nephew Kyle's Chrysler LeBaron caught on fire in the parking lot of Lantern Lake, with sweet-tempered Kyle sleeping it off in the front seat, sure to have been burned alive if not for Ethan's intervention. The senior center, where Ethan serves Thanksgiving dinner each year before coming home to celebrate the holiday with his family, still has a banner up in the rec room: *Three Cheers for Ethan.* Ethan himself would have already torn down that banner if the very idea didn't chill some of the seniors to their bones, for the residents of the center sleep better with the knowledge that Ethan is watching over them.

He is truly an extraordinary person in many ways, even in the eyes of his wife. Jorie Ford gazes at her husband the way another woman might appraise the sunrise, with equal amounts of familiarity and awe. She had wished their son would resemble Ethan, but Collie Ford is pale and fine-featured, like his mother, with blond hair and blue eyes and a sweet, cautious nature. Collie is cool where his father is hot, easygoing and, at twelve, tall for his age. Still, he's shy in spite of his parents' love and support; he's prone to let other boys edge right past him, at school and on the playing field, even though he has more brains and talent; it makes no difference that he's bigger and stronger, he's content to remain on the sidelines. He's an A student happy with Bs, an outfielder who should be pitching, too good-natured, it sometimes seems, for the deceptions and the difficulties of those who excel in the world.

You know what his problem is? Ethan says as they lie in bed on this morning with the window shades drawn up and the bees in the garden drifting over blooming roses and phlox. Jorie is eating a strawberry and it has turned her mouth red. *You baby him.*

Oh, please. Jorie laughs. *You're just jealous. You want me to baby you.*

That's true. Ethan slides his hand between her legs and she feels those pangs begin. *Baby me,* he tells her, so near that every word burns. *Give me what I want.*

Jorie thinks of lily of the valley, hyacinths, star-of-Bethlehem. She thinks of the night they had made Collie, a starry August evening at Charlotte's family's vacation house at Squam Lake. Jorie is sure her son was conceived there because a big white moon rose into the sky, a lantern in all that darkness, and she had cried when they made love. Afterward, she had stood out on the porch while Ethan slept and as she searched out the first summer star, she'd made a wish that things would never change between them.

I have to get going, Jorie says now, pushing him away. She feels absolutely derelict to still be in bed at this hour. *I'm so late, Charlotte will kill me.*

Jorie rises and stands squarely in the sunlight, her long hair turning from gold to platinum. She has never lived anywhere but Monroe, nor would she want to, even though this is a town in which there are more apple trees than there are houses. She had once believed she could predict exactly how her life would turn out, but then she met Ethan. There were several local boys who'd been after her, and she'd imagined that someday she'd give in and marry one of them. She still feels sheepish when she runs into Rick Moore, who she dated all through college. But bygones are bygones, and Rick himself is married now, with two boys of his own, and he teaches over at the middle school, science and health. Why, Collie will probably be in his class next year. There are no hard feelings, and when they meet accidentally, on Front Street or at the annual Little League barbecue at the end of the season, Rick and Jorie are always polite; they hug each other and pretend that neither one remembers the way Rick cried when Jorie broke up with him.

16

Time has drifted by lazily, and Jorie is amazed to see just how late it is. There won't be much headway on the Starks' construction today; no plumbing will be installed and no measurements for the new tub will be taken. By now Mark Derry has grown tired of waiting and has decided to leave a note for Ethan on the back door. *Hey, asshole—where the hell were you?* is the message Sophie Stark, aged twelve, will find tacked up when she gets home from school.

In point of fact, Ethan is getting dressed at the very moment Mark Derry is pounding his missive into place, using a nail he'd found in the dirt, used to add iron to the soil and encourage the hydrangeas to turn a deep indigo. Ethan Ford has never been one to rush, not even when he's late. He takes his time and knows what he wants. He believes it's his duty to live his life in the right way, and he never grouses when emergency calls come in on cold, icy nights. If he's old-fashioned, so be it. He figures he owes something to his neighbors. He has never once turned down a friend when asked for a loan; Mark Derry and Warren Peck both know from personal experience that when Ethan writes a check he doesn't even ask what the advance is for. Trying to thank him for all the good he's done is another matter entirely. He flatly refused a public ceremony after he'd rescued the McConnell girl, which would have greatly pleased the mayor, Ed Hill, who's always looking for a chance to promote his own favorite cause: a

17

third term in office. Ethan is known for the sort of conviction only a man who's been blessed can possess. What can he want, when there's nothing he's lacking? Why should he rush through this life, when he's lucky enough to have everything he needs? He runs one hand through his dark hair now as he gets ready, without bothering to look in the mirror. He knows who he is, after all. Lucky as a man can be, that's Ethan. Lucky, through and through.

Outside the window, the last milky petals from Mrs. Gage's cherry tree are aloft in the air, weaving through the blue light, settling on rooftops and lawns. Jorie has gone into the kitchen to fill a thermos with lemonade to ensure that Ethan will have a cool drink to enjoy later in the day, when the sun is high and the heat is all but unbearable as he carts old cabinets out of the Howards' kitchen. Jorie smiles at what is already becoming a memory of how impulsive they've been today. She is the sort of woman who doesn't need to tell her most private business, not even to her best friend. She has never been tempted to admit to Charlotte that she always thinks of lilies when she and Ethan are in bed. Sometimes, at the height of their passion, she opens her eyes and is amazed to find white sheets and walls rather than the vivid fields she's imagined, brilliant with orange and yellow, as if sunlight itself had been caught behind her eyes.

Someone once told Jorie that plants you least expected were members of the lily family, asparagus, for instance, and onions, both of which she plans to add to her garden, a large patch of earth in the backyard. Jorie doesn't like to boast, but her garden is perhaps the best in town, yielding bushels of beans every year, and fire-red tomatoes, and such generous amounts of blueberries that Jorie often grants her neighbors free rein to pick as much as they'd like for jams and jellies and pies.

Jorie is thinking about her garden, how pretty asparagus plants will be against the fence, how faithful onions are once they take hold, when she hears someone at the front door. Right away she thinks something's odd. It must be a stranger come to call, because everyone knows the Fords always use the kitchen door, which opens to the driveway and the garden. The postman, Bill Shannon, brings their mail around the back, and even Kat Willams, Collie's friend from down the block, knows not to use the front entrance.

I'll get it, baby, Ethan says. He's come into the kitchen, to grab his key ring, stopping only to reach into the cookie jar for some petty cash he'll use to buy lunch at Hannah's later in the day. He looks happy as he heads for the hall. Jorie hears him open the door, and then she hears nothing. The silence is unnatural. It's as if Jorie has been thrown headfirst into the cold embrace of the sea and water fills her ears. Rattled, she drops the coffee cup she was about to refill, but she doesn't hear it break on the hardwood floor. She just leaves it there, in pieces, and hurries down the hall. She's moving through water, drowning in green waves. There are some people who insist that every time one door closes, another door opens, but this isn't always the case. There are doors that are meant to stay closed, ones that lead to rooms filled with serpents, rooms of regret, rooms that will blind you if you dare to raise your eye to the keyhole in all innocence, simply to see what's inside.

Jorie takes note of the way he's standing at their own door, her husband, Ethan, whom she loves more than anything in this world. He's so rigid, anyone would think he's been shot. She glimpses the other men who have gathered on the porch, and as she recognizes them, local men one and all, she wants time to stop, then and there. She is reminded of another summer's day, when she wasn't more than eight years old; it was a hazy afternoon, and she'd climbed one of the apple trees in the orchard that was then behind her mother's house, acres of Baldwins and McIntoshes and delectable Empires, known for their delicate pink blossoms. She looked up at the sky, mesmerized by the thick, lazy white clouds, and for a minute she truly believed she could reach up and take all that she saw into her arms. She had wanted heaven for herself; she was greedy and hopeful in equal measure, convinced she could have anything her heart desired, if only she'd grab for it.

When she fell, she was reaching out for those clouds, but there was nothing between herself and the earth save the pale and heedless air. She broke her leg in two places, and she still remembers the pure shock of falling to earth, the foul taste of her own blood in her mouth as she bit through her lip. It was the season when the orange lilies appear in Monroe, wildly, randomly, in every ditch and thoroughfare, as it is again now. All these years later, Jorie still always tastes blood when the daylilies bloom, and here in the doorway to her own living room, on this fair and glorious day, she knows why she's never chosen to grow any of those lilies beside her own door, no matter how beautiful they might be. They only last for a single day, and then, no matter what a person might do to save them, they are fated, by God, or circumstance, or nature, to fade away.

True

THE FIRST THING I noticed was that he could walk past a mirror without casting a reflection. My grandmother always told me that a mirror can shine back a person's dishonesty, but what did it mean for a man to have no reflection at all? Something bad, I knew that for certain. Something people should stay away from. I carried my knowledge around inside me until it started to hurt, like a splinter in my finger, throbbing and too tiny to see. Every time I went into their house, I avoided the living room, where there was a big mirror framed in gold. That was where I'd seen him turn to look at himself. He didn't seem surprised to find that nothing was there, only empty glass the color of dishwater. He didn't even flinch.

I told Collie that the living room was too fancy for my tastes, with their nice furniture, and that anything too nice made me nervous because I was bound to break something. Collie believed me because he knows I'm clumsy; he didn't guess I had my fingers crossed behind my back. I told my best friend— my only friend—a lie right to his face, and that was just the start of my deception. I like nice things, as a matter of fact. The fancier the better, that's the way I see it. I want to grow up to be rich, so no one will think they're better than me, the way everyone at school does. All the same, I had the strangest feeling every time I went in that house, although we stayed clear of the living room where the mirror was, and Collie's mother was always so nice to me, going out of her way to tell me things that are obviously false, like how I would be beautiful someday, when anyone can tell that will never happen. Not if I wait for a hundred years.

Of course, I made certain not to be there when Collie's father was around. I could tell when he was about to arrive the way some people say they can sense when it's likely to rain. I was like a dog who knew when his master was getting close to home, only in reverse. Instead of sitting by the door panting, I did the opposite and got out of there fast. Usually, I went out the side door and headed across Mrs. Gage's yard, which separates my house from Collie's, darting past the cherry tree and the willows. Sometimes, when the sky was dark or when the wind was howling, I ran. If Collie tried to stop me, if he said, *Come on, Kat, stay,* I told him I had a migraine. No one can deny a headache. I know that for a fact because my sister, Rosarie, who just turned seventeen, has migraines and you can't talk to her when she gets them. She lies on her bed with a cold cloth over her forehead and the lights turned out, and we have to tiptoe around her like she's the Queen of Sheba. My mother brings her orange juice and Excedrin tablets, and when it's really bad some sort of medicine my sister shoots into her arm that makes her go limp, like a rag doll, and then she sleeps for ten hours straight, which, if you really want to know the truth, is a big relief for us all.

Lying on her bed, with the lights out and her dark hair tangled on her pillow, my sister actually does look like a queen. I'm always jealous when I stand there watching, though I know she's my sister and I'm supposed to want the best for her. I wish I felt that way, but I don't. At such times, I am tempted to pour vinegar over her clothes or sprinkle her with sugar water, so when she awakes there will be ants entwined in the strands of her hair and she'll smell bitter. It's a terrible thing to feel this way. My jealousy is bound to clog my veins and turn me even uglier than I already am, which is what my grandmother says is the unhappy but well-deserved fate of envious people. When this happens you can see it in someone's face if you look closely, a faint and poisonous green rising up through the skin. *That's envy,* my grandmother tells me. *Make no mistake about it. That's their price to pay.*

I am named Katya, after my grandmother, but they have always called me Kat, and I've always been curious, probably too much so for my own good. Rosarie says I shouldn't ask so many questions. She tells me a girl who can't mind her own business will wind up with nothing but enemies, but I don't care. My sister is five years older than I am, and in that time she has learned everything she needs to know to get whatever she wants. The meaner she is, the more beautiful she becomes. It's not fair, but it's true. She shimmers when she stamps her feet and insists on having her way. She glows when she pulls my hair or calls out a stream of curses.

When I lie on the floor and watch her get ready to go out on Friday nights, I have to admit I'm impressed by her beauty. I find myself doing whatever she tells me—I run to get her mascara, I lend her my hair clips, I search the kitchen for spring water so she won't have to wash her face with ordinary tap water like the rest of us. I'm her slave and I don't even like her. I can only guess what it's like for some unsuspecting individual to see her for the first time; it's perfectly understandable how fast somebody like that could fall under her spell, how easily they might be taken in by what is only skin deep.

Rosarie pretends to be good when it suits her. She comes home at midnight, the time of her curfew, kisses our mother and grandmother good night and goes upstairs, as if she were the last person on earth to consider breaking the rules. But as soon as everyone's asleep, she climbs back out her window, like a blackbird, finally free of us, flying down Maple Street, with her long hair trailing behind her. She goes off with her boyfriends, taking as much delight in breaking their hearts as she does in winning them. Everyone knows she swims in Lantern Lake with no clothes on and steals flowers from Mrs. Gage's perennial beds and lipsticks from the pharmacy. She torments the other girls in town by not caring what they think of her. When it comes right down to it, the only opinion that matters to her is her own.

In the morning, when Rosarie finally gets out of bed, she combs her hair. She yawns and doesn't notice what falls out from among the strands: fireflies, petals, white moths, heartache. When some new boy follows Rosarie home, our grandmother never lets him past the front door. She shakes her mop at the lovelorn boys in our yard and tells them they're too young to be pining after someone, especially if that someone is our selfish Rosarie. As far as my grandmother is concerned, those boys are nothing but moths caught up in a spider's web, but I have compassion for them. I bring them Cokes with ice and listen to their sad stories; I offer them consolation, along with cookies and chips. Someday they'll think fondly of me, the ugly little sister who sat beside them on the grass, or maybe they won't remember me; they'll only recall the sweet sodas they drank as they looked into Rosarie's window, hoping for a glimpse of her beautiful face.

You would think that what has happened in our family would show up in my sister in some way, that her complexion would turn yellow, or her dark eyes would be dulled, or her red mouth would fade to an ugly white pucker, but none of that has happened. Unfortunately, the same is not true for me. You can see everything in my face, which is why people tend to stay away from me. The ones who are frightened by what they see call me names behind my back, and I don't blame them. Even the biggest fool could take one look at my miserable complexion and sorrowful features and know well enough to avoid me. Even someone like that could see bad luck written all over my face.

Some people might guess I took a dislike to Collie's father to get back at my own father for leaving us the way he did, and that I was looking for somebody to hurt, but that wasn't the case. My father made certain choices because he was sick. It was too bad that my sister was the one who found him. My grandmother and I were up in the attic, going through the belongings she'd brought when she came to stay with us. If it had been me who opened the garage door, everything else would have been easier. I would have known that he loved us, now and forever, but my sister didn't understand, and our mother's reaction was worse. She didn't speak for six weeks after our father died, not even when Rosarie burned his clothes on the back patio. Rosarie poured lighter fluid over everything and lit it up so high that the leaves of the mimosa trees caught on fire and Collie's father, who is a volunteer fireman, with one of those blue globes he sticks to the top of his car, which allows him to speed to the scene of a fire, jumped over Mrs. Gage's fence and came running to ensure that our house wasn't burning to the ground.

This year the leaves of the mimosas have come back blackened, black feathers hanging from the branches, falling on the slate and on our bare feet as if there were a flock of blackbirds living above us. Collie and I sit on the patio to study the mimosas almost every evening. We don't have to speak about the way my father died; we don't have to talk at all. Silence doesn't frighten us. We can just look at each other and recognize that there is pain in this world, even on beautiful nights when twilight settles in our backyards, sifting through the grass and the hedges. We take a blanket out there and look up through the black mimosas; we call out the names of the constellations we know until we're too tired and dizzy to look up anymore.

I probably would have been on the patio gazing at stars that night if Collie hadn't come down with a fever. But he was home in bed, and it was no fun being alone in the dark. As a matter of fact, it was kind of scary, with those sour black leaves and so many stars you could never hope to count them all, not if you tried for a thousand years. My sister had a new boyfriend, Brendan Derry, who seemed to think that Rosarie belonged to him, and he wanted her to spend every second of her free time with him. Poor Brendan didn't have a clue that he'd be gone before long, another speck in my sister's romantic history. Still, Rosarie liked a good time, even when she was breaking somebody's heart, and I knew she wouldn't be back for hours. I felt free to go into her room and turn on the TV she'd gotten as a Christmas present from one of her boyfriends the day before she dumped him. None of us remembered his name anymore, but the TV worked great.

I threw myself down on her unmade bed without bothering to take off my shoes. Rosarie was the lazy sister, she was the rude sister, but she was the sister who had everything, and I was the one watching TV all alone. I had brought a bowl of popcorn with me to her room, even though I knew Rosarie would kill me if she found a single kernel in her bed. Frankly, I didn't care if popcorn accumulated on the sheets. I could be mean, too, after all. I could be selfish and thoughtless when I tried, or at least that's what people around here said. Maybe that's because everybody was crying at my father's funeral except for me. When you do things like that, when you stand there and shut your mind until all you can hear is the humming of bees, people think you don't have any feelings. They think what they see is what you feel deep inside.

As I sprawled out on the bed with nothing to do but eat popcorn and envy my sister, my mother came in to say good night. She was still pretty, and she wasn't old, but she wasn't the same as she used to be. She hardly ever talked anymore. Just the bare essentials. Just *Pass the green beans* and *You have a dentist appointment* and *Don't forget to shut the front door when you leave.*

Sometimes I'd catch my mother staring across the yards, watching Collie's parents as they worked out in the garden, laughing and having so much fun. I knew what she was thinking. She'd been shortchanged, with my father and all. She was forty-six years old and living with her mother and her two thankless daughters, and how had that happened? Once she'd figured that out, she'd probably start talking, but for now, she was keeping it simple. She sat on the edge of Rosarie's bed and ran her hand through my hair, even though her fingers caught on the snarls at the base of my neck. Those knots hurt, but it had been so long since anyone had touched me, I didn't complain. I have terrible hair that sticks up where it shouldn't and makes me even uglier than I already am. When I see Rosarie's beautiful long dark hair, I want to pull it out, and every time I feel that jealousy, I know my true self. In spite of everything Rosarie's done and how selfish she is, I'm far worse than she'll ever be.

After my mother went to bed, I stayed in Rosarie's room, eating popcorn and making a mess. I could feel myself curdling; I was a sour pudding, a recipe made of envy and spite, green at the edges. When I feel that kind of badness inside me, I am capable of anything. I really am. I opened the window even though it was raining. I did it on purpose, just to see something of my sister's be ruined. I let raindrops splatter all over Rosarie's pillow, and her white quilt, and her night table where she keeps her jewelry box, the one my father gave her for her sixteenth birthday, a gift she now says is nothing but a piece of junk.

I had the TV on, but I was busy sorting through my sister's jewelry, the tangled gold necklaces various lovestruck boys had given her, the earrings missing crystals and beads, the silver rings she wore on all of her fingers. When his picture came on, I wasn't really listening. I just looked up and there he was, as if the image that should have been cast in the mirror had somehow arisen on my sister's TV screen. I reached over and turned up the sound. It was one of those real-life crime shows, and although I had missed most of what they'd said about him, I did hear his name. It wasn't Ethan Ford, that was the strangest part, it was something entirely different, but that was definitely his face, the one with no reflection, so I wrote down the number to call.

I sat on Rosarie's bed for a while, and after a time I went out her window. By then it had stopped raining, and the streets were wet and shining, as if stars had been mixed in with the asphalt. My father did what he did because he didn't want to drag us through any more pain, but it seems I'm the only one who understands that he acted out of love, except for our family doctor, Dr. Abbot, who said that courage took place in all sorts of ways you could never even imagine. We were standing in the driveway after my father's funeral when Dr. Abbot said that, but I don't think anyone else heard him. They were heartsick, stuck in their own disbelief, but not me. I always expected the worst. I was born to be that way, and when it came to Collie's father, I have to say I wasn't as surprised as somebody else might have been to discover that Ethan Ford wasn't everything he pretended to be.

I went down to Hannah's Coffee Shoppe on the corner of Front Street and Lincoln Avenue. I could see Rosarie in there, having a grand old time with her friends. Brendan Derry was all over her; he looked so proud and pleased with himself, but that wouldn't last. By next week he'd start to appear chalky, he'd cry himself to sleep and wonder what on earth he'd done wrong. I thought about talking the situation over with Rosarie, confiding what I'd seen on TV, but she always made me feel stupid, so after a while I just decided by myself. I went to the pay phone in the parking lot and made the call. When I got home, my

31

grandmother was waiting for me. She was sitting in the kitchen with the black candles she'd found in my room and the rest of the supplies I'd sent away for, and she wasn't happy.

"What is this supposed to be?" she asked me, but she knew. The manufacturer's advertisement swore that if used properly these items would dissolve the curtain that separated this world from the next, but I wasn't so sure. I had been trying to contact my father for nearly a year, and so far I'd had no results.

"Nothing," I said, which was pretty much the truth.

"You can't change what's meant to be," my grandmother told me.

My grandmother was usually right about such matters. I sat down and had a cup of tea with her and thought about her advice. My hands had been shaking ever since I'd gotten back from the phone booth outside the coffee shop, but my grandmother didn't seem to notice. I feared I might just have changed what was meant to be with the phone call I'd made, or maybe my seeing Collie's father's photograph on TV and calling in was a part of what was meant to be in the first place, and now I'd never know which one it was. Not for sure. I'd simply have to live with the doubt hanging over me.

"You, for instance," my grandmother went on, "were meant to be beautiful."

I laughed. "I don't think so."

I had found if you didn't expect much, you weren't disappointed as much. That's probably why I liked Collie; he was the opposite of me. He saw the best in everybody. When I tried to get him to hate someone at school, he'd shake his head and laugh, and there wasn't anything I could do to get him riled up and vicious the way I was sometimes.

"If you know something bad about someone, do you have an obligation to turn them in?" I asked my grandmother when she came to sit down at the table with me.

"Sometimes." That was the kind of answer my grandmother always gave, the kind that gave you room to move around in but didn't quite offer you any peace of mind, so that the answer wound up being more work than the question had ever been in the first place. She knew there were things that could never be explained, and that people had obligations in this world. When my father got sick, she moved here from Hartford, Connecticut, and she must have left her cat behind, the one she loved so much, because Rosarie is allergic to dander. She left almost everything to take care of us, and I had to wonder how many people would be willing to do that.

I guess if I had one good quality it would be my loyalty. I take after my grandmother that way. I had never turned my sister in no matter what she did wrong. I had found plenty of evidence in her room when I was snooping around and trying on her clothes. I'd discovered marijuana and condoms. I'd examined her birth control pills and the packets of love letters that were filled with details I didn't understand, but I never did tell a soul. On this night I stopped off in Rosarie's room to think things over; the truth was, I went there because my room was too childish for the sort of things I had to think about. I guess I was mad at my sister or wanted to get back at her in some way for sitting in Hannah's, sharing a plate of French fries with a boy who was in love with her and having fun when I had to make a decision that could ruin people's lives. I must have been angry, because before I left her room to go to bed, I locked her window so she couldn't sneak back in.

When she came home later, Rosarie had to climb in through the bathroom window, and in the process, she slipped in the shower and broke a bottle of her favorite bath oils. She came marching into my room, smelling like vanilla and steaming mad. She pulled my hair and called me a traitor but I didn't care. As far as I was concerned, she could pull most of my hair right out of my head and I wouldn't be the worse for wear. I'd probably look better bald than I did ordinarily.

"You're going to pay for what you did," Rosarie told me, and I was afraid she was right.

That next week I had a terrible feeling in my stomach. I wouldn't go over to Collie's. I kept telling him I had headaches, the way my sister did, and I kept a cold compress on my forehead whenever he came over to watch TV. Instead of paying attention to any of the programs we tuned in to, I was mostly keeping an eye on him, thinking about how good he was and how he'd never hurt anyone and how he always expected the best from everyone. After a while, seeing his father's picture on TV felt like a dream, and climbing out my sister's window to call in and report him seemed as though it had happened to someone else entirely. I was starting to forget the whole thing. It's amazing what you can block out when you really try. Although some things stay with you no matter what; they affect everything that you do. My mother, for instance, no longer parked her car in the garage. She wouldn't even open the door. Squirrels could be nesting there, the roof could be falling in, and she still wouldn't go near. Some things you carry around inside you as though they were part of your blood and bones, and when that happens, there's nothing you can do to forget.

One day we got off the school bus on the corner of Maple and Sherwood Streets and I knew something terrible had happened, only this time to Collie. It was a hot day, and Collie and I had done our homework on the bus so we'd be free. It was the last week of school, and the day was as hot as August, with the sky a shimmering blue and the leaves turning dusty the way they did in the heat and so many birds singing you could hardly hear yourself think over their calling. I knew something was wrong because the Fords' front door was open, and they never went into the house that way. Someone had left so quickly, he hadn't even bothered to close the screen.

When we went inside, it felt like one of those houses you see in films of disasters, how everything is always left exactly as it was at the moment when catastrophe struck. There was a bowl of strawberries on the counter, leaking red juice onto the wood, and a coffee cup left in pieces on the floor. Above the sink, the clock was ticking, too slowly, it seemed, for the time to be right. Through the window, I could see Mrs. Gage's cherry tree, sprinkled with the last of its snowy white flowers. Collie went through the house, room after room, calling for his mother, but anyone could tell that no one was home.

"This is weird," Collie said when he came back to the kitchen. His face was so good it made you want to cry. "She always leaves a note when she goes somewhere."

Someone else might have called Collie a momma's boy, but I didn't make judgments like that. How could I when I had been such a daddy's girl? I would have been nobody's favorite if not for my father, who cared about people's true selves, not what they looked like or how mean they might appear to be.

"Well, she must have been in a hurry." My heart was beating like crazy. I figured this was the way a criminal's heart must start pounding whenever he told a lie or acted like he hadn't been responsible for something he knew damn well he'd done.

I suggested we go to my house, where my grandmother probably had her soap opera tuned in. Whenever we watched it with her, my grandmother would tell us what was going on in the story, which she'd been tuning in to for more than twenty-five years, and her narration was always much more interesting than what was actually happening. We had fun trying to figure things out before the truth was revealed—who would run away together, who'd come down with amnesia, who would find true and undying love—but that day I felt sick just looking at the TV. I wished I hadn't been watching that night when Ethan Ford's picture came on. I wished I lived in another town, someplace where nobody knew me and I didn't have any obligations to do the right thing.

Collie's mother didn't come for him until it was very nearly dark. She knocked on the door too hard, the way people do when they're in a hurry, or frightened, or when their world has just fallen apart. When my grandmother went to let her in, she took one look at Collie's mother and said, "Jorie, what happened?"

Jorie Ford stood in our doorway and you could see how wrong something was from the expression on her face. Her hair was knotted and her clothes were wrinkled, and when my grandmother gave her a little hug, Mrs. Ford started crying right there, half in and half out of our house. It happened fast, and then she pulled herself together just as fast. She was still upset, but she wouldn't let any tears fall. Not in front of us. Not with Collie there.

"What is it?" my grandmother asked.

Collie and I were sitting on the floor in the front room, sharing a bag of potato chips my grandmother had told us would ruin our dinners. Right before his mother knocked on the door, Collie had turned to tell me something; his face was animated and it seemed as if he was going to say something funny, he always had dozens of jokes, but he never did speak. When he saw that his mother had arrived, Collie got up and went to her. As soon as she put her arms around him, Jorie Ford started crying again. You could tell she didn't want to, she was trying with all her might to hold it back, but sometimes it's impossible to do that. I know that from personal experience. You have to turn yourself cold as ice in order to stop yourself, and then if anything falls from your eyes it will only be blue ice crystals, hard and unbreakable as stone.

I could tell from the way my grandmother was watching Collie and his mother that she was thinking about how quickly things could turn from good to bad. I would bet she was reminding herself of how precious every peaceful moment was, which is what she told me after my father died. She said that we had to savor whatever time we had in this world and believe in the ultimate goodness of the universe, but I had never been much of a believer. If anything, I believed that things got worse before they got better. I believed good people suffered. I believed I had lost my father, and I didn't really care much about the goodness of the universe without him in it. I never said any of this to my grandmother. I would never do that. People who have faith were so lucky, you didn't want to ruin anything for them. You didn't want to plant doubt where there was none. You had to treat such individuals tenderly and hope that some of whatever they were feeling rubs off on you.

My grandmother asked if there was anything she might do to help. Considering the fact that Jorie had brought dinner over for us for two weeks straight last summer, there had to be something we could do to return the favor, for this was clearly her time of need. But Jorie shook her head; there was nothing. The sky was turning murky by then, a marine blue dipping into darkness around the edges. You could smell cut grass and heat even now. Tomorrow, the town pool would be opening, and Collie and I had plans to get there early, but I could tell we wouldn't be going. There would be races and diving contests, the way there always were on opening day, but it wouldn't matter. Not to us.

"Don't listen to anything anyone tells you," Jorie told Collie. She sounded fierce when she spoke to him. "Do you hear me?"

"Yes, ma'am," Collie said.

Some other boy might have started asking questions, but Collie wasn't like that. He had a serious look on his face, and you could tell he'd do exactly as his mother said.

"Everything will be fine," Jorie assured him.

But from the way she was standing in the doorway in that deepening night, it was clear she wasn't sure of that herself; she was just trying to sound like she was.

"At least come in for dinner." My grandmother reached to draw Collie's mother inside our house, but Jorie took a step back. She didn't want to be touched and she didn't want anyone to be kind to her. She was filling herself up with ice, and when a person starts doing that any human contact can be dangerous.

"We just want to be alone." Jorie's voice was ragged and her mouth looked sour. She was usually so nice to everyone. She brought my grandmother vegetables from her garden, armfuls of lettuce and snap peas so fresh Rosarie and I argued over who would get the larger portion. As soon as these rude words were out of Jorie's mouth, you could tell she was sorry. She stepped forward and put her arms around my grandmother. "I didn't mean that. I'm not myself," she told us both, and we nodded as if we understood, then watched as she and Collie walked across Mrs. Gage's lawn to their own house, where all the lights were off and all the windows had been left open.

My grandmother and I went out to the porch and stood there in the dark. I could tell we both felt like crying, but for different reasons. One by one the lights turned on in Collie's house, but I already knew: his father wasn't there. They'd come to take him away while we were at school, and maybe that was for the best. Maybe it's better not to be at home when such things happened. Close your eyes and count to ten whenever sorrow strikes you, that's what my grandmother recommends, although in my opinion even ten thousand isn't a high enough number. But tonight, my grandmother didn't offer any advice. She only circled her arm around me, and she didn't even tell me not to be afraid of the dark the way she usually does. We could hear the leaves on the mimosa trees moving. We could hear the caterpillars that would turn into white moths before long. Soon enough it would be exactly one year since my father died. The night before it happened, he stood underneath this same sky and told me he would always love me, no matter what. He said that if somebody really loved you, you would always hear his voice somewhere inside your own head.

"That poor woman," my grandmother said of Jorie.

We couldn't see them anymore. Their door was closed, and it was just as if they'd never even been standing here with us and we'd been alone the whole time. It's like that when people leave you behind. You get to wondering if you ever had them in the first place. Still, it was a beautiful night, and my grandmother went out to the lawn that had been in bad shape since last summer, uncared for and littered with weeds. She picked a pod of milkweed and blew on it until the seeds lifted into the sky. She has always told me that you could blow your bad fortune away by doing so, and as I watched the milkweed drift upward into the sky, I wished I still believed in things like that. I wished I could fly our troubles away.

The Conjurer

CHARLOTTE KITE SMITH, STOOD up by her best friend and her soon-to-be-ex-husband on the very same day, is a smart woman, one who is well aware that there are some losses an individual simply has to accept. She believes that bad fortune is a wake-up call and that most people would do well to have their eyes open. Those who were dreamers often wound up as sleepwalkers and Charlotte is not about to become one of them. She's a practical woman who's learned not only to curb her resentments, but has managed to temper her hopes for the future as well. Today during her physical, for instance, she wasn't surprised when her doctor suggested a biopsy for the lump that she'd found. Nothing has worked out quite as she'd expected; why should her body be any different? She had thought at this stage she'd have half a dozen children, when in fact she's living in her house on Hilltop alone. Through the years she's learned not to assume that she's already had her portion of bad luck, even though she lost her parents when she was barely out of high school, one following the other in a matter of months, and has recently gone through a prolonged and complex breakup with Jay. In Charlotte's opinion, suffering is not the border on the outer edges of one's life, but the cloth itself, elegantly stitched on one side, crude and miserably sewn on the other.

But who can dwell on such disappointments? Certainly not Charlotte Kite. It's a beautiful evening, far too rare and fine for her to waste feeling sorry for herself. When she looks out the window of her house high on Hilltop, she can see the whole town before her, a grid of deep blue shadows and sparkling light, as though diamonds have been thrown down in the hillocks beyond the trees. Tonight, Charlotte runs a cool bath to wash away the scent of chocolate and rum that clings to her from the day's baking. She's used to spending her evenings alone, but perhaps her loneliness is the reason she continues to work at the bakery so faithfully, though it is now one in a chain of many and can handily be run by accountants and bakers who know the recipes and the business far better than Charlotte herself does. Still, she does not wish to pass her days alone as well as her nights. It's a big house she lives in, built at the turn of the century as a wedding present for Ella Monroe, whose father founded the town and left a ring of apple trees a mile wide around the old abandoned house where he once lived, smack at the end of King George's Road, a location that was wild frontier at the time, when it wasn't unusual for bears to eat their fill from the orchards and bobcats to claw at the bark of the saplings.

Charlotte's house is so large there are rooms she hasn't been in for months; the entire third floor, which might have been perfect for a nursery, has been closed down and even the cleaning service won't venture up there. Too many spiders, they complain. Not enough light.

So many of the girls Charlotte grew up with had been jealous when she'd married Jay Smith at the age of nineteen, the year after her parents died, but those girls are now grown women who consider themselves lucky that Jay passed them by. He seems to be a man who's constitutionally incapable of fidelity; in the interest of a peaceful parting, Charlotte has decided that in his case adultery should not be viewed as a lack of character, but rather as a hereditary defect, clearly evident in Jay's father, who, at the age of seventy-eight, is still chasing the ladies, marrying for the fourth time only weeks before he entered a nursing home.

Jay can't even be depended upon to come and pick up the last of his belongings, which was supposed to have been done this evening. Charlotte had hoped they might have one final dinner together to celebrate the end of their fruitless union. It's true, every now and then she wonders if his passion for her could ever be reignited, about as likely a possibility as a bear knocking at her front door and asking directions to Hamilton. When Jay doesn't show up, Charlotte takes her bath, and afterward phones in an order to the Pizza Barn. By now, she doesn't have to give her address. The counterman knows who she is; he even asks if she wants extra cheese, per her usual. When the delivery boy, Brendan Derry, arrives, Charlotte tips him twenty dollars. She does it not to spite Jay, who is notoriously cheap, but to see the grin on Brendan's face. How lovely that someone can feel joy over such a little thing. How wonderful to know there are still some people in this world who can manage to be happy.

Charlotte eats pizza out of the box on the floor of her bedroom. Because of the size of the house, she likes to cocoon in the one room where she feels most comfortable, and so she's there, munching on crusts and going over some paperwork, when she happens to glance up at the eleven o'clock news, thereby learning that her best friend's husband has been arrested for murder that very morning, in the doorway of his own house. Charlotte's initial reaction to the news is helped along by the slices of pizza she has consumed, far too many, as well as the hour, far too late for someone who wakes at five A.M. But perhaps what makes Charlotte ill is the mere idea that on a perfectly ordinary night, as june bugs hit against the window screens and the whole world smells of honeysuckle, there is no protection from disaster.

Whatever the cause, Charlotte goes into the bathroom; she holds back her red hair and vomits, then washes her face with cool water. When she returns to the bedroom, she searches her closet for a crumpled pack of cigarettes she keeps for occasions such as this. Quickly, she lights up, then grabs the phone and dials Jorie, whose number she knows so well she could recite it in the depths of her sleep. The TV is still on, filling the bedroom with wavering light. It's turned on in houses all over town, as well, illuminating living rooms and bedrooms in the old section of town and up here in Hillcrest. Even those residents who usually go to bed early stay up late on this strange and singular night; they wake their husbands or wives and say, *Look at this,* mostly because they find themselves doubting their own vision, obscured by the snaky blue images on their TVs, wondering if their sight is failing.

But what they see on their screens is real, there's no denying that fact. It's a portrait of Ethan Ford in an old photograph, when he was a good fifteen years younger, a likeness that glides through the air, circulating past apple trees and telephone wires, drifting through town like a fine rain over people's rooftops. This handsome and familiar man, boyish but still recognizable, startles people as they walk to the bathroom to brush their teeth and makes them forget the simplest of tasks. Cats are not put out for the evening, sleeping children are not checked upon, husbands and wives are not kissed good night.

Residents of Monroe are stunned by the possibility of something amiss. This is a safe village, far from the crime of Boston, and yet tonight many will lock their doors, some for the first time in years. They'll use bolts they had previously judged to be pointless and make certain to secure their windows in spite of the fine weather. Not that everyone in town believes what they see on the news. Warren Peck's father, Raymond, who helps his son out at the Safehouse Bar every now and then, and whose wife Margaret's heart attack might have been fatal had Ethan not been so quick to arrive on the scene, applauded when Warren threw a pitcher at the TV perched above the bar during the news broadcast, so outraged were they by what were obviously bald-faced lies. Neither old Raymond nor Warren took the time to think about how the TV screen would splinter, however, smashed into thousands of shards, leaving customers to find slivers of glass in every bowl of peanuts and cashews set out during happy hour the following week.

Charlotte lets the phone go on ringing even when it becomes clear that Jorie isn't going to answer. She sits on the floor next to her bed, smoking one cigarette and then another, thinking about the last time both couples had gone out together, to DiGorina's Restaurant in Hamilton. Ethan and Jorie couldn't seem to stay away from each other that night. Their behavior was nothing unexpected for people in love—a few kisses, hands on each other's legs, whispered jokes no one else was privy to—

but sitting there with Jay didn't make their display any easier for Charlotte. She remembers thinking how unfair it was for Jorie to have wound up with everything. They'd both had hopes, hadn't they? They'd both deserved happiness, and yet their fates hadn't been measured out in even amounts. Charlotte recalls exactly how sharp her envy had felt that night, little pinpricks that caused her great pain.

When her own phone rings, she grabs for it, hoping Jorie is calling. To her surprise, it's Jay. He apologizes for not showing up, but then he was always good at excuses.

"I caught the news over at the Safehouse," Jay tells her. "What a bunch of bullshit."

"It's all a mistake."

"They've got the wrong man."

For once, they agree on something. It's quite a shock to both of them, and they laugh.

"Too bad we couldn't have a conversation when we were married," Jay says.

Charlotte can hear the crowd at the Safehouse. She can close her eyes and visualize Jay standing at the phone beyond the bar, his head bent close so he can hear.

"You were never around when we were married," Charlotte reminds him.

"That does make it difficult," Jay concedes. "How's Jorie?"

"Not picking up the phone."

"Poor kid." Jay has always had a soft spot for Jorie. *I don't see her complaining,* he'd said to Charlotte on more than one occasion and Charlotte had always fought the urge to spit back *Of course you don't. She's got nothing to complain about.*

Charlotte lights up another cigarette and inhales.

"Are you smoking?" Jay asks.

"Do you care?" Big mistake. Never ask a question you don't want an answer to. And never tell bad news to someone who's already walked away. She had mentioned her doctor's appointment to Jay the last time he came by to pick up a suitcase full of clothes, but he clearly doesn't remember, and why should she expect him to? They have been little more than roommates for quite some time.

"My life's my own business, right?" Charlotte says. "If I want to smoke, I can puff away."

"That's right, honey," Jay says, and for a moment Charlotte isn't sure whether he's speaking to her or to some other woman at the Safehouse, some lovesick paramour, perhaps, who doesn't know any better than to wait around for a man like Jay.

Charlotte laughs at herself and whoever else is foolish enough to respond to Jay's charms. "I pity whoever falls in love with you."

"So do I," Jay says cheerfully before he hangs up.

Charlotte pulls on a pair of jeans and a tee-shirt and takes her cigarettes from the night table. She goes downstairs, through the darkened hall, then into the kitchen, which Ethan remodeled two years earlier.

He'd done a great job, installing granite countertops, along with cherrywood cabinets that open without a sound, and a floor fashioned from terra cotta tiles. The truth of it is, there were days when Charlotte had rushed to get dressed in order to hurry downstairs in the pale morning light and drink a cup of coffee with Ethan before she went off to work. Listening to the birds who were waking in the trees, standing so close to him, she was afraid he would hear her heart pounding. Throughout the day her thoughts would return to him, and she couldn't put aside the way she felt when she brought him to mind, a mixture of deep pleasure and guilt.

As for Ethan, he never seemed to notice her attraction to him. He treated her as though she were his wife's best friend, which, of course, was exactly what she was. In a way, she'd been relieved when he'd finished with the job, and she'd never bothered to call him back when it turned out the sink had been installed incorrectly, phoning Mark Derry, the plumber, directly to ask if he'd stop by and make the repairs. She hadn't wanted to see Ethan in her kitchen again or feel her pulse quicken when he was close by, and from then on she avoided him. Maybe she'd been afraid of what irretrievable thing she might say or do, distrusting her own uncultivated desires as if they were a flock of wild birds let loose, the sort you could never catch once they'd been freed, not if you chased them to the farthest corners of the Commonwealth.

Tonight as she locks her house before heading over to Jorie's, Charlotte thinks about the brittle wedge of resentment she'd felt earlier when Jorie hadn't shown up at the bakery. She had planned to tell Jorie about the lump that she'd found, for she'd needed an optimist's embrace, and Jorie always managed to see the best in every situation. Now Charlotte understands why Jorie never arrived. She'd been down at the county offices, on King George's Road, caught up in the turmoil of something gone so haywire, no one in the town of Monroe ever would have imagined the way her day would begin and how it would end.

The newscaster had said Ethan was being detained in regard to a murder that had taken place fifteen years earlier, not that Ethan Ford was his true name. It was nothing more than an identity he'd purchased for two hundred dollars. The real Ethan Ford, the one whose social security number this man had been using ever since his arrival in New England, had died in his crib thirty-nine years ago on a summer night in Maryland; he had not lived past his first birthday. Now, as the evening cools down, Charlotte walks out of her house and across the lawn beneath a ceiling of stars and confusion. If she believes what has been reported tonight, then perhaps anything is possible. She might turn onto Front Street and fall headlong into the ether. She might take a single step and find there are constellations swirling beneath her feet as well as up above, in the black and endless sky.

Usually, most houses were dark at this hour, but tonight people in Monroe were staying up late; even those who believed in early to bed and early to rise were drinking coffee and trying their best to puzzle things out. They're caught up in something they've always believed couldn't happen anywhere close by, not in Monroe, where there are only eight men on the police force and no one frets when children play outside after dusk. Those who knew Ethan Ford best of all—his friend Mark Derry, for instance, or the lawyer Barney Stark, who's been his fellow coach at Little League for the past six years, or the valiant members of the volunteer fire department, who have time after time entrusted their lives to him—feel as though they'd been hit hard, right in the stomach, so that it is now impossible for these men to draw a breath without pain.

Barney Stark assumes he'll step in as Ethan's attorney, just as he had two years ago, when the Jeffrieses over on Sherwood Street sued Ethan after their house burned down. True enough, Ethan had refinished their basement and, therefore, the Jeffrieses had been quick to blame the blaze on the insulation he'd installed. That Ethan had helped to extinguish the Jeffrieses' fire, putting his own life at risk, meant nothing to Roger Jeffries and his wife, Dawn. They were days away from a court date when the insurance company found that the fire had started in the Jeffrieses' teenaged son's bedroom. The case was dropped when the boy himself, a gawky, shy sixteen-year-old, finally admitted he had fallen asleep while smoking in bed.

Like everyone else close to the Fords, Barney hasn't had any luck reaching Jorie. The wires have been jammed since the newscast, with Jorie's sister, Anne, setting her phone on automatic redial. But after a while, even single-minded Anne realizes that Jorie has decided not to answer, and figures it's best to wait until morning. Barney, however, does not yield so easily. He's a worrier, a good and thorough man, the sort of individual who gets in his car and drives over to the Fords', just to make certain he isn't needed. Lights have been left on inside the house, but the curtains are drawn, and no one answers when Barney knocks at the door. He smells something he doesn't recognize. Honeysuckle, perhaps. A sweet summer night. From what he can gather from the newscast, there is some evidence that connects Ethan to a murder in Maryland—he was in the town where it happened and abandoned his truck there, a vehicle that recently had been pulled out of the sludge when a local swimming hole was drained—but this is circumstantial evidence, the sort of half-truth that gets innocent men sent away for crimes they would hardly be able to imagine, let alone commit.

"Hello," Barney hollers to the shuttered house. "Anyone home?"

One yard away, the younger of the Williams sisters sits on the porch, not fifteen feet from the spot where her father killed himself last July. Kat Williams watches Barney with narrowed eyes, arms encircling her knobby knees.

"Do you know if anybody's home?" Barney waves to make sure he's made contact, because you never can tell with Kat Williams. She's the kind of child who makes Barney nervous, a wild card you can never trust to act like a child, alternately older and younger than her age. Thankfully, Barney's own daughters are calm, predictable girls, although he's none too thrilled that his eldest girl, Kelly, is friendly with Kat's sister, who has a reputation for her rude behavior as well as her beauty. Sorry to say, but when it comes to Rosarie Williams, Barney can see nothing but trouble ahead. "No one's answering when I knock," Barney calls to the girl who's watching him.

"That's because they don't want to see you," Kat calls back across Mrs. Gage's lawn. Kat has been catching fireflies, and there is a jam jar at her feet that glitters with light. Tonight there were so many fireflies flitting across the lawns and among the leaves of the hedges, Kat hadn't even needed to chase them, the way she and Collie usually did. She'd just opened her hands and they'd flown right in. "You'd better go away."

"What makes you think they don't want to see me?" Barney has a wave of anxiety; he feels the way he used to, back in school, when he was always the last to know when someone was making fun of him.

"If they'd wanted to see you, they would have

opened the door," Kat Williams says reasonably. "Wouldn't they? They wouldn't keep ignoring you."

Kat has Band-Aids on both her legs that she's fiddling with; she isn't pretty or athletic, and she has a peevish expression on her face, but she doesn't miss much, and in this case, she definitely has a point. In Barney's estimation, Kat Williams probably has the makings of an excellent attorney. She's a smart cookie, that much is evident. Barney prides himself on his ability to read people. If anyone can judge who's being forthright, it's Barney, whose own daughters call him the Great Detecto behind his back. The Stark girls know they can't get away with the slightest fib in their house, not even those small, white lies, such as who left the dirty dishes in the sink or who was responsible for a rash of long-distance phone calls.

In court, Barney can easily distinguish between who's telling the truth and who's not. What people say about a liar not being able to look you in the eye isn't true. A liar will stare at you and tell you he's a polar bear or the king of France; he'll swear on his dear mother's life that he's an innocent man. No, Barney can gauge when the truth is omitted, because if you watch closely you'll see that a liar's eyes tend to move back and forth, as if, while he speaks to you, he's already looking for the pathway to his escape. All liars are ready to break and run. They don't sit on their porches, glaring at you, globes of fireflies at their feet.

55

"Maybe you're right," Barney calls to Kat Williams.

"No maybes about it." Kat's mouth is set in a thin line and her shoulders are hunched over. Her certainty touches Barney. He thinks of his daughters, sweet girls who've never had to suffer a day in their lives. Kat Williams knows too much about sorrow. It wasn't that long ago when Barney used to see Aaron Williams out here in the evenings with his new lawnmower, most often tackling Betty Gage's lawn along with his own, simply to be neighborly. Barney supposes Mrs. Gage has to hire someone these days, most likely one of those boys trying to get close to Rosarie, although it seems as if no one's been mowing the Williamses' lawn lately; it's a patchwork of weeds and black brambles. Vines have begun to grow over the shrubbery, weaving in and out of the polite quince leaves and the well-mannered rhododendrons. Rose canes are dark and bare, even though the growing season is said to be excellent this year.

As Barney is appraising the neglected yard, Kat Williams is called in by her grandmother, who first came to stay when Aaron Williams took ill. Looking out the window, Katya has glimpsed a strange man lurking on the sidewalk and she glares at Barney with pale, cold eyes.

"Evening," Barney calls to her.

But Katya doesn't recognize him, although he'd often come to call during the last weeks of Aaron's life. Those days were a blur, best forgotten, and all Katya sees is a man posted in front of the Fords' house. Immediately, she takes him for the sort of rubbernecker who gets a thrill from the sight of other people's blood. They had a taste of that themselves last summer. People would stand on the sidewalk and stare at the garage, they'd drive past slowly, observing the house the way other people might study a natural disaster, a hurricane, perhaps, or a flash flood. Late at night, there were some who threw stones and shouted threats, and then, like the cowards they were, ran away to hide in the bushes as soon as the porch light was switched on. It's no wonder Katya waves her hands at Barney as though shooing away flies, without so much as a hello.

"Go home," she tells him. "Learn to leave good people alone."

Kat Williams grins at the lawyer before she goes inside, and Barney knows exactly what she's thinking.

What did I tell you? None of us want you around.

After the Williamses' door slams shut, Barney feels he should go after them and explain that he's only come to help. He's a good-hearted man who hates his actions to be misunderstood, too frequently the case when he's at home with his wife, Dana. What he wouldn't give for someone to talk to, to have someone who would really listen to the way he feels, deep inside. He lives in a house of chattering girls where there is never a moment of quiet until everyone is asleep. It's only at those moments, while his daughters and his

57

wife are dreaming, that he often realizes he hasn't said a word all day.

Looking down Maple Street from his post outside the Fords' house, Barney spies two cats in the road, lolling in the moonlight, as though they own the night world, two feline kings yowling at each other as they vie over the nesting birds in Mrs. Gage's cherry tree. There is no traffic, but an empty street can be deceiving. The reporters aren't here yet, but they will be soon. A figure walks through the dark, and Barney realizes it's Charlotte Kite who's approaching. You can spot Charlotte anywhere because of that red hair of hers, and now she lights up the dark with both purpose and distress. She's smoking a cigarette, although Barney cannot recall having seen her smoking before. He often sees her at the bakery when he stops there on his way to his office; he's all but addicted to the cinnamon Danishes, even though he knows he could stand to lose a good fifty pounds.

Although he's several years older than Charlotte and Jorie, he remembers them well from high school. Pretty girls he never would have stood a chance with, not even if they could have gazed into the future to predict he'd attend Harvard Law School and go on to live in one of those big houses in Charlotte Kite's neighborhood out beyond Horsetail Hill. They wouldn't have looked at him twice, not if he'd had a million dollars in his pockets and had gotten down on bended knee, begging for their attention. He'd had an especially big crush on Charlotte, an embarrassing fact he's never mentioned to anyone. Certainly, he'd never dared to act on his pathetic desire, or ever imagined she might one day respond. He may have been a loser back in school, but nobody could call him stupid, not then and not now.

"Hey, there," he says to Charlotte as she approaches. Charlotte's expression is cloudy when she sees him; whether this is caused by the smoke from her cigarette or a haze of suspicion isn't clear. "Barney Stark," he reminds her.

"Right," Charlotte says, looking at him for further explanation.

"I'm here in a professional capacity. Just checking in."

"Are you saying they're going to need a lawyer?" Charlotte moves a little closer, even though there's no one nearby who might overhear.

"Innocent people need lawyers, too," Barney reassures her.

Charlotte is relieved. She herself has recently spent a small fortune on legal fees, and her only crime was marrying Jay. Of course they'll need a lawyer. Charlotte has never paid Barney Stark any mind, but at this moment, in the dark, standing on the sidewalk facing Jorie's house, their conversation feels oddly intimate. "You're absolutely right. He'll have to fight those crazy charges."

The Williams girl has left her jar of fireflies on the porch steps. Yellow orbs of light whirl against the glass.

"Will you look at that," Barney says. He's talking too much and he knows it, but he may never get another chance to have Charlotte Kite listen to him. He might as well take advantage of the moment, for it will surely never come again. "So bright you could read by the light of those bugs."

"Well, they'll be dead by morning."

Charlotte turns and looks him over. Barney lives two blocks away from her, in one of the brand-new pseudo-Victorians on Evergreen Drive, built a good century after the Monroe family went bankrupt and sold off parcels of land, but frankly, she doesn't know much about him. She does take note of his Lexus, however. It's a rather surprising choice for a large, plain man such as Barney, but perhaps he needs to show off his success. It's all coming back to Charlotte; he was one of the kids people used to make fun of in high school. He was heavy and plodding and far too shy to ask out any of the girls. Now he's rich and has three beautiful daughters, and Charlotte has nothing. "I'll bet you're one of those expensive lawyers."

"Well, I am," Barney admits. "But I'm good."

"I'm happy to put up some money for Ethan and Jorie. If it comes down to it."

Charlotte tosses her cigarette onto the sidewalk and red sparks rise upward. She may seem a little hard, but she's anything but, and Barney isn't the least bit surprised by her offer.

"I'm sure they'd appreciate that." Barney thinks of his daughters, safe in their beds, and he knows he won't be able to sleep tonight. He's something of an insomniac, and he often spends nights in an easy chair pulled up to the window in the living room. From the heights of his house on Evergreen Drive, beyond a hill where there used to be nothing but orchards, the very spot where Ella Monroe herself was married so long ago, he is always surprised to see a few lights blinking in Monroe after midnight. On street after street, there are sleepless, unhappy people, much like himself, trapped like fireflies inside their own houses.

"I think I see Jorie." Barney has spotted a shadow in an upstairs window. The curtain moves in the breeze. A few faded cherry blossoms dip through the sweet, dark, honeyed air, and Barney inhales deeply. He thinks of the first time he saw Charlotte Kite, when she wasn't more than fourteen. He thinks of the way her red hair gleams in the sunlight in the mornings, as she stands behind the counter in the bakery. He realizes that Charlotte smells delicious, her aroma much sweeter than the honeysuckle in the night air, as if she could never wash the scent of chocolate or the granules of sugar from her skin. Oh, how he wishes he could tell her what he's thinking. He knows he has a foolish look on his face, the stupid expression of bliss.

"I've got an extra key," Charlotte declares. "I'm going on in."

When she starts up the walkway, Barney keeps

pace with her, but Charlotte quickly sets him right. "I don't need any help, if that's what you were thinking."

"Oh, no, of course not." Barney recalls that she'd said something like this to him once before, ages ago, when they were in school. Charlotte had dropped her books in a rush to get to class, and he'd knelt to help gather some of the fallen papers. She'd looked him straight in the eye and told him not to touch anything. He'd felt as though she'd burned him with a single remark. His fingertips had puckered and blistered afterward, and he'd had to dust his hands with baking soda to ease the pain, and tonight he feels the same way all over again. She can burn him with one word. Even now.

"I know Jorie better than anyone," Charlotte says. "I can handle it."

In fact, she has handled everything in her life. Charlotte is not and never has been the sort of person to say please any more than she is likely to say thank you, and she has very little pity for the meek and the mild. Still, tonight she feels a strange sort of empathy for Barney, with his expensive, ill-fitting suit and his Lexus parked at the curb. Moonlight spills across the lawns on Maple Street and what looks like little stars are floating right past, a wave of milkweed spores, luminous and mysterious as they drift through the dark. Charlotte can see that she's bruised Barney Stark somehow. He's the kind of man who wears his heart on his rumpled sleeve.

"All I mean is that you don't have to waste

62

your time here anymore. I'll take care of everything." Echoing Kat Williams, she adds, "Go home."

Charlotte uses her key and slips inside. It's an odd sensation, standing in the front hallway of the Fords' house. Charlotte always goes around the back, and for this reason it seems that she's stepped into a stranger's home.

"Jorie?"

Charlotte doesn't want to be one of those statistics, some neighborly soul shot through the heart when all she's doing is trying to help.

"Anybody here? It's me, Charlotte."

She goes into the kitchen, where she finds a box of cereal left out on the counter, along with two unwashed bowls. A mess such as this isn't like Jorie, who is always so house-proud. As Charlotte continues on, she doesn't have to look outside to know that Barney Stark is still there, waiting to make certain no one needs him before he goes home. A man such as this is a mystery to Charlotte. Why, he's as much a riddle as the Sphinx in the desert. She cannot even imagine what it might be like to have a man who would stand by you, who'd love you for whoever you are.

The staircase is dim, and Charlotte keeps a hand on the wall to guide her. As she goes up to Jorie and Ethan's bedroom, she feels a bit like a Peeping Tom, treading softly, roaming through the place uninvited, even though the house belongs to Jorie, who's closer to Charlotte than she is to her own sister. The night is so strange she can't help but wonder if they've all been hypnotized. There have been cases of people who shared the same dream, and maybe that's what's happened. Perhaps Charlotte and Barney Stark and Jorie are asleep, entering freely into one another's dreams, walking down the same imagined empty streets, watching the same nonexistent news broadcasts, having conversations they would never be party to during the shining hours of daylight. If one of them wakes, surely the rest are bound to follow, jolted out of their slumber, panting for breath, frightened by how close they've come to disaster.

But when Charlotte peers into the bedroom, Jorie doesn't have her head on the pillow, her breathing shallow, the way a dreamer's is whenever the dream feels as real as everyday life, dreams of bread and butter, and of lives gone wrong, and of quiet houses where couples sleep through the night. No, this is no dream. Jorie is sitting on the edge of the bed, wearing the same clothes she's had on since morning, her face drained, her beautiful golden hair lank as straw. Collie is the one who's asleep in the big bed, but anyone can tell his rest is fitful, for he turns and pulls the quilt closer, then groans, a fluttering boy noise that causes a catch in Charlotte's own throat.

"What you heard isn't true." Jorie's voice is low, so as not to wake her son. All the same, there's something in her tone that sounds desperate.

"Of course it isn't." Charlotte usually

expects the worst of people, but she's more than willing to make an exception in Ethan's case. There has to be someone worth trusting, hasn't there? One man among them to whom even a disbeliever like Charlotte can pledge her faith. "The whole idea is insanity. Jay called me from the Safehouse, and everyone down there is outraged. Don't worry about what people are thinking. Everyone knows they've got the wrong man."

"Really? Well, our friends were the ones who came to get him," Jorie says with real bitterness. "Hal Roderick. Adam Sorrell. Dave Meyers."

These men have worked with Ethan on dozens of occasions, pooling the resources of the volunteer fire department with the police whenever there's an accident on the highway, or a heart attack phoned in, or a stretch of woods left in flames after a fierce lightning storm.

"Dave himself stood out on our front porch and read Ethan his rights. As if he had any!"

Charlotte and Jorie have known Dave Meyers, now the sheriff of Monroe Township, since grade school, and although that hadn't stopped him from arresting Ethan, Dave certainly wasn't able to look Jorie in the eye. *I'm sorry,* he'd muttered, as if his apology was worth anything.

As Jorie speaks of the morning's events, her voice rises dangerously, and Charlotte nods at Collie, who starts in his sleep. The women retreat to the window seat Ethan built last year, making use of some old oak paneling he'd removed from the tumbled-down Monroe house, abandoned long ago on the outskirts of town. Jorie moves the curtains aside, and from where they sit she can spy a man on the sidewalk, peering up at them. It's still hot outside and the man keeping watch wipes his face with a handkerchief.

"Don't worry. It's only Barney Stark." Charlotte leans her elbows on the casement. Just as she suspected, Barney has stationed himself on the walkway. He's taken off his loosened tie and stuffed it in his pocket, but he still looks awkward and overdressed and worried. Charlotte waves, and Barney cautiously waves back. "He's come to see if you need help," Charlotte tells Jorie. "The big oaf."

"How do we get rid of him?"

The women look at each other and laugh.

"Easy enough. I could always get rid of him." Charlotte motions to Barney that he can go. "Come back tomorrow," she calls. "Jorie will be fine till then."

"Tell her I'll meet her down at the holding station." Barney certainly doesn't wish to use the word *jail*. He's a polite, well-bred man whose mother was extremely proud of him up until the day she died. "At nine."

Charlotte turns to Jorie. "The jail at nine A.M. And remember," she adds when she sees the wash of anxiety cross Jorie's face; again Charlotte is thankful for Barney. "Innocent people need lawyers, too."

"Right." Jorie pulls at her tangled hair. She is frighteningly pale, as though her flesh has turned to fish scales, her blood to ice water. "They say he was in the same town where some girl was killed, but what does that prove? How many people pass through Monroe every day? Does that mean they've all murdered someone?"

"It means nothing." Charlotte is quick to agree.

Collie is deeply asleep now; he turns and flings one arm over the side of the bed. Awake he is close to being a teenager, and the man he'll become is evident in his rangy appearance. Odd how children look so much younger when they sleep; perhaps their slumbering forms are what prompt adults close by to try their best to protect them from every evil under the sun.

"I had him sleep in here tonight because I didn't want him to be scared. Now I think I was the one who didn't want to be alone."

Jorie had cried in the car as she drove home from the jail, wanting to get it all out before she picked up Collie. Then she'd gone and broken down in the doorway of the Williamses' house like a common fool, some poor woman who was at the mercy of whatever the fates might bring. She'd made herself stop, then had brought Collie home where she sat him down in the kitchen and told him that his father had been taken over to the county offices on King George's Road. It was nothing for them to worry about, a few questions about a crime committed years ago, a thousand miles away, by someone else entirely. Life wasn't fair sometimes, and this was one of those times. Sooner or later it would be sorted out, but until then they'd just have to get through it; they'd have to hold tight and wait for Ethan to be cleared of any charges. They'd have to stand by him till then.

It had been a horrible day for Jorie, most of it spent in a hallway at the county offices. She had tried to talk to Dave Meyers and to Will Derrick over at the county prosecutor's office; she'd tried to make some sense of what was happening, but she'd gotten absolutely nowhere. When at last she demanded to see Ethan, who'd been brought down to a cell in the basement, she'd found she could not breathe. It was panic she was feeling, this drowning sensation that overwhelmed her. It was fear caught in her lungs where there should have been air, plain and simple as that.

Go home, Ethan said to Jorie when she came to stand outside his cell.

He wouldn't look at her, not even when she reached in through the bars.

Don't you hear what I'm saying? I don't want you to see me here. Don't you understand that?

She'd started crying then, stunned by his resolve and by the stark reality of the situation. Ethan had relented at last; he'd rested his head against the metal bars, and Jorie had done the same, and when she closed her eyes she could imagine they were far from this horrible place where they stood.

We'll figure it out tomorrow, Ethan had promised Jorie before she left, and she had

believed him, but now, sitting here with Charlotte, there seems too much to ever figure
out. Jorie gazes at Collie's sleeping face, at the
pale skin, the fine features, the way he breathes
so deeply as he dreams. She had been so sure
of her everyday life—you wake up, you make
coffee, you send those you love off to school
and to work, there is rain or it's sunny, you're
late or you're on time, but no matter what, those
who love you will love you forever, without
questions or boundaries or the constraints
of time. Daily life is real, unchanging as a well-
built house. But houses burn; they catch fire
in the middle of the night, like that house
over on Sherwood Street where the son was
smoking in bed and everything disappeared
in an instant. No furniture, no family photos,
only ashes. Well, it's ashes Jorie tastes now,
ashes in her mouth, on her hands, beneath her
feet. The fire had come and gone, and she
hadn't even known it. She'd just stood there
while it swept through the door.

When Jorie goes to the bathroom to wash
her face and comb her hair, Charlotte follows.
The night is like any other night of disaster,
with every fact filtered through a veil of disbelief. The rational world has spun so completely out of its orbit, there is no way to
chart or expect what might happen next.
Charlotte is reminded of the time in high
school when their friends Lindsay Maddox and
Jeannie Atkins were in a fatal car crash over
on the highway. Everyone had difficulty getting over the shock of the accident, espe-

cially Jorie, who stopped eating and missed several weeks of school. It seemed so unfair that Lindsay and Jeannie would never get to finish senior year; they'd never graduate or kiss another boy or fulfill the promise of their lives. There is still a marker at the spot where the accident happened, and although Jeannie's family moved to Florida, never to return to Monroe again, Lindsay's mother continues to bring wreaths of flowers on the first of every month, bands of everlasting and sweetbrier and roses that she twists through the fence, unaware of whether or not there are thorns.

Every time Charlotte drives past, she remembers that she's lucky. She was supposed to go with them that night, but her mother made her stay home because she was recovering from the flu and had a slight fever. Charlotte thinks about that whenever she's home alone at night. She thinks about it right now. Good fortune can turn out to be bad, Charlotte knows that for a fact, and the luckiest among us can be ruined by chance: a simple wrong turn, a metal fence, a man who drives through town on a cold, foggy night.

In the harsh bathroom light it's impossible not to notice the toll today has taken on Jorie. Still, she's beautiful, even now. Charlotte understands why Ethan fell in love with her the first time he saw her. Charlotte herself was standing right next to Jorie, but she might as well have been invisible. She still remembers Ethan's expression as he approached; the way he wanted Jorie was all over his face, his attraction as obvious as a drowning man's prayer for solid land.

"Do you ever think of what your life might have been like if we hadn't gone to the Safehouse that night?" Charlotte asks. They're headed down to the kitchen, so that Charlotte can make them a pot of tea. "We could have gone bowling instead, or to a movie. One changed plan and your whole life would have been different."

"It would never have happened that way," Jorie says with conviction.

"You think you were meant to be with him? No matter what?"

"I know I was." Jorie sounds much more like herself now. She always had an assured manner, even when they were girls. That was one of the things Charlotte envied, how Jorie never seemed torn apart by doubt. "He hadn't decided to stay in Monroe until the night we met. Did you know that? He was on his way to New Hampshire because a friend of his was working in Portsmouth and told him there was a lot of work to be found there. He was in Monroe for exactly one night."

After the tea is ready, Charlotte decides to fix her friend some toast as well, having rightly assumed that Jorie hasn't thought to eat supper. She suggests that Jorie go to the living room and lie down on the couch; Charlotte will bring in a tray. While the bread is browning, Charlotte takes the opportunity to tidy up the kitchen. She's glad she hasn't mentioned that her doctor insisted upon a biopsy; Jorie has more than enough to worry about. Charlotte refuses to think about her own problems as she washes out the cereal bowls and sweeps up the last shards of the broken coffee cup and gets the silver tray she gave them as a wedding present. She will think about this house, instead, about this kitchen. Everything here is top of the line, hand-crafted cabinets, a stainless steel stove that would suffice for a restaurant, slate countertops that shine with silvery mica. Ethan must have gotten it all at cost, but anyone can tell he designed this kitchen for the woman he loved. It's the curved arches of wood above the windows, fine carpentry that must have taken weeks, that speaks of his devotion. It's the inlaid pattern of light and dark squares on the floor, fitted with such care that the wood appears seamless, black and white bark grown together on the very same tree.

When she really thinks about it, Charlotte knows nothing about Ethan before that night when they first caught sight of him in the Safehouse. He arrived out of nowhere with no baggage and no tales to tell. Whatever he'd said about himself they would have gladly believed, for the past hadn't mattered much back then. Charlotte and Jorie were both so young that all they cared about was the future. They couldn't get to it fast enough, the sweet, unexplored empire of their dreams. And why shouldn't they look forward? The present hadn't seemed particularly interesting. Charlotte was working in her family's bakery after her parents had passed on, just about the last thing she'd ever planned to do, and Jorie was teaching second grade at the Ella Monroe Elementary School. At that point, they were both convinced that love was a figment of other people's imaginations, an illusion fashioned out of smoke and air that didn't really exist, at least not in Monroe, Massachusetts, where they were acquainted with every available man and more than well aware of every flaw and every strike against him since kindergarten.

That night at the Safehouse, their meeting had truly seemed like fate, the way Ethan looked at Jorie, the way he asked if he could buy her something to drink, then had guessed what she wanted was white wine, as if he already knew her preferences. Jorie wasn't the sort of girl who was inclined to take a man home on their first date, not even if she'd known him her whole life long, but she brought Ethan up to her apartment, and she's never once regretted a decision that some might call impulsive and others might cite as the best irrational act of her life. Here she is, thirteen years later, asleep on the couch when Charlotte brings in the tray of tea and toast. Jorie is Ethan's wife, no matter what lies anyone might tell. She has pledged herself to him, now and forever, and on this moonlit night, she is dreaming of those lilies the flower shop on Front Street sets out on the sidewalk at Easter, flowers that look far too delicate to last, but if planted carefully in the garden will come back, season after season. Some things return, no matter what, like the constellations in the summer sky or the mourning doves that alight in bushes and trees in the gardens every year at this time, so that the last days of June are always accompanied by cooing and whispering: *What can happen, what will happen, what is meant to be.*

Knight of Swords

IN THE MORNING, MEN in jail will try to sleep their time away, dreaming of home and happiness, staving off waking for as long as possible. What they wish for is a spool of invisible thread with which to sew up their eyes; what they want more than anything are soft pillows, upon which they can rest undisturbed as time falls past them in endless waves. There is just cause for this desire for sleep: the dream is often more real than what a man might find when he opens his eyes. The dream is everything he once had, and foolishly threw away. Dinner set out on the table, the scent of summer, the woman who loves him waiting at the screen door. Awaken, and green light streams in, like fish skin, and the air is foul, overlaid by industrial-strength air-freshener that, no matter how strong, cannot erase the scent of fear. Fear, like heat, rises; it drifts up

74

to the ceiling and when it falls down it pours out in a hot and horrible rain. A man has to train himself to sleep through such circumstances; otherwise every drop is a drop of fire from the first level of hell, wet cinders in his eyes, his heart, his lungs.

Ethan Ford is especially ill-suited to this environment. He's a man who likes his own bed, and his life set in order. Locked up, he's unable to sleep for more than a few minutes at a time, and he's therefore deprived of his dreams. He can feel the enormity of what has happened inside his chest, feverish bands that encircle his ribs. His mouth is always dry, and the dryness cannot be relieved, not by water, not by ice, not by dreams of the blue ponds of his youth, spring fed and deliciously cold, so clear you could kneel down and drink right from the shore. Since the moment when he opened the front door to see Dave Meyers and the other men from the sheriff's office standing there, Ethan has had a weightless feeling. It's as though everything that has been holding him to earth has been cut away; all that remains are white bones and whatever wisps of cloth might cover him.

A sleepless night can last an eternity, and because of this Ethan has had plenty of time to decide what to do. He has already made up his mind by the time Barney Stark sets off for the jail promptly at eight the following morning. By then, Ethan has walked to hell and back while his neighbors have been dreaming in their comfortable beds. Hours later, he's still burning. Touch him, and you burn along with him. Touch him, and you feel his pain.

When at last he hears someone in the hall, Ethan cranes his neck to see who's approaching, hoping only that it's not his wife. He will not have Jorie witness his degradation in this cell again. The mere idea is anguish to him, and he'll do whatever he can to prevent such an occurrence or, at the very least, postpone it. Naturally, he's relieved to find that his visitor is only Barney Stark.

"Hey," Barney calls as Dave Meyers leads him to the cell. Usually, Frankie Links or one of the other guards would have this job, but today Dave has come in on his day off to ensure that Ethan will get proper treatment. Still this is always an awkward moment, men trying to act as though nothing unusual is occurring when one individual is locked up and the others are free. "I got us breakfast." Barney rattles the paper bag he's brought with him. He's already stopped at Kite's Bakery, where he picked up two coffees to go and a sack of sugar crullers, along with his favorite Danishes. Barney asked Jorie to meet him at nine because he needs a little time alone with Ethan to walk through some of the details Ethan will no doubt want to spare his wife. How much a trial can take out of you, for instance, if circumstances should come to that, and how damned expensive such an undertaking can be, particularly if investigators charging by the hour are needed to track down witnesses who, in the span of fifteen years, might have gotten to be just about anywhere.

Barney figures something sweet might help this information go down, hence the pastries, but that's not the only reason he stopped at the bakery. He had hoped to see Charlotte, and although he was disappointed to find she wasn't there, he wasn't surprised. His guess: she's spent the night over at Jorie's, fielding phone calls and chasing off unwanted visitors, such as himself. Anyone can tell that's the kind of friend Charlotte Kite is, and if there was one thing Barney respected, it was loyalty. Loyalty is the reason he's here, for his practice doesn't run to complicated criminal cases. Ethan and Barney may not be the best of friends, but they've coached baseball together and their knowledge of each other is at a deep level. Each knows how the other deals with failure, and with false hope, and with the absolute and fleeting bliss of an eleven-year-old hitting a fly ball over the fence.

Driving here, Barney had eaten one of the Danishes he'd bought at Kite's, and he brushed the crumbs from his suit jacket as he signed in for his visit. He knows the officers on duty, he's grown up with most of them, and he doesn't blame them for their hangdog expressions. It was Ethan Ford they had locked up in the holding tank, not some drunk who'd had one too many at the Safehouse and had been temporarily corralled for his own protection while he slept it off.

"I'm not happy about this," Dave Meyers

tells Barney as they walk down the corridor to the holding area.

"Nobody's happy about this, Dave," Barney agrees.

When the door to the cell is unlocked, Ethan stands to greet Barney, but he's not interested in breakfast. "Just coffee, thanks."

Barney shrugs and hands the bakery bag to Dave. "Knock yourself out." Barney knows that Dave can never get enough to eat, yet, unfair as it may seem, he's as lean as poor Barney is heavy. As soon as Dave leaves them alone, Barney lets Ethan know that even though his practice is primarily family and estate law, the least he can do is get the ball rolling. He can access the court documents, including the Maryland demand for extradition. Barney is talking about the intricacies of the law, a subject he loves, listing the steps they'll have to take to fight the transfer south, when he notices Ethan isn't listening. Distracted, Ethan appears to be studying the shadows of the bars that fall across the linoleum floor. The kind of disinterest he's displaying is never a good sign. Either he's confused, or he's given up, or, worst of all, he simply doesn't care about his own fate.

"I know this is a lot to take in," Barney says. "Hopefully most of it will make sense in time."

Ethan's face is unshaven and his black hair looks blue in the shadows. Remembering the coffee Barney brought him, Ethan picks up the cup. His hands shake as he removes the lid.

He's aware that Barney is trying to help, but he can't focus on that now. "I've got to talk to Jorie first."

"Sure." Barney understands. "She's coming at nine."

"You've got to help me with something." Ethan gulps his coffee, hot as it is. What difference does it make, since he's burning anyway. He's got the pent-up demeanor of a man who's got to have his way, at least when it comes to the matter he wishes to discuss. "I can't have her see me in here."

"We can move you into the sheriff's office for some privacy. I don't think Dave has to worry that you'll climb out the window and take off."

For the first time, Ethan looks directly at Barney, just a glance, a quick one, but it's not the kind of expression Barney would have wished for. All the same, he claps his friend on the back.

"Hey, relax. I've been here before. You think mistakes don't get made all the time? It will take time and money and effort, but eventually, we'll set things right."

By now, Ethan has drained the coffee and is tearing the cardboard cup apart. He does it systematically, so that the pieces are all the same size. Barney doesn't like this either. Some people become really quiet when they're confined, but others get wired, you can see how keyed up they are and how it might be possible that they would do almost anything in order to escape: punch a police officer, bolt and run, grab an old friend and put an arm to his throat, threatening to break his windpipe with a single move. Ethan has turned out to be the wired kind, and innocent or not, this sort of behavior will not put him in good standing with anyone.

Barney calls to Dave Meyers and explains that Ethan would like to speak to Jorie privately. This isn't an unreasonable request, and of course the sheriff agrees. Dave's got two children, a seventh-grade girl named Hillary, and Jesse, an athletic boy who's just finishing up sixth grade, in the same class as Ethan's son and Barney's daughter. As a matter of fact, Jesse Meyers is on their Little League team. He's a good kid, with a lot of power in his arm, and they'll probably turn to him more and more often this season. Ethan is the one who practiced with Jesse all last year, and as a result, Jesse's pitching has greatly improved. From Dave's rueful expression, it's clear that he knows about the extra effort Ethan has put in with his son.

"I wouldn't have done it this way if it was up to me." Dave knows he should keep quiet, but he feels the least he owes Ethan is an apology. "The pressure's coming out of Maryland, and let me tell you, these guys are a royal pain in the ass."

"I'll bet." Ethan is quick to let Dave off the hook, and why shouldn't he be? These two men have worked together many times, most often when both the police and fire departments are called in to oversee an accident on the interstate. Last month, they had been part of a team that had worked for hours to free a teenaged driver from a pickup that had become a burning pile of scrap. Once the kid had been taken to Hamilton Hospital, they'd gone off together to the Safehouse, having quickly agreed it was not just their right to get drunk, it was their duty.

"Take your time," Dave tells Ethan now. He goes to the window and raises the shade in an attempt to make the room a little less gloomy. As he does, he remembers how blistered Ethan's hands had been that night at the Safehouse when they shared a few drinks. Ethan had grabbed onto the hot metal door of the kid's truck without a thought for himself during the rescue, and hours later he still hadn't noticed how badly he'd been burned. "Take as much time as you want," Dave tells him, and although he's the sort of man who hates to break the rules, Dave's surely not about to pay heed to the twenty-minute visitation limit. Not when it comes to Ethan.

"Thanks." Ethan runs a hand through his hair. He blinks in the stream of sunlight that pours into the dingy office. There's still a whole world out beyond the confines of the block of county offices, including an old field of meadowsweet crisscrossed by crumbling stone walls. Anyone can see how much Ethan Ford wishes he were there; if only he could walk through the wild grass and wait in the sunlight for his wife to arrive. In thirteen years, they've hardly spent a night apart. Other men might

81

yearn for such things, for freedom and soli-
tude, but not Ethan. He cannot begin to
imagine how he will ever manage to sleep
without her.

"If there was something I could do to stop
this, I would," Dave Meyers mutters before
he goes. Once a guilt-ridden man starts talking,
he can never seem to hush, and this is the case
with Dave, who has never been particularly well
suited for his job. The rules and regulations
are one thing, but the personal heartbreak is
something else entirely. "They're hoping to
take him back to Maryland by the end of the
week," he tells Barney.

"Not if I have anything to say about it,"
Barney replies. "I'm going to petition the
court for a probable-cause hearing, and the
least they'll have to do is respond to it. That's
not going to happen by the end of the week."

Once they're alone, Ethan turns to Barney.
It's impossible to read his dark eyes. His
complexion is chalky, or maybe it's the dreadful
lighting that bleaches the color from his skin.
"You think you're going to save me."

"Of course I am." Barney grins his big,
wide grin, the one that shows his teeth and
which was, unbeknownst to him, the reason
the kids in school always laughed at him and
called him a hyena. Well, he has laughed his
way up to Evergreen Drive and that enormous house of his, and now those same kids
who'd abused him so mercilessly are the first
to phone Barney the minute their own kids get
busted with marijuana or slapped with a

drunk-driving charge. He's the one they come to when there's a nasty divorce or an estate hearing, or when they simply want someone trustworthy they can talk to. "I save people for a living, Ethan. That's what I do."

Jorie's car pulls into the parking lot, and as soon as Ethan spies his wife, he's no longer paying attention to Barney. He tucks in his shirt and rubs one hand over his dark growth of beard. He's a man in love, and he wants to look his best. He wants these few moments alone with Jorie before things get any worse.

"Here goes," he says. "Wish me luck."

Barney goes out into the hall, and waves when he sees Jorie. "Don't look so worried." He gives her a hug. Jorie's face is drawn, and it's clear she hasn't bothered to comb her hair. "Did Charlotte stay with you last night?"

Jorie nods. "I used the back door and dropped Collie at my mother's. Charlotte went out the front and dealt with the reporters. They appeared from nowhere, and they won't go away. They've got a van of some sort parked in the Gleasons' driveway across the street."

Barney is pleased that Charlotte understands exactly what she needs to do to protect Jorie. He thinks about what an idiot Jay Smith was, as far back as in school. Everyone in town knew he was fooling around except for Charlotte, and there were several times when Barney came close to writing her a note, something gentle, yet honest. But Barney never knew how driven he was by self-interest, and in the end, he decided that the outcome of Charlotte and Jay's marriage was in the hands of fate.

"I'll try my best to keep Ethan out of Maryland, and I'm asking for bail to be set. With a little luck, I'll have him home in twenty-four hours."

"Twenty-four hours?" Jorie looks even more distraught when she hears what Barney had assumed would be good news. Twenty-four hours of absence between Barney and his wife, Dana, is a matter of course. There are times when they meet in their own living room and Barney realizes they haven't spoken in days, and the worst part is, neither seems to care.

"Go on. He's waiting for you. And stop worrying. That's my job."

Jorie has been anticipating this moment, but now that it's here, she finds she's afraid. The hallway seems perilous; the distance she must travel suddenly appears vast. What will she discover when she opens the door? Perhaps Ethan has changed overnight, grown sharp teeth, perhaps, or claws. Surely her fears are the product of a terrible night, for like her husband, Jorie has barely slept. She only closed her eyes for a fitful moment or two, and even then she dreamed of shadows, blue shapes shifting across her own garden, swooping down at her, darting so close she could see their eyes, cold and indifferent and dark.

She takes one last step, then opens the door to Dave's office. Instantly, she knows it's all right. He is still the same Ethan, her dear husband, the love of her life. Jorie rushes to him and collapses against him, and Barney reaches to close the door, allowing them the privacy they so rightly deserve.

"Jorie," Ethan says once she's in his arms. The word sounds like a prayer and, indeed, it is her name that has allowed him to get through his night of hell. He has walked through the fire with her name on his lips; he has drunk of it and found sustenance in it, until at last he was carried to the other side of the black river. He has contemplated this moment, re-envisioned it again and again, and now at last he's in it. He's already started kissing her, slowly and softly at first, and then desperate, earth-shattering kisses that make her sob. *Baby,* he says, *I don't want you to cry.* But that's what she's doing, she can't stop herself, seeing him like this, falsely accused and stolen from their lives.

Ethan brings Jorie to Dave's old leather couch and pulls her onto his lap. He cannot let her go. But time is vanishing; they can't hold on to it, or stop it, or bargain for more. They gaze at each other, their yearning for each other and for the lives they've led until now is so painful, they can barely look at each other. Jorie rests her head against her husband's chest and listens to his heart. The rhythm is racing, but then it has always seemed to her that Ethan's heartbeat was faster than any other man's. He has the stamina of two men, the good looks of three, the heart of at least half a dozen. Sometimes when she watches him sleep, Jorie feels that he may indeed be an angel, drawn to earth by her selfish needs and desires. Perhaps she's trapped him here beside her, to sleep in her bed, and eat her dinners, and go off to work, when he was meant to be elsewhere. True love, after all, could bind a man where he didn't belong. It could wrap him in cords that were all but impossible to break.

"Barney says it will take twenty-four hours to get you out. I'm guessing it will be less once the court realizes how foolish this is."

"Let's not think about time."

It is then that Jorie notices what grows directly outside Dave Meyers's window. There is a row of orange lilies, all facing east, drawn to the strength of the sun. *Blood lilies,* Jorie thinks. She gets up and goes to the window, drawn there just as certainly as the lilies are drawn to the sun. Outside, there are dozens of blue jays, picking through the damp grass. She thinks about how surprised she was when Collie told her that a jay's feathers had no blue pigment, and she blinks at the riotous blue blur as the birds take flight. There are fields of wild lavender beyond the sheriff's station, and the birds are always attracted to the purple blooms. It's the time of year when fledglings are especially susceptible to hawks, but they come to feast in the fields anyway. Jorie turns away from the world outside; she lowers the window shade and welcomes the darkness. Her universe is contained within this room. Fair skies and blue jays no longer concern her. Not anymore.

Ethan has been watching Jorie carefully. With every move she makes he can feel how time is coursing past them, shaking the floors and the ceilings, rattling their world. He can't get enough of Jorie, he can't let her go, and yet he's afraid that may be exactly what he's about to do. When Jorie turns back to Ethan there's something in his eyes she doesn't recognize. Then, all at once, she knows what it is. It's fear. It's the one thing she doesn't want to see. Everything looks blue in these moments: the walls, and Ethan's face, and the shadows that are cast upon them both, blue as hyacinths, lasting as heaven.

"People are going to say a lot of things about me," Ethan tells his wife, as if this weren't occurring already. Down at the Safehouse and at the bakery, in the schoolyard and in the streets, his name has been repeated so often it has become an incantation, calling the bees from the fields, until there is a buzzing sound drifting over town, a low rumble that informs every word that is spoken aloud.

Though Jorie has heard none of this gossip, she knows people in a small town often feel the need to meddle, and she laughs, her voice sweet and clear. "Honey, don't you think I know that? People are always going to talk. That's human nature."

Ethan thinks over the right way to tell her. He has thought it over for years, but the time has finally come, so he'll just have to say it as best he can. "I mean real bad things, Jorie. Things you won't want to believe."

"How bad could it be?" Jorie sounds light-hearted, but that's not the way she feels inside. Fear is contagious. It doubles within minutes, it grows in places where there's never been any doubt before. "Are they going to tell me that you have another wife down in Maryland? That you want a divorce?"

"No." His love for her is nothing to joke about, and he's stung by her mocking tone. Still, Jorie goes on teasing him.

"Maybe you've got a family you left behind. Three kids who called you Daddy before you moved up here and met me."

"There's only you and Collie. You know that." The thought of his son having to endure the taunts that are bound to arise makes Ethan's color deepen. His son's discomfort was the last thing he'd ever want.

Jorie knows what he's thinking, she can see the haze of guilt, the worry, the look on his face when he gets like this, for he's a man who always puts others' needs before his own. "Don't worry. Collie will be fine just as soon as you get home."

Ethan gazes at his wife with gratitude and with sorrow. He never wants to stop looking at her. Jorie can feel his desire, on her face and her shoulders, in her blood and her bones, how much he longs for her. How many women have that, after all? They were destined to be together. Otherwise he wouldn't even be in New England; he'd be a good two thousand miles from here. Although, in truth, he wasn't on his way to New Hampshire the night he met her, as he's always told her. There was no job, and no friend up in Portsmouth. These were lies he made up on the spot. He told Jorie what he thought she wanted to hear, but that doesn't mean anything he said was true. In fact, he was headed for Las Vegas on the night they'd met, for he'd gotten it into his head that a man could start fresh there. He'd be one of thousands of individuals who'd made mistakes and could still manage to roll through town with no past and nothing to prove.

He'd spent quite a while working on the Cape, making good money, and at last he'd had enough to drive out west. At any rate, that had been his intention, but the thought of the desert had made him thirsty, and he'd pulled off the highway at the exit past the hundred-mile marker, where there is always a wreath tied to the fence in memory of Jeannie and Lindsay, those ill-fated high school girls who'd been such good friends of Jorie and Charlotte's. He skirted town on the twisting back roads, driving aimlessly until he saw the neon sign for the Safehouse. It was a sleety, bleak night, and the new truck he'd bought when the job on the Cape was through skidded on the bumps of King George's Road, but he kept driving fast. He needed a drink and he needed it badly; it was as if the Nevada sun was already striking his windshield, and maybe that was why he was so parched.

He figured one last stop in this godforsaken Commonwealth wouldn't kill him. He hated Massachusetts, the dark frozen months, the cross, melancholy citizens. He'd grown up on the Eastern Shore of Maryland where the well water was a thousand times sweeter, the land was green and gentle, and everything that fell from the sky wasn't intended to destroy man and beast alike. He rolled down his window and let the sleet come in sideways, and he told Massachusetts to go to hell; he'd be gone by morning, headed toward sunshine and hope. Still, he had his overpowering thirst, so he parked in the lot of the Safehouse and went on in before he even knew the name of the town in which he'd arrived. He strolled up to the bar and ordered a beer, and while he waited for the bartender to slide the foamy glass toward him, he turned to the right, and that's when he saw her, her golden hair shining, pure sunlight in the blue shadows of the roadhouse.

He knew that if he didn't walk away right then, just forget about the beer and his terrible thirst, he might not walk away at all. He had a decision to make in an instant, or else he could easily find himself trapped in some no-name Massachusetts town where November was one of the foulest months on the planet, with ribbons of ice and lead-blue nights and a gloom that spread out from Front Street to the highway, where the handful of pink roses Ethan had spied had been tied to the fence in memorium of the high school girls who had died.

Memories were not what Ethan was after that night, nor was it love he was looking for. He still recalls thinking he needed to head for the door. He told himself that while he was unzipping his jacket, while he placed his money down, while he grabbed his beer and walked straight to her.

I should be on my way to New Hampshire, he said to her. The lies came easy to him; it was the truth that was giving him so much trouble. *And I probably would be, but instead I'm standing here looking at you.*

Oh, really? What would make you do that if you've got someplace better to be?

When she'd laughed, he'd stood there at her mercy, unable and unwilling to turn away. Her hair was honey-colored and long, and her eyes were a clear, startling blue that could stop a man in his tracks. Ethan could tell she was feeling the same thing he was from the way she was staring back at him and from the color that rose in her cheeks. She wasn't shy or cool, and she didn't play games. The friend who was with her, Charlotte Kite, tugged at her sleeve and tried to get her to join some old high school pals and play a round of darts, but Jorie paid her no mind.

Go on without me, she'd told Charlotte, and Ethan knew there and then that she was the one. All his life he'd been closed up, like a locked door, like a cellar, and here it was at last, in the place where he'd least expected to find it, the key to everything he'd ever wanted, shining and golden. True love had appeared in front of him, in a roadhouse resembling scores he'd already passed by. He understood immediately that he would never leave this town again; no matter what its name might be, this was his address from this day on.

You don't think you'll regret standing here with me? He smiled at her then. Not the calculated grin he knew drove women crazy, but the real one, the one that showed his soul. *You don't think you'll kick yourself later for not staying with your friends?*

He peered through the knot of customers, strangers he couldn't care less about. A mass of faces, that's what they were to him, people he never wished to know. They were throwing darts and whooping it up, and although they were nearly the same age he was, they seemed ridiculously young to him. He might have looked good, a handsome well-built man in his twenties, but he was a hundred years old on this night, with shoes worn down from traveling, and only the last bits of cinder left for a soul. He gazed at this beautiful, innocent girl before him and he was well aware of how much he wanted her. All the same, he gave her one last chance to walk away. *Your friends look like they're having fun. You should probably go join them,* he told her, though it pained him to speak this sentiment aloud.

Jorie hadn't bothered to look behind her to see those young men and women she'd grown up with. She met his gaze instead. *They're not having fun.* She had moved closer to him, and he'd had to lean close in order to hear what she had to say over the noise of the place. *They just look like they are.*

For thirteen years he has lived in Massachusetts, the place he despises more than any other. He has tolerated a steel-blue sea that is so cold in July it can freeze a man's blood. He has put up with snowstorms and ice in December, with Augusts so muggy the humidity forces dogs to take shelter beneath the drooping, dusty hollyhocks, where they pant in the heat. In Maryland, hollyhocks lasted long into autumn, skies were blue until Christmas, and when snow fell it was soft and tender, coating both hedges and fields. Throughout the years, he has risen every morning and gone to work no matter the weather or the circumstance; he has mended fences and cleared the old oaks from the woods behind the high school so that the ball field could be added. He has brought turkeys down to the senior center on Thanksgiving and has walked through fire for his neighbors without a thought to his own safety, so that among the other volunteers at the firehouse he is known for his own brand of wild bravery. He has cried at the birth of his boy, he's given thanks to God, he's walked the leather off his shoes at night when he goes out to ramble through the neighborhood after Jorie is asleep and at peace with the world. He has wished on stars and on his child's life, but nothing takes the past away, he knows that now. The past stays with a man, sticking to his heels like glue, invisible and heartbreaking and unavoidable, threaded to the future, just as surely as day is sewn to night.

Later, when darkness has fallen and his neighbors are out on their porches, gazing at the starry sky, thankful for the lives they lead, he will be in a cell that measures twelve by fourteen feet. He will be sitting on the edge of the hard bed with the harsh taste of regret rising in his throat. He can feel his loneliness already, so it is doubly painful when he takes his wife in his arms. He is a passionate man, but never before has he given her everything in one kiss, completely and utterly, his heart, his life, his soul. As for Jorie, she loves him in a way she never imagined possible. She would be here in his place, if such a bargain were possible. If allowed, she would never view the doves in her garden or spoon ice cream into a bowl on a summer day; she would never see her son's face again if that's what it took to keep her husband safe.

Dave Meyers opens the door to politely remind them that Ethan's time is up. Ethan begs for five more minutes, and because Dave is a decent man, he gives in to this last request. It's all the time Ethan has to spit out the words that have been caught in his throat like a bone, and perhaps that's just as well. Every year it has been harder to keep the words down; they have twisted into a fishhook that has served to keep him silent and bleeding at the very same time.

Jorie looks at her husband, afraid for what is to come when he goes down before her, on bended knee. All at once she knows that they are only at the beginning of their sorrow. Her beautiful hair is knotted, and her face has no color. She vows that nothing he can tell her will make a difference; nothing will change the way she feels inside. He needn't explain anything, he needn't speak, but Ethan has to get these words out or he'll bleed to death. He tells her the truth, and the way he sees it, the truth is a simple thing: he is not the same man anymore. Yes, that's his name on the warrant from Maryland, the one he was born and raised with, but if he were to drive by his younger self, hitchhiking on the road beside fields of red clover, he'd pass that boy right by. He wouldn't recognize that selfish individual who thought he was entitled to anything he wanted, who whistled as he walked through fields of lettuce and soybeans and corn on the night he killed a girl, stopping only to change his clothes and to gather a handful of strawberries, which were so ripe and so delicious every bite only served to remind him of how good it was to be alive.

Two

Blackbird

ON THE ANNIVERSARY OF my father's death, I went out to the garage with three black candles, a lighter I had stolen from Rosarie, and a photograph of my father taken when he was so handsome and young no one would guess fate would be so cruel to him. Last year at this time the weather had been bad, muggy and overcast, but tonight you could see every star, you could spy Venus looking back down at you, like a ruby in the sky. It was such a beautiful night I found myself hoping for things no one should ever ask for. Ever since last summer, I'd had only one wish, and it burned within me until it was the only thing I felt or knew or wanted.

My father was the vice-principal of the Ella Monroe School, which is why there's a bronze plaque with his name on it outside the building, and why my mother won't go there anymore, not even last spring, when she was called in by the acting vice-principal, Mr. Percy. I'd had some trouble with several girls in my class who had offered their opinions about the way my father died and then weren't pleased with my reaction. I could be pretty vicious when I had to be, more than most people might expect. But my mother refused to come in for a conference, and in the end, Mr. Percy had no recourse but to meet her at Kite's Bakery, where they drank coffee and never got around to discussing my poor social development and the way I'd thrown certain individuals' notebooks into the toilet.

Mr. Percy could have no more given my mother another dose of bad news than he could have slapped her in the face. After that meeting, he never called again. He understood that my mother was willing to do just about anything to bypass the school and that plaque with my father's name on it. She would circle around to Hamilton and drive back on the service road that runs parallel to the highway, just to avoid the vicinity. She still had not ordered the memorial for my father's grave, and we all knew why: she couldn't bring herself to see his name written in stone. Some people believe that if you don't open your eyes to sorrow and you don't talk about it, you can pretend it never happened. You can go on about your business and not even notice that a year has gone by, time enough for there to be nothing left except heartbreak and bones.

When I went into the garage on the anniversary of my father's passing, I didn't bother to turn on the light. I wasn't afraid, not of anything in the world beyond ours at any rate. Last summer, my father showed me every constellation in the summer sky, including the rising scorpion, which stung everything in its path, man and beast alike. He showed me that courage wasn't simple. The final weeks of his life were spent lying down, in bed or on the couch or in his hospital room. He was fading, disappearing into the white sheets and the piles of pillows. He was evaporating right before our eyes. After a while, he seemed like half of himself, but that half still loved me.

I was trying to learn how to play the recorder back then, and I spent hours practicing beside his bed. His eyes shone whenever he watched me, even though I was terrible and gave up the recorder soon afterward. I couldn't even look at a recorder anymore, and my grandmother sent a note to the music teacher to excuse me from participating in class. I sat in the cafeteria while everyone else was practicing, covering my ears and thinking about my father, but I couldn't go backward in time past his illness. I was having trouble remembering the person he used to be before he was sick, or even conjure up what he looked like when we used to go skating together and he would lift me up into the falling snow until we were covered with crystals and our breath turned to ice whenever we laughed out loud.

Tonight, it was hot, starry and blistering and

clear as could be. Most people in town would surely turn on their air conditioners in order to get a decent night's sleep, except for Rosarie, who believed recycled air is bad for the complexion, and Ethan Ford, because the last town referendum voted down air-conditioning the jail. Usually, the week of July Fourth in Monroe is great fun, with fire-works set off in the high school field fol-lowing a cookout and a parade along Front Street, the best part of which is when the fire trucks turn their hoses on the crowd and spray everyone with water. But this year, everything was different. The firemen decided not to be in the parade, out of respect for Ethan Ford, and Collie and I didn't bother to go, which was probably a big mistake. Instead, I convinced him to visit his father. Looking back, I realize I should have known better. Collie didn't want to go and I could tell from his expression that he was scared when I brought up the subject. I should have let it be, but I had the idea that if Collie saw his father, his spirits would lift and he'd be back to his old self. As it was, Collie was hardly talking. He had a funny look in his eye, like he didn't believe in anything. You'd say something simple to him, such as, *I'm starving* or *Let's go swimming,* and he'd look blank, as if he wasn't speaking the same language anymore. Once, I saw him throw a rock at one of the reporters posted in Cindy Gleason's driveway, and although I could easily picture myself taking such a course of action, it was the sort of thing Collie Ford would never do, at least not before this summer.

The truth was, I had my own selfish reasons for wanting Collie to see his father. I wanted to make sure I hadn't made a mistake in reporting Ethan Ford the way I had. Innocent men are punished each and every day, and I didn't want to be the cause of someone spending the rest of his life in jail for no reason other than my own stupidity.

Come on, I said to Collie. *I'm sure he'll explain everything to you. Somebody probably called in to report him, and at this point they regret it like crazy.*

But for someone so good-natured, Collie wasn't that easy to convince. *I don't know. My mother said she'd take me to see him when things settled down. If they ever do.*

He told me how his mother locked herself in her room at night so he wouldn't hear her crying, but he heard her anyway, and that lately he couldn't get to sleep until the sun began to rise. When I heard how bad things were, I felt like the worst liar on earth. I felt like I was the criminal. What I'd done didn't seem any different from pulling the switch on the train tracks, and now no one would ever know what path the Fords' lives might have taken if I hadn't seen him on TV and made that call. I waited for Collie to say something more, maybe to curse whoever turned his father in, but he didn't say anything, and after a while, the moment when I might have admitted my part in his father's arrest passed. In an instant, the opportunity to confess was gone, down the well, falling fast into unreachable waters. I thought about the way it was when you swam across Lantern Lake and tried to call to someone on the other shore, how your voice drifted up and disappeared into the treetops, how you might as well have no voice at all.

If nothing else, you'll feel better seeing him. Wouldn't your mother be glad if she knew he'd explained everything to you? The real killer is probably wandering around Maryland right now knocking on people's front doors. We could probably help, you know. We could put out fliers or something. We could do something to get him out.

I guess I was convincing, because after a while Collie said, *Let's go,* and we took our bikes and went along the service road. All those orange lilies were blooming, thousands of them perched along the highway like a flock of tangerine-colored birds. It was hot and the heat whipped across our faces, and Collie let me lead the way, like he always does. We rode hard and fast, suddenly in a hurry to be somewhere. On the other side of the chain-link fence there was the highway that led to New Hampshire and Maine, and the cars speeding by threw bits of black gravel into the steamy air. I thought about all those people headed somewhere and how there were some of us who never got to where they wanted to be. I wished my father and I had driven to Maine last year and had sat on the edge of a lake to watch the stars. I wished we'd had one more day together. That's all.

When we got to where the county offices were, near the end of King George's Road, we left our bikes locked to a tree, since we figured if there were any criminals in Monroe, they'd probably be somewhere in this vicinity. This is where people went if they had a speeding ticket or if they'd been caught with marijuana, like Brendan Derry was last year, but it was also the place you came to if you needed a marriage license or a permit to expand the deck in your backyard. The buildings looked the same out here, the jail and the courthouse and town hall. We stood staring at the white concrete blocks, framed by hawthorns and maples and shady linden trees. You could hear the parade if you listened carefully. All those kids in my music class were playing their recorders like crazy, and the sound made me want to put my hands over my ears. Collie's face had a funny look to it. He shaded his eyes and watched some crows cross the horizon. He was sunburned, and his hair was so blond it was almost white.

What's wrong? I said.

I don't like it here, he told me, and, actually, I felt a chill myself. The sky was still blue, but the day was fading, and something was making a whispering noise. It was the hawthorns above us that sounded so strange, the way their leaves crackled in the heat, as if they were made of paper, and wouldn't last another day. I started to think this visit was a bad idea; we'd definitely miss the cookout at the high school, and we probably wouldn't get to the field in time for the fireworks either, but it was too late to turn back. Dusk was falling, and there was a violet haze hanging over the highway. When I swallowed my throat hurt, but I acted like it was the most normal thing in the world for Collie to be visiting his father in jail.

I've been in there, and there's nothing to be scared of. It was true; my grandmother and I had brought Rosarie here last month to take her road test, which she had promptly failed for the third time even though the motor vehicles clerk couldn't take his eyes off her. *They're just some stupid office buildings,* I assured Collie.

And yet the closer I got to the county buildings, the worse I felt inside. I felt faint, the way Rosarie gets when she has her headaches. Once we were through the door, we followed the signs to the secured annex, which is what they called the jail. There were two guards there, and they told me I couldn't go with Collie. I'd have to wait in the hall on a bench. Collie looked panicked, but he didn't say anything when one of the officers took him down to the jail. He looked like he wanted to turn and run, but he didn't, because that's not the kind of person Collie is. It's the kind of person I am, though; for two cents I would have run all the way home, and I was dizzier than ever. I felt like I'd ruined so many people's lives, I couldn't even keep count anymore. I couldn't even breathe, not without feeling there was a knife in my chest.

Out in the hallway, I put my head between my knees and when a woman from the motor vehicles department peered out of her office to ask if I was all right, I said no. I begged her for a paper bag to breathe into, because that's what Rosarie does when she gets this way. Unfortunately, I only felt worse after breathing into the paper bag. I am usually easily embarrassed, but right then I would have stretched out on the tile floor, so paralyzed by my own actions I could no longer move; if they wanted to get rid of me, they'd have to carry me out. I guess I was thinking about the fact that my father waited until the day after July Fourth to do what he did. Even then, he was trying his best not to ruin things for us any more than he already had. But the truth was, it was worse this way. I knew that the whole time I was watching fireworks last year, dud after dud in the humid air, my father was counting the hours until he could be released.

When Collie came back, he looked awful. He looked worse than I felt, so I got off the bench and followed him down the hall, and I didn't say a word. Outside, it was nearly dark, but still hot. In spite of the temperature, Collie seemed frozen. He dug his hands into his pockets, and his lips were pinched and blue. It was as though he'd been trapped in a freezer the whole time I'd been sitting on the bench in the hallway trying my best to breathe. I had to stop myself from reaching out and touching him to test if he felt as cold as he looked.

What did your father say? I asked.

Collie glared at me and he made a strange sound in his throat, as though something was supposed to be funny, only it wasn't. He didn't seem like himself. Not one bit. He turned away from me and wiped his eyes with the tail of his shirt. I knew I had made a big mistake in talking him into coming here, and that he might never forgive me. All the words I had inside that I could have used to tell him how sorry I was drifted away before they'd been spoken. That's what it's like when true silence comes between two people. Hot and empty and hopeless. Collie pulled the lock off his bike, and he didn't even say good-bye; he swooped across the parking lot, then pedaled as fast as he could, only he wasn't going in the direction of where we lived. He was going out toward the highway. He was riding like a crazy person, and when he reached the fence, he sort of crashed into it, then he got up and left his bike where it was and he climbed over the fence. He jumped down into the tall grass, and two mourning doves started and flew out of the brambles, higher and higher, and then I couldn't see Collie anymore. One minute I was watching him, and the next, he was gone.

I was wearing a black blouse that I'd bor-rowed from Rosarie because I had thought it made me look older and a little less ugly, but now the cloth felt like needles. It was prickly against my skin. I felt as if I should be burned at the stake, or banished, or cooked in hot oil. Everything I did was wrong, even when I tried to do what was right. I got on my bike and went over to the service road that trailed the highway. You couldn't hear anything but cars over there. The sound drowned out your thoughts, and maybe that was just as well. I looked through the fence, but Collie had disappeared and all I could see was a steady stream of traffic and the green borders of grass on either side of the asphalt.

I kicked out some of the dents in Collie's bike, enough to allow the wheels to roll; then I walked both our bikes home, although it hurt my arms to do so. By now, stray Roman candles were being set off in backyards and along the lakeshore; the echo of celebrations rumbled across the sky, leaving trails of ashy fire. It was so hot, and I had to walk clear across town, so by the time I got home I was drenched with sweat. I stood under the sprinkler my grandmother had switched on to water the faltering perennial garden my father had planted a few years ago, back when we thought we had all the time in the world. I snapped off two of the flowers that had managed to bloom and kept them for later. I went upstairs, dripping water over the carpets, and when I got to my room I pulled off my clothes. I stared into the mirror and I didn't even recognize myself. My arms and legs were too long, and because of the way my hips stuck out you could see my bones. I wanted to look the way I did when my father was still here, but I wasn't that person anymore.

I left Collie's bike on our front lawn, but he didn't come for it. I kept an eye out for him as I ate the dinner my grandmother had made for me, but he never showed up. I knew that Collie's father hadn't told him what he wanted to hear, and maybe I should have been glad that I hadn't turned in an innocent man, but I wasn't. I wished I could ask my sister what to do, but Rosarie was out with Brendan Derry. She had bragged that Brendan had worked overtime in order to rent a boat and take her out on the lake to watch fireworks. Poor Brendan might be having the time of his life right now, but the only thing I could think of was how when she told him it was over, he'd come here in the evenings; he'd stand on the corner of Maple and Sherwood and stare at her window, hoping for a glimpse of something he'd never have again, not that he'd had Rosarie in the first place.

Everyone expected me to go to the fireworks with Collie, the way I always did, but when I called him his mother told me he was sick and had already gone to bed. I didn't really care about the fireworks anyway; I was too old for them and I knew it. Still, it surprised me to find how much I hurt inside, as if I were made out of glass and pieces of me would just go on shattering until no one could put me together again.

I went out to the garage after my grandmother had gone to bed. I didn't have to worry that my mother might notice me sneaking around. She had started working again, back at the admitting room at Hamilton Hospital. People said she was the calmest woman you'd ever met and that she was made for the job. You could walk into the ER bleeding buckets, you could have your bones sticking through your flesh, and my mother would just ask for your insurance information and page the emergency nurse. She dealt with tragedy the way other people's mothers cut up apple pie. Hillary Meyers experienced this firsthand when she toppled off the balance beam in gym class last year; she cracked her jaw so badly that her teeth were falling out and she had to hold up a towel in order to catch them, but she said my mother didn't act any differently than she used to when I was in second grade and Hillary was in third and she used to come over for lunch, back when she and I were friends.

Try to keep the blood on the towel, dear, my mother told her. Hillary stopped panicking then; she figured her injury must not be too bad since my mother was so calm, even though her own father, the sheriff, who was used to car crashes and holdups, was sitting beside her and crying. It wasn't until Hillary looked at her battered face in the mirror the next day that she realized how awful her injury had been. I wasn't surprised at my mother's response. After all, she'd appeared to be completely unruffled throughout my father's illness. She took him to his doctor appointments and sat with him during his endless chemo treatments and never once let on how bad it was. She must have known from the very start there was no hope, but she never let anything negative show through, a skill she had probably perfected in the ER.

We're going to visit our friends at the hospital

today, she'd announce, as if they were going to the market or the flower shop, when the truth of the matter was, my father couldn't breathe anymore, he couldn't eat or talk to us or even open his eyes in the glare of the sunlight.

Don't be noisy, Pop's sleeping, my mother would tell us, and we'd be assured that our father was resting, gathering his strength. For the longest time, I thought everything was improving because of the tone of my mother's voice, I trusted her completely. Then one day I opened the door to their room when she said he was napping, and I saw him lying there, eyes open, lost in pain, and I knew not to believe her anymore.

My mother and Rosarie had been out shopping at the mall in Hamilton, and so Rosarie was the one who opened the garage door when they got home. You could hear her screaming no matter where you were. My grandmother and I were unpacking boxes in the attic, and my grandmother cut off the tip of her little finger with the sharp paring knife she'd been using to slice through masking tape. Collie told me he was in his yard helping his mother in the garden, and when he heard the sound of Rosarie's cry, he knew someone had died. He stood by the blueberry bushes and hoped it wasn't me. Now it's his mother who stands in the garden every night. I can see her from my window up on the second floor. I can look out and watch her crying and know it's my fault.

Making that phone call is just one mistake

in a long line of errors. I should have known better than to talk Collie into seeing his father. I should have known my father was dying. You wouldn't even guess anyone was buried where my father is; there's no marker, only an unbroken square of grass and a border of lilies. My mother insisted on these lilies after my father died, and it was the one and only time I've ever seen her have a fight with a stranger. She informed the people at the cemetery that she wanted a border put in, and she didn't care how much it cost. But it wasn't so easily done. We were advised that the families of the other individuals interred in that area would have to agree to the planting, and that was when my mother lost it. She told the funeral director to go to hell. She hoped that one day someone he loved would be denied one final bit of respect and then he would know how it felt to be left with nothing. My mother sat down in the dirt where my father had been buried and she cried so many tears I sometimes think the lilies that grow there now arose from her sorrow, and that the petals last no more than a day because they also must fall, like her tears.

I brought along everything I needed for the anniversary when I climbed out Rosarie's window. Up above, the sky exploded with color. The earth was shaking every time fireworks went off at the field, and black ribbons of dust fell across rooftops. I had several strands of hair and an envelope full of nail clippings with me and the two flowers I'd picked earlier that my father had tended. I had looked through the boxes in my mother's bedroom closet until I found my father's hairbrush, and a photograph that was taken so long ago my father didn't look much older than Rosarie.

It was still so hot that the concrete path across our yard burned my bare feet; june bugs drifted through the air. I took a deep breath before I slipped inside the garage. I didn't turn on the light and after I closed the door I went directly to the place where it happened. I lit the black candles and set out all the ingredients I brought with me: the strands of my father's hair taken from his hairbrush twisted together with mine, the nail cuttings, the watch I took from his night table drawer, the photograph from when he was young. I wasn't certain that I could bring my father back to me, but at least I could hear his voice. I imagined him as hard as I could. I thought about us standing on the porch gazing at stars and remembered how he looked sleeping in his bed, with his blankets as white as snow. I still didn't want to believe that a person's whole life could change in an instant, in the time it took to walk out to the garage.

All of a sudden, something seemed to be happening. I could hear the scrape of wood as the door was pushed back. I hadn't expected to have any success until after midnight, when July Fourth became the fifth, and the anniversary officially began, but it was happening now. I closed my eyes and tried to steady myself, but my heart was racing. *Are you here?* I said.

My voice sounded strange. It was thick and hot, the way it was on the day he died. I heard somebody coming toward me, and I hoped I hadn't upset the natural order of things, calling to my father the way I had, and then I realized I didn't care what I upset. I just wanted my father back. I wanted him now.

When I opened my eyes, I felt dizzy. In some strange way, I felt a shudder of hope, as though I were a true believer. I wanted a world without end, a new order of things in which my father could walk through the door of our garage even though I knew he was gone. I wanted him to tell me his pain was nothing more than a memory and that all he wanted was for me to be happy, but that's not what I got. It was my sister who'd come into the garage, and now she stared at me as though I'd lost my mind.

"Hey, dumb bunny." My sister sat across from me on the floor. Candlelight glimmered over her face. "Are you trying to burn the place down? Or are you just trying to prove that you should be locked up for your own good?"

I still had the chills even though it hadn't been my father who'd appeared to me. I had almost felt him near. I'd almost heard his voice. The candles flickered, and I felt a sharp ache in my chest.

"I thought you were at the lake with Brendan." I sounded guilty and breathless, as if I'd been caught doing something unforgivable.

"I was, until he bored me to death. I decided I'd rather drown then spend another minute with him."

I realized that my sister was dripping wet. She told me she had jumped out of the rowboat and had swum to shore; she'd laughed as Brendan called out for her across Lantern Lake, not caring how he humiliated himself.

"It's a good thing I got back here." Rosarie wrung out her dark hair, and green drops of water fell dangerously close to the lighted candles. The fire hissed and smelled like the lake where my father and I liked to skate as soon as the ice was thick enough. We'd wait for November, and rejoice over December; we'd long for January on hot nights like this one. "What exactly is it you think you're doing?" my sister asked.

"None of your business. And even if I did tell you, you wouldn't understand."

"You poor, pathetic creature." My sister shook her head. "Of course I understand. You're celebrating the anniversary of your father's suicide. That is sick. Do you know that? That is one of the saddest things I've ever heard."

"Why don't you go away and never come back?" I could feel the aching in my chest get even sharper, but I didn't care. "Then everyone would be happy."

When I started crying, Rosarie didn't say anything. I bent my head, hoping she wouldn't see, but my shoulders were shaking, and she knew what I was doing. What difference did it make if she teased me for being so stupid? What I wanted, I could never have, and after a while I didn't care what my sister saw. I just cried.

"I once read about a woman who lost this man she loved, and she tried to bring him back by sewing his bones together. You know where she wound up?" Rosarie said knowingly. Even her eyebrows were beautiful, arched and black like crows. "The nuthouse."

I guessed she was referring to the psychiatric hospital out past the lake. I'd never really thought about people being there, trapped behind the stone walls. I wondered how they felt on hot nights like this one. I wondered if they'd lost people, too.

Before I could say anything, Rosarie took a cigarette from her purse and lit up. After she exhaled a plume of smoke, she put the hot match to her skin and looked at me, defiant. Even through my tears I could see the red mark she was making was only one of many. There was a long line of burns up and down the inside of her arm, in the place where the skin was most sensitive.

"Amazing, isn't it?" she said to me. "I don't get hurt."

"Maybe you're the nut case," I ventured. Who smokes after her father dies of cancer? Who puts hot matches on her flesh and laughs when you call her names, the way my sister was doing? "What made you come in here anyway? I thought it was too creepy for you."

"It's not so bad." Rosarie looked around with her big dark eyes. "For a death trap."

117

Everything about her was sharp on the out-side. Her fingernails, which she'd painted cherry red. Her perfect, white teeth. Most of the time she was fearless, but the one thing that had scared Rosarie all this year was the garage. If somebody needed something, fur-niture polish, for instance, or a screwdriver to fix the storm door, and they wanted Rosarie to go get it, they could forget about it. My mother was the very same way. Throughout the winter, our car had been left in the driveway, and every time it snowed we'd had to dig it out; sometimes it would take hours, but Rosarie and my mother didn't seem to care. Nothing could force them to open the garage door. Now Rosarie seemed to have gotten over her fear, and she looked even more smug than usual.

"I got a ride home from the lake with a reporter," she told me. "Once I got away from Brendan." She shivered at the mention of his name. "Can you believe that Brendan actually thought I was going to run off and marry him?"

"You got a ride with a stranger?"

"Who happens to work for the *Boston Globe*. He asked me my opinion about Ethan Ford's arrest. Everything I said will be in the paper tomorrow."

"Who cares about what you have to say?"

"Well, he sure did. And he took my photo. He said to look for it on the Metro page. I just wish my hair hadn't been wet."

I had always thought my sister had no opin-ions, other than ones that had to do with herself. It must have been the photograph that had convinced her to talk to the reporter, the notion that everyone in town would be gazing at her face while they had their morning coffee.

"I told them an innocent man had been locked up and that the American system of justice needed to be completely overhauled."

She was serious. "You know nothing about the American system of justice," I reminded her. I would have laughed if I hadn't then recalled the look on Collie's face after he'd seen his father. For no reason I started thinking about the mirror in the Fords' front room and how gray the glass was, like a lake with no bottom, a river with no shore.

"The point is, I'm going to be in the newspaper." My sister could not have been more pleased with herself. "So whether or not I know what I'm talking about doesn't really make a difference, does it?"

I had always thought my sister was the smart one; now I had to rethink my assessment. "Everything makes a difference."

"Oh, yeah?" Rosarie blew cigarette smoke upward, into the rafters, and the air turned blue. She eyed the ingredients I'd spread out on the concrete. "Well, tell me what difference this crap is supposed to make."

"It's to call him back," I admitted.

I thought Rosarie would laugh, I thought she'd tell me I was an idiot and needed to be locked up and not released until I was a functioning adult, but instead she just said, "Watch this." She held her hand above one of the candles. She kept it there for longer than I would have thought possible. The flame flickered and spit and turned the center of her palm a sooty charcoal color, but she didn't flinch. Maybe she was right. Maybe she didn't feel pain.

"I have news for you," Rosarie informed me once she'd taken her hand out of the fire. Anyone else would have been crying; they would have been searching for some salve or a pail of cool water. "He's not ever coming back, Kat. You know that, right?"

Maybe it was the fact that she said my name, something she almost never did, or the superior expression on her face, but I just got mad then. I reached over, even though the candles singed my sleeves, and before I could stop myself, I slapped her.

Rosarie gasped and put a hand to her reddened cheek. Even I couldn't believe what I'd done. Rosarie sat on her heels, too shocked to hit me back.

"Why did you do that?"

I shook my head. In all honesty, I didn't know. I expected my sister to pull my hair the way she usually did when she wanted to hurt me, but instead she came around and sat next to me while I finished crying. Then she waited while I gathered up my worthless ingredients and tossed everything in the trash. I blew out the candles and threw them away, too. We pulled open the sliding door that no one had used since my father died, and when we did, nothing unusual happened. It was just like every other garage door in town. We could smell cut grass even though no one had mowed our lawn all summer. We could see the moon. There on the lawn were the two bikes I'd walked home from the county offices. Rosarie had a last cigarette while I brought Collie's bike into the garage, just to make sure no one stole it. If I lost one more thing in my life, I'd probably disappear myself.

I propped Collie's bike up against the wall, then went back to stand beside Rosarie. I was thinking about Collie, about how good he was and how fixed his mouth had looked when he rode away from me toward the highway, as if he didn't want me in his life anymore.

"Do you think anyone ever winds up with the first person they fall in love with?" I asked my sister.

"You'd better hope not. Look at Mom and Dad. Childhood sweethearts." Rosarie shook her head, and I could smell the smoke and the lake water in her hair. "What a mistake."

"They were happy."

"Operative word?" My sister shimmered in her wet clothes and her face was pale. "*Were.*"

"How many times have you been in love?"

I had never dared to ask a question like this before, but tonight Rosarie seemed to have forgotten who she was talking to.

"Too many times. And every one has been a big disappointment." Rosarie seemed softer than usual. She had already crossed Brendan

Derry off her list, and after spending half the night alone in his rented rowboat, he surely knew he was history. All the same, having her photograph in the newspaper wouldn't begin to satisfy my sister. Even being beautiful wasn't enough for her. "Nobody loves me the way I want to be loved."

But I knew that someone had loved us both so much he hadn't wanted us to see him suffer. He had loved us completely, as much as a man could love anyone, and what had it brought us? Nothing but sorrow and emptiness and heartache. By then, my sister must have completely forgotten who I was, because she draped her arm around me. We stood there together, like people who didn't hate each other, grateful for the dark. We'd both missed the fireworks and everything else, so we looked up at the constellations my father had taught us a few summers ago, when there were record sightings of meteor showers. Back then, we brought blankets out to the grass and stayed out past midnight, each of us trying to be the first to see Antares, the red heart of Scorpio.

"Make a wish," Rosarie said as we stared at the stars, but I'd already made mine and it hadn't come true.

"No, you," I told her.

Rosarie smiled thoughtfully. "All right," she said.

She really was the most beautiful girl on earth, especially on this night. You'd never even guess she had all those burns on her arm or that she was trying so hard to feel something. She closed her eyes and her breathing settled, and I could tell she was also wishing for something she would never have, and that no matter how beautiful she was, she wasn't any different than me.

The Labyrinth

COLLIE FORD IS AMONG those few individuals in town who have chosen to ignore July despite its many temptations, the fine, cloudless mornings and lazy, expectant afternoons. There will always be those contrary residents who abhor good weather and couldn't care less about the buttery sunlight, or the cicadas calling from the hedges, or the long days that wash blue and bluer still as the day turns into evening. Hannah Phillips, for instance, who runs the coffee shop, has a sun allergy that keeps her inside even on her afternoons off, and when she does venture out, she's always well protected by a baseball hat and a long-sleeved shirt, no matter how high the temperature. Alarmed by how dizzy she becomes during the heat of the day, Mrs. Gage gardens only in the mornings. Mark Derry hasn't had a moment of free time all month, especially now that he's taken it upon himself to make sure Ethan's jobs are completed, hiring a jack-of-all-trades named Swift from over in Hamilton to finish up the carpentry. As a boy, Mark lived for summers; he was a champion swimmer, but lately he can't remember what it feels like to dive into the cool waters of Lantern Lake. He's jealous of his son Brendan, and the rest of the teenaged boys in town, who are ready and willing to tempt fate by jumping in headfirst from atop the highest rocks, ignoring their parents' warnings of how easy it would be to drown in these waters before anyone heard their panicked cries for help. Bill Shannon, the postman, has always prided himself on facing any sort of weather, from the stormy to the sizzling hot, has been warned by his doctor about the high risk of skin cancer for mail carriers, and nowadays Bill has taken to hiding from the sun at noon, making himself comfortable on one of the benches across from the coffee shop, reading the newspaper and figuring that people in town will just have to wait for their mail delivery until the cooler part of the day.

Collie Ford is among this group who've been searching out dark, empty places. He's been avoiding people with nearly the same alacrity as the voles in his mother's garden dodge the traps set out among the strawberries. Collie has been spending much of his time at the library on Liberty Avenue. In the old building built of stone and ruddy bricks, a July afternoon spent curled up in one of the leather armchairs in the reading room is no different from a sleety February evening. Most often,

Collie stations himself behind the periodicals rack, where the librarian, Grace Henley, has placed a huge fish tank on display. As Collie watches the gills of the angelfish moving in and out, he wishes he were underwater as well, so deep no one would ever find him. He wishes he were a thousand miles from Monroe, Massachusetts, a place he has quickly come to despise. He could not be far enough away, mile upon mile, league upon league. What he wouldn't give to be walking on the moon right now, running on its pale, cruel surface, stones in his pockets and in his shoes, stone heart and lungs and limbs.

Collie doesn't want to talk to anyone, but when he looks out the window, tall and arched with bubbly green glass fixed within the sashes, he spies Kat Williams. He can tell Kat is waiting for him; she's sitting with her back up against the oldest apple tree in the village, a rare Westfield Seek-No-Further, which always blooms months after all the other trees in town and has grown on this spot since 1790, planted a hundred years before the cornerstones of the library were set down. These Westfield apples are tough-skinned, good for nothing other than the most humble of pies, and every October, rotten fruit rains down upon the library's lawn, much to the librarian's dismay. Local boys use the cores to pelt one another, and many of the old windows have been broken by such hijinks, the green glass splintering into thousands of pieces. Grace Henley always places the offending applescruff on display atop her desk, along with a jar used to collect funds for a new window, which is why the light streaming into the stacks is clear and sharp on some afternoons, and at other times gauzy and dense, as if water were pouring in through the windows, siphoned from the muddy bottom of Lantern Lake.

Collie has been thumbing through an old edition of *The Boy's King Arthur,* illustrated by N. C. Wyeth, but now, seeing Kat on the lawn, his reverie is shattered. It doesn't matter that Kat has always been his one true friend. He doesn't want a friend anymore, that's the problem. He wants his aloneness; he wears it like armor. He used to pride himself on his honesty, but something inside him has changed. Instead of returning the book to the shelf, Collie slides it up the front of his shirt, like a common thief. The spine of the book feels cool against him. The pages whisper as he holds the book close to his chest, right to the place where it hurts most of all, the place, he imagines, where his heart used to be.

Luckily for Collie, he left his bike by the back door of the library; he can slip away unnoticed. He shoots outside, then gets on his bike and pedals fast, the heat waves slapping against him, the sharp sunlight nearly blinding him. He'd had to go into Kat's garage to get his bike this morning, and that hadn't been easy. He'd held his breath, run in, grabbed it, and run back into the sunlight; but as it turns out, the damage he did to the wheels makes the bike wobble uncertainly and the metal rims dig into the front tire. Still, the bike allows him to round the corner before Kat can look up, her view obscured by the last of the pink-tinged blossoms on the apple tree. As he races down Liberty Street, Collie has the strangest thought: he will cut down that apple tree. The idea comes to him all at once, and as it does, it seems as though he was predestined for this singular act of destruction. He can hear the tree falling inside his mind. He can imagine how the bark will shudder, how the splinters will pierce his hands. For some reason, this venture seems as right to him as it is wrong. It feels like the only thing that can clear away the facts that are stuck in his head, the words his father said that won't leave him alone, no matter how hard he tries not to think.

Collie's chest has been hurting ever since his father confessed to him; the heaviness that has settled inside burns and makes him want to run away to someplace frozen and blue, but it also makes him want to chop something down to its roots. Even if he tried to be the person he was before he went to see his father, it would be impossible. That person is gone. As Collie rides his bike through town, he isn't thinking about fishing at the lake or playing baseball with his team, the way he might have been only a few weeks earlier. He is thinking of his mother, locked in her bedroom, convinced he can't hear her crying. He thinks of the reporter who chased him this morning after he retrieved his bike from Kat's house and took off for the library.

I just want to talk to you, the reporter had shouted as he tried to keep up with Collie. *Hey, you little shit,* Collie had heard called out behind him as he'd ridden farther and farther away. *Slow down.*

He has been in flight ever since, and now as he avoids Kat Williams and swoops down Mayflower Street, taking the curb at top speed, Collie feels, for one brief moment, as though he is soaring through the sweet blue air. He hits the asphalt with a thud, then turns onto the dirt path that leads behind the high school in the direction of King George's Road. If he hadn't stopped to look out at the field, Kat never would have been able to catch up with him. The bike she's riding used to belong to Rosarie, until Rosarie announced it was too inferior for her to bother with. Kat, on the other hand, enjoys the bike, perhaps because she'd been with her father when he bought it. It had taken almost two hours before he'd finally settled on something he hoped Rosarie would like, but Rosarie hadn't been particularly pleased with his choice. *Three speeds?* was her only comment.

Kat, on the other hand, likes the way this bike chugs along. A person got to really see things if she wasn't racing through life. As she rounds the corner onto Mayflower, for instance, Kat notices there are cosmos in several of the yards, tall stalks of purple flowers abuzz with honeybees. As she approaches the high school, she sees a boy watching a baseball game. On closer inspection, that boy turns out to be Collie, and the sight of him makes Kat aware of her own pulse drumming in her ears. She pulls up next to Collie and leans forward, hooking her fingers though the meshing of the fence. She knows he's been avoiding her, so she doesn't look at him. She is trying her best not to scare him away. "Isn't that your team?" she asks mildly.

It is indeed the Bluebirds out in the field, down by a landslide in the fifth inning. Kat herself is not a team player. The only sport she could ever manage is ice skating, and this winter she couldn't even bring herself to do that. Every time she went down to the lake, she thought she saw her father, over by the bench where there were always oatmeal cookies and hot chocolate, where fathers knelt beside their children to help lace up skates.

On this hot and gorgeous July day, the Bluebirds are being slaughtered by the Braves from Hamilton; they haven't scored a single run. Perhaps the loss is unavoidable; though not showy, Collie has always been the most consistent player on the team. His father has spent thousands of hours with him in this very field, throwing ground balls and curve balls, but those hours are evaporating into shining and unrecognizable bits of time. Collie has already decided: he's never playing baseball again.

Kat appraises the Bluebirds. "They sure could use you. They're terrible."

"I don't care if they win or not."

"Did you see my sister's picture in the

newspaper?" Kat asks. "I don't understand why anyone would be interested in her opinion, but she looked great."

"I care even less about that than I do about baseball."

Collie can feel the sun on his head, his neck, his arms. He can smell grass and the rich, damp scent of the field. If his father was coaching today, he and Collie would be coming up with a strategy to turn the game around. *Swing to the right,* his father would say, or *Hit short and surprise them.* Collie thinks about King Arthur and how he tried so hard to be a good man, and how he'd been betrayed; how in the end, he had failed at everything he had tried to accomplish. Somewhere inside himself, Collie knows that he's taken the book from the library shelf to make sure no one else will be able to read this story; no one should be fooled into believing in a kind of honor that doesn't exist, not then and certainly not now.

Kat turns to tell Collie that the Bluebirds don't seem to know the first thing about winning, and when she does she sees that he's crying.

"Baseball is stupid, anyway." Kat's heart is pounding, and she has a metallic taste in her mouth. "Everything is stupid when you really think about it. People get up every day and they act like whatever they do is so important, but they're all just going to die in the end, so none of it matters."

"Shut up, Kat." Collie blinks and looks out over the field. He has broad shoulders and is a truly fast runner; he's a natural athlete, but now he seems folded up on himself.

As Kat Williams studies her friend, her pure, cold heart is breaking for him. People who are good are at risk, that's what she's figured out. She knows that Collie's father told him something that is too terrible to talk about. She has the feeling that people who've done what Ethan Ford did are sent away for a very long time. They don't come back until they can walk past a mirror and their reflection can be seen once again.

"Let's go swimming." Kat wants Collie to say yes so much her throat hurts. She wants to go backward in time, to the hour before she made that phone call. She wishes they were still eleven, or perhaps even ten. Rosarie has informed her that by the time seventh grade is over, Collie will no longer be her best friend. *You're crazy,* Kat told her sister, but Rosarie only smiled, sure of herself as could be. *Wait and see. He'll be wanting something more from you then.*

Maybe it's thinking about what Rosarie said that gives Kat an idea of how she might bring Collie back to her. She swallows hard. Once she says it, she knows there'll be no returning to who they used to be.

"We can go to the pool if you want. Or we could go to the lake." She lowers her voice, not that there's anyone who could possibly overhear. "I'll go in with no clothes if you do."

Collie glances at her, but his eyes seem flat. Any other boy would race Kat to the lake right then and there, he'd bind her to her promise and watch bug-eyed as she ran naked into the cold water. But Collie's not any boy, and Kat can see she hasn't managed to shock him or even to interest him. She hasn't managed anything at all.

"I don't think so." Collie's face looks different, older, somehow, and more pinched, as though her offer has disappointed him, as though disappointment is the only path he knows. "I'm going for a ride."

Kat understands he means alone. She knows where he goes when he leaves the library; she's followed him out to the end of King George's Road, past the hospital, to the abandoned house she herself showed him a few summers back. People don't come out here much, in part because the land abuts the psychiatric hospital. But anyone interested in local history knows this dilapidated house had once been the grandest in the county, with the land for miles around belonging to the Monroes, acres of Christmas apples and sugary Nonesuches and crinkly Blue Permains, pippins that are said to have skin the color of plums. But that was long ago, and none of the Monroe family remains, no matter how much acreage they owned; raccoons have taken up residence in the ruins, along with wood rats and voles. None of these creatures have frightened Collie away, however. He spends hours there, Kat knows, time he no longer wishes to spend with her. She can't bring herself to look at him when he turns his bike toward the road.

Instead, she stares straight ahead, at the dust rising when Jesse Meyers rounds third base, the first among his peers to do so. A hot breeze comes up to ruffle the leaves of the linden trees, and Kat shudders, then huddles against the fence. Some people say the dead can speak to you whenever the wind blows. *Listen carefully,* that's what people say. *Listen and you'll hear everything you need to know.*

Collie has hurried away without noticing that the book he filched from the library has fallen out of his shirt, tumbling onto the grass. Kat bends to retrieve it. She glances at the illustrations, then turns to the back of the book. It hasn't been checked out for over three months. Stealing is not like Collie; it's more the sort of thing Kat would do, so she tosses the book into the basket attached to her bike, an accessory Rosarie has always ridiculed as childish. The least she can do is take the blame for this one small act of thievery, even though she knows she'll never be able to make up for the hurt she's caused him.

Out in the field, Barney Stark has spied the children through the haze of floating milkweed. The sight of Collie biking away makes him feel like running to catch up so he can promise everything will turn out all right in the end. But this isn't a promise Barney is able to make, so he stays where he is, coaching third base, exactly as he has every Saturday for the last six years. This afternoon is different, of course, for Barney is coaching alone. He knew something irrevocable had happened in that moment when

Dave Meyers opened the door to his office and there Jorie was, sobbing, her hands covering her face, the sound of her wailing drawing them in, like a riptide. It was dark in the office, the shades drawn, the air murky. Ethan Ford had glanced over; his face was ashen and Barney had known what they were up against right then. Here before them stood a guilty man.

"Give me two minutes," Barney had begged Dave, and once Dave left them alone, he'd turned to Ethan. "Don't say anything. Do you hear me?"

Ethan shook his head. He had the clear, unworried countenance of a man who didn't understand the measure of his own actions. "I just told Jorie. Now I want to tell you."

"Yeah, well, don't. Don't say another word until you have proper counsel, because whatever you say can't be taken back, and I don't want to be in the position to have to testify against you." Barney had glanced over at Jorie, whose hands still covered her eyes. "Do yourself a favor," Barney said to his neighbor, a man he was beginning to wish he'd never met. "Keep your mouth shut."

Ethan has always done most of the coaching, and maybe that was why the Bluebirds have headed toward a losing streak ever since his incarceration. He was a man who had infinite patience, even with players who seemed constitutionally unfit to catch a ball. He'd go over basics, again and again, without ever losing his temper like some of the coaches you saw, browbeating eleven-year-olds every time

134

a ball was fumbled. Now they are on their own, and under Barney's guidance, the Bluebirds are failing. A mantle of gloom hangs over the field, and some of the players haven't attempted to catch the ball, even when a hit is headed straight toward them.

Barney's youngest daughter, Sophie, comes running over as the sixth inning approaches. Sophie is an upbeat kid and Barney's greatest joy, but today she seems wary and out of sorts. All the kids are in a bad humor, as a matter of fact, so at the end of the game, when they have lost and shaken the hands of their opponents, as Barney insists they do no matter how bitter their defeat, he gathers the players together in the bleachers.

"Most of you already noticed that Mr. Ford isn't here today," Barney says. It's getting near supper time, but the sky is still China blue and the temperature is as hot as it was at noon. Usually when Barney calls the team together he has to hush them a couple of times, maybe even threaten to call off next week's game until he has peace and quiet, but now they face him expectantly. They look so young and confused, Barney can hardly bring himself to go on. Most have already heard bits and pieces of rumors they can make little sense of, and Barney, more than anyone, knows the gossip will only get worse. "At the moment, Mr. Ford is having some legal difficulties that make it impossible for him to coach."

Joey Shaw raises his hand, and the sight of his earnest expression makes Barney want to turn around and jog down to the Safehouse, where, for once in his life, he might manage to get good and drunk. Instead, he nods to the boy. "Yes, Joe?"

"Will he still be our coach when he gets out of jail?"

Barney is walking the thin line between preparing these kids for the truth and protecting them, if even for one more day. Ethan Ford no longer has any chance to have bail set, let alone return to coaching Little League.

"We'll have to wait and see. In the meantime, we'll just play our best."

This answer satisfies no one, especially as the Bluebirds' best is nothing short of disastrous, but Barney dismisses his kids, telling them they played hard and honest, which is the most anyone can ask for.

"Everyone knows he's in jail for murder, Dad," Sophie says as they load the equipment into the trunk of the car. "Most people think he's innocent, but some people are waiting to hear all the facts before they make up their minds. They want to see how he pleads and what his alibi is."

"How does everybody know this?" Barney studies his daughter. Before long, she'll be going out on dates, and he'll have to worry about whom she's with on Saturday nights, the way he does with Kelly and Josie. His older girls have grown distant, more interested in their friends than in him, and he dreads the same thing happening with Sophie once she hits adolescence with full force.

136

"Everyone knows everything, Dad." Sophie sighs. She looks like her mother, especially when she's exasperated, but she has an empathy and a warmth her mother lacks, at least in relation to Barney. Sophie is one of those girls who has always seemed older than her age. Her brown hair is plaited into a single braid that falls past her waist and she has a lovely, serious face. "It's like when Kat Williams's father killed himself. You and Mom thought it was a big secret, but everyone knew. Even the little kids who were supposedly being shielded from the horrible news. They all knew."

"Little kids like you?"

"Dad!"

"Sorry." Barney opens the cooler he always brings to games and fishes out the last two root beers for them to gulp down as they watch the sky deepen into azure, then damson, then inkberry blue.

"I'm older than you think," Sophie says. "You should tell me when things happen to the people we know."

Barney mulls this over while he finishes his root beer. He wonders if she'll feel even more betrayed when she finds out he hasn't told her the whole truth. "Okay. I'll try not to keep you out of the loop."

"Does that mean you're going to tell me if he's guilty?" It's the question she and every other kid on the team want to ask, but Sophie is the only one with enough nerve to actually do so. Barney thinks of the way she looked when she was born, how tiny she'd been and how amazed he was that he could be party to the creation of something so perfect.

"Lawyer-client privilege." This way he's not lying to Sophie, at least not directly. "In other words: none of your beeswax."

They get into the Lexus, which Sophie thinks is ostentatious, a car Barney cares about far more than he should, especially when he runs into someone from high school out in the parking lot behind the courthouse.

"Like I said. You think I'm a baby." Sophie is huffy and refuses to talk to him as they drive home. But when they get to the house, she helps Barney unload the equipment, and they're horsing around by the time they're headed for the door, tossing a ball back and forth, each trying for more height with every throw, aiming for the branches of the crabapple tree they walk beneath on the way to the house.

The remains of a pizza and some salad have been left out on the kitchen counter. Barney eats standing up, bolting his food. More and more often, he finds that he feels like an intruder in his own home, and there are times when he has the sense that he's blundered into the wrong house, that he was never meant to live in the posh neighborhood of Hillcrest, and that the life he's been leading is an experiment of sorts. Mark Derry is still working on the bathroom, and there is a fine film of plaster dust everywhere, a small price to pay, his daughters insist, for another shower and tub. Still, the dust in the house and the pipes left on the front lawn remind Barney of the house he grew up in, a cramped ranch knocked down years ago when the county offices were built, a place he is more nostalgic for than he'd ever imagined possible.

Dana Stark comes into the kitchen when she hears the racket as Sophie takes some mugs from the cabinet, then slams the refrigerator door, having collected a bottle of root beer and a pint of vanilla ice cream so she can fix one of the brown cow floats her father always enjoys.

"What's happening with Ethan Ford?" Dana asks. She and Barney met in law school, and of the two, she was clearly the better student. Barney was surprised when she gave up working so soon after Kelly was born. Dana has an especially suspicious nature, which would have given her an edge had she chosen to practice law.

Barney nods to Sophie. "Don't you want to know if we won the game?"

Dana takes one look at her daughter's face; it's all she needs to determine that the Bluebirds have lost. "Better luck next time, kiddo."

"She's psychic," Sophie says with her mouth full. "Sees all. Knows all."

"Chew your food," Dana suggests. "Otherwise, I predict you'll choke."

"Fred Hart's coming down from Boston in the morning. He's taking the case," Barney tells his wife.

When Sophie takes her dishes to the sink and is out of earshot, Dana says, "I'm glad it won't be you. It could be a real stinking mess if he happens to be guilty."

"I heard that," Sophie calls. "I heard every word."

After dinner, Barney gets back in his car, having decided to call on Jorie. But the truth is, he's hoping he'll run into Charlotte Kite again. Maybe if he saw her he could forget what he knows to be true about Ethan, at least for a little while. Funny how often he spies Charlotte in the neighborhood, and tonight it happens again; Charlotte is backing out of her driveway, so Barney slows to below the speed limit, then follows her car down Hilltop, through the posts that mark the entrance to the neighborhood, cruising behind her all the way across Front Street. At the stop sign on the corner of Maple and Westerly, Charlotte reaches out her window and signals for Barney to pull alongside. She has had a hellish day, first meeting with her doctor, then spending hours waiting to have her arm pricked, over and over, in the pre-surgery unit of Hamilton Hospital. She has blue circles under her eyes and her auburn hair is carelessly pulled away from her face. All the same, Barney Stark smiles when his car pulls up next to hers.

"Are you following me?" Charlotte asks him.

"I was going to see Jorie." Barney is aware of the lump in his throat that he always feels in Charlotte's presence. He is known throughout the Commonwealth for his oratory skills and can argue against the best of them, but whenever he sees Charlotte words escape him; he is as mute as a bear walking through the apple orchards on the outskirts of town, and just as single-minded.

"Uh-uh." Charlotte shakes her head. "*I'm going to see Jorie.*"

"That goes to show you. We're very much alike." Barney Stark is staring at her, and he doesn't seem the least bit concerned that he's blocking the street, not even when a car comes up behind them. It's Warren Peck, the bartender from the Safehouse, who is said to be as angry as he is distraught over Ethan's arrest. Barney waves, then signals for Warren to drive around. "You've got plenty of room," Barney calls.

"What do you think this is? A damn parking lot?" Warren shouts, and then he hits his horn and lets it blare until he disappears down Westerly.

"We are nothing alike," Charlotte says through the window of her car. She thinks about the way Barney Stark used to galumph around the hallways in high school. She thinks about the moony expression he has on his face right now. They are worlds apart, that's the truth, and they always have been, and yet whenever Charlotte sees Barney something strange happens: she finds that she says whatever comes to mind, no matter how personal. Except for her health. She's definitely not talking about that. "I heard you refused to be Ethan's lawyer. I thought you were his friend."

"I don't do criminal cases at that level. But Fred Hart from Boston is an excellent lawyer."

"Are you saying that Ethan needs an excellent lawyer?"

Barney appraises Charlotte, fully appreciating both her insight and her common sense. "The situation will be cleared up. That's what the law is for."

"I thought the law was meant to punish people."

There's a Volkswagen honking madly behind him, and when Barney peers into the rearview mirror, he sees Grace Henley's familiar face. Barney signals for the librarian to go around his car, but Grace is stubborn; she won't cross over the yellow line. Instead, she continues to lean on her horn. Barney has no choice but to drive on with Grace Henley beeping at him like crazy.

"Just as well," Charlotte tells him. "We can't both visit Jorie at the same time without her thinking we're ganging up on her. This time, it's my turn to check up on things."

"Right." Barney feels exactly as he used to back in high school; whenever he saw Charlotte he felt elated in some odd way. Her presence made him far more aware of everything around him, and it still does. He notices the inky coloring of the darkening sky; he spies the halo around the lamp lights and the thin wafer of an ice-colored moon already rising in the sky. "You're right," he says, with such a strange expression on his face that Charlotte feels puzzled long after he has driven away.

"Guess who's been following me?" Charlotte

lets herself in through the back door to Jorie's, the way she always does. "You'll never in a million years guess who."

Jorie, who's been loading a day's worth of dirty plates and cups into the dishwasher, is relieved to find that someone wants to discuss a topic other than Ethan. She would hate to have to lie to Charlotte outright, but she's not prepared to discuss the truth, not even with her dearest friend. She turns from the sink and nearly manages a smile. "Barney Stark."

"There's something wrong with that man. He's absolutely peculiar." Charlotte has had a nervous stomach today, and because she's starving she starts in on a box of wheat crackers left on the table. "He said he was coming to make sure you were all right, but I got the distinct impression that I was the one he was after. Why would he do that?"

"Barney Stark has always been after you; you just never noticed."

Jorie turns her attention back to the dishes. She and Charlotte have been friends since nursery school, and their friendship has always been easy, but now things have changed. They've started to keep secrets from each other, and although they have each other's best interests at heart, in staying clear of the truth they've begun to forge a long, blue hollow where before there was only candor. If Jorie could speak, she would cry out that she's drowning in a thousand different ways, on dry land, in her own kitchen, prey to an undertow so dirty and deep she's unable to call for help.

This is her best friend at the table, the woman who knows her dreams better than she herself does. But a nightmare is a different case entirely, it's a box of black shadows and vicious red stars, something to keep carefully closed, lest the ground below be broken in two.

"If that's true, it just goes to show you what a fool Barney Stark is," Charlotte says, for who but a fool would love a woman like herself? Her luck is about to take another terrible turn; she is on the edge of the terrible kingdom of illness. Charlotte's biopsy will confirm what her doctor suspects, that the lump in her breast is malignant. Sitting in Jorie's kitchen, Charlotte already knows this, she's certain of it in the way people in this part of the country can tell when snow is about to fall simply by taking note of the stillness of the air, or the huddled sparrows on the lawn, or the cold blue bark of the lilacs. All the same, Charlotte keeps her secret close, a painful ember tucked beneath her skin.

"How's Collie?" she asks. Collie was the one child whose presence on earth Charlotte did not resent while she was trying, and failing, to get pregnant.

"Locked in his room. He won't even open the door for Kat Williams. She's been hanging around, waiting for him. I finally had to tell her to go home. Not that she necessarily listened to me." Jorie goes to her window and lifts the curtain. She gazes at the trailing peas in her garden, the flowers drooping in the heat. "I think she's still camped out in our yard."

"What about you?" Charlotte has come to stand beside her friend. "Are you all right?"

"Oh, yeah. I have to be, don't I?"

Jorie is relieved that Charlotte doesn't go on and on about Ethan's innocence, the way her mother and sister did earlier in the day when they came to pledge their support. Jorie's mother, Ruth, vowed to mortgage the girls' childhood home on Smithfield Lane, along with everything in it if need be, to help pay the legal bills. Anne, always so chilly and disinterested, had hugged Jorie, insisting she was on her side, one hundred percent of the way. Jorie had thanked her mother, she'd kissed her sister, and when they'd left, she watched them walk down the path with a liar's distance between them. She could no more bring herself to tell her family the truth than she could report that the sky was now the earth and that the blue vista above them would forevermore be the stuff they walked upon. How could she tell them that wrong had become right and everything they once believed now needed to be restrung on another cord entirely, glittering pearls of faith that have turned out to be nothing more than a strand of worthless stones.

"I'm fine," she vows again tonight, as she sends Charlotte on her way, although when she hugs her friend at the door, Jorie is no more substantial than a bundle of sticks. She'll break if she's held too close; she'll fall into splinters right there in the doorway.

"Will you call me if you need me?" Charlotte asks, but already the door has closed behind her. Charlotte walks along to her car slowly, like a woman trekking through snow even though the weather is fine and golden, with the pale evening sky falling into the darkness of the night. It is long past supper now, the time when the families in town are safe in their houses, glad that they have nothing more serious to worry about than woodchucks in the garden, mice in the basement, peeling tiles in the hall. Out in the heavens, the harp star is rising in Lyra, higher and higher, a beacon in the night. The air smells fresh, the streets are empty, and only the loneliest individuals in town are seated at the Safehouse bar, ordering a tonic for what they think ails them, hoping in vain to discover a cure for the way that they feel inside.

It is the hour Jorie once longed for, that blue hour when she and Ethan would stand in the kitchen with the lights turned off, stealing a kiss before they finished the evening's chores. Now it's a time like any other, long minutes, tedious seconds, nothing more than flat time moving forward, like it or not. Jorie has taken to forgetting the simplest things—dinner, for instance—and so now she brings a tray upstairs. She knocks at the bedroom door, and when Collie doesn't answer, she leaves his supper in the hallway, nothing fancy, just a grilled cheese sandwich and a bowl of tomato soup. Decent enough fare, but wasted all the same, as she knows he won't eat.

Perhaps Collie wants to sit in his room

until the present blows over them, beyond rooftops and orchards, until it's gone so far away they can once again open their windows and doors. But Jorie knows her poor boy can wait forever, he can sit in his locked bedroom until he is an old man, and this thing that has befallen them will not go away. It has come to settle; it is here to stay. They could talk about this if they could talk at all, but as it's true with Charlotte so it is true with Collie as well: keep a wicked secret and soon enough there'll be no choice in the matter. Before long, they'll have lost the ability to speak.

Down at the firehouse on Worthington and Vine, twelve sorrowful men sit around the table, with untouched tumblers of seltzer set out before them. One seat is empty, and the other men avert their eyes from the chair Ethan Ford always took at the head of the table, as if he came by his leadership naturally. Each of these men, Mark Derry and Warren Peck included, can think of a time when Ethan saved a life, when he did something they themselves were afraid to risk. They half expect him to walk out of the night and take his accustomed place, the way time and time again he has walked out of the fire, but there is no one at the door, and the weathervane atop the firehouse, a wild racing horse that breathes metal flames, guards an empty street.

As for Jorie, she knows Ethan won't be coming home. He won't be turning onto Maple Street in the dark, tired from an evening with his friends after a hard day of work, ready for her arms. Jorie has always been an optimist, the sort of person who has looked for the best in people and found it. Now she chides herself for being gullible; she wonders if it's in her nature to be fooled. When she and Anne were children, she had believed anything her sister told her. Anne insisted there was a hole in the ground that reached to the other side of the earth and Jorie had been naïve enough to treat this bit of nonsense as if it were a fixed and unalterable truth. Even when Charlotte told her such a thing was impossible, she couldn't be swayed from the notion.

If a person dropped through such a hole, Jorie had whispered to Charlotte, why, she'd travel right through the molten core of the globe and come out on the other side, trapped in a foreign land where she knew neither the customs nor the inhabitants. This is where Jorie feels she has landed. She goes downstairs, then traipses into her garden, barefoot, feeling the warmth of the day's sun in the earth even though night has fallen. In every summer before this, there have been neat rows, with each meandering sweet pea vine tied to a wooden post. Now, after only a few days of being ignored, the garden has been taken over by weeds and there are Japanese beetles clinging to stalks and stems. In days it's become an unrecognizable landscape. If Jorie had been asked which way was north and which way south, she couldn't have ventured an answer, although she has staked out every inch of this garden each spring as soon as the ground is soft enough for her to work the soil. She doesn't know the geography of this place where she's landed, she only knows every moment here hurts. Breathing the air is enough to cause serious damage. Walking is like treading on glass.

I'm not that man anymore, that's what Ethan said to her, that's the secret she keeps, from Charlotte and everyone else she loves, the words that opened the door to this realm where right is wrong and every pavement is sharper than crystal. His eyes were black, the same eyes that had gazed upon her every night as she got ready for bed. *The person who did those horrible things deserves to be punished for his mistakes.* That's what he told her. *But listen to me: I'm not him.*

It is as though a shadow had been stitched to the soul of the man she'd been married to all this time, a specter sewn to his feet and his fingertips, black, deceitful netting that can only be seen in certain light. The pale daylight washing in through Dave Meyers's window, for instance. The moonlight in her very own garden. Look in that light, and you can't help but see what's there before you.

Baby, just understand. I'm a different person now.

Is it possible, Jorie wonders on this ordinary summer night, for good people to go crazy all at once? Could such an individual lose sense of what was real and what was right, precisely the way another man might lose his way in the woods? Could he take a girl's life and keep on walking, with every footstep as good as a mile, and every mile the length of a lifetime? For that is precisely what Ethan Ford has done. He shed his past as though it were a second skin, abandoned on a road in Maryland, left to shrivel up in the sun until it was nothing more than a fine powdery dust to be carried about on the wind, then deposited in marshes and fields along the blue shoreline. Afterward, he'd been led to Massachusetts by destiny, that's what he told her. He'd been brought to the Commonwealth for a purpose, to start anew, to walk through the cold January days, to shovel snow, to raise a child, to be the first to arrive whenever there was a fire in the village, to give thanks for the lives he's helped save, to praise each new day, grateful for the distance between himself and Maryland.

Jorie crouches down in her garden, then sits back on her heels. Tonight, the whole world seems to be calling out in a voice she can neither understand nor recognize. Crickets are singing and june bugs buzz through the air; even the moonlight seems to have a sound, like clear glass shattering under the pressure of the hot, dark night. Soon enough, the truth will be everywhere, it will fall like hail and crack their lives open. But for now, the air is heavy and fragrant. Trout lilies and hyacinths bloom along the paths, their sweetness nearly tangible in the dark. Jorie reaches to pick beetles off the leaves of her zucchini vines. The moonlight falls like a curtain over rows of lettuce, and radishes, and the tender tomato plants, thick with green fruit which emit the scent of sulfur when anyone brushes against them. There are the straggling peas, left to their own design, and the strawberry plants Ethan and Collie brought Jorie one Mother's Day, flat after flat of heart-shaped plants. Jorie makes jam once a summer, and no matter when she chooses to boil the fruit, it turns out to be the hottest afternoon of the year. Somehow the heat of the day infuses these batches of jam with a peculiar sweetness, so that each spoonful spread upon muffins or toast in the morning can recapture the perfection of summer for a single mouthful of memory.

With so much moonlight illuminating the yard, a person can take note of details that might not be revealed on any other night: how soft, pink clematis climbs along the fence, how the water in the stone birdbath turns silver at this hour, how the wings of the beetles clinging to the vines are a shiny blue-black, glimmering scarabs trying their best to eat their fill before daylight. Oh, how Jorie wishes she could evaporate in the moonlight the way dew vanishes in the glare of full sun. Night after night she has slept with a shadow, an impostor formed out of ashes who rested beside her on clean white sheets and kissed her beneath the same apple trees she walked past when she was a girl. She never made anything of the winter evenings when he went off by himself or took note of the way he often looked behind him, as if there was danger even when traversing the most familiar of streets. She never wondered about a history devoid not only of parents, but of aunts and uncles, cousins and friends.

But perhaps no one would have noticed such things. Perhaps Jorie is no more or less observant than anyone might have been. For although it is dark, she spies something white fluttering at the edge of her garden. It's as if a single icy bloom has grown up in the last few hours, there to console her. Jorie walks through the rows of vegetables, then leans down to see what's been left behind. It's only a piece of wrinkled paper. What she thought were petals are merely lines of blue ink. Jorie reaches for the paper the way another woman might pick a single rose. She recognizes the mark of a young girl's handwriting, and she thinks of Kat Williams, standing here in the garden, peering up at Collie's window until she was chased off like a sparrow or a jay.

I'm sorry I called after I saw him on the TV show. I shouldn't have done it, but now you know and there's nothing I can do to take it back. I wish I hadn't done it, because I think I ruined your life.

Jorie smooths out the paper, then closes her eyes and listens to the june bugs. In their humming she can hear the rattle of her own destiny; it is coming after her, like it or not. This is the way things happen: a girl watches a show on TV and everything falls apart. Such are the consequences of a single act, no matter what you might wish afterward. Surely if circumstances had been different, Jorie would have walked down another path, but this is the course her life has taken, and it has led her to this place, a world where some people tell you too much and others tell you nothing at all. Here in her garden, the Japanese beetles glitter like stars and the sky is endless and black. It is impossible to stop some things, rainfall, for instance, and love at first sight, and the slow and steady path of sorrow. Jorie's life as she's known it is over. Tonight, in the old section of Monroe, Massachusetts, where people have never locked their doors before this summer, in a town where there are more apple trees than can be counted and the children have always slept peacefully, Jorie is well aware of what has happened. She can close her eyes, she can dream for a hundred years, but one thing remains certain: now she knows.

The Unwise Man

WHEN HE TOLD HIS wife the truth, he felt as though he were recounting the story of another man's life. Who was Bryon Bell, anyway, but a boy who had been a sleepwalker? Who was he but a soulless being left behind in a shallow grave in the rich Maryland soil? In his short lifetime, he had loved nothing but baseball and himself, although in time he learned to despise both. He was a small-time individual, but a big shot all the same in a town as humble as Neptune, a tiny speck of a place on the outermost edge of the Eastern Shore, where the bulrushes grew to be as tall as a man and fish crows and grackles wheeled through the sky, ready to steal whatever catch the fishermen might bring home on any given day.

Bryon himself was a fisherman's son who hated the sea. He was contrary and vain, the sort of boy who smiled politely, then did whatever he pleased, no matter the cost or the consequence. His father had died young, disappearing into a storm, and although his mother doted on him, she often watched her son as though he were a stranger who had come to call only to stay on, uninvited, to take over the house. Here was a child who destroyed whatever he touched; everything near him turned into ashes. By the time Bryon was twelve, he was rifling through his mother's purse for money and staying out half the night. At sixteen, he quit school and could be found down by the docks, as much an opportunist and a scavenger as the fish crows screaming from their perches on the pilings. As he grew older, he grew more handsome and more selfish as well. After a while, the boys Bryon had grown up with refused to be on the same baseball field with him, for he played not just to win, but to hurt his opponents. And yet the girls in town seemed unable to refuse him, and the way they looked at him only served to raise his opinion of himself. People said that Bryon Bell carried a mirror in his pocket. *The better to see himself,* that's what they whispered. *The better to know exactly who he was.*

As the years went on, the girls in Neptune became wilder in their pursuit of him. They drove by his house at odd hours and telephoned day and night, until his poor sleep-deprived mother got in the habit of leaving the phone off the hook. Such girls knew they were fools; surely they'd only be hurt by Bryon, like the others before them, yet when he smiled, even the smartest girls in town grew convinced that no matter what had happened in the past, this time he would remain true. They paid for his new clothes and for the gas in his truck; they loved him in their own single beds after he'd sneaked through their windows in the hours past curfew, or they went with him into the woods, where the loblolly pines howled at night, like men trapped in the darkness, fated to stand in the same place for all eternity.

By the time Bryon was seventeen, two local girls had tried to commit suicide because of him, and a third was up in Baltimore, at a home for unwed mothers. None of this bothered Bryon Bell in the least; he looked at girls and saw only sweet little fuckboxes, there for him to use, no hearts involved, no souls, and, most assuredly, no responsibilities. In time, the girls in town wished on him a sort of curse: they hoped he would one day know the sort of love they themselves had experienced the first time he kissed them, the cruel and desperate variety that always accompanies yearning for someone you're bound to lose.

Throughout his youth, Bryon worked odd jobs, learning a carpenter's trade, but he knew he was meant for more than a town where there wasn't a single movie theater and a person had to drive a good half an hour before he found a decent bar. He dreamed of baseball, of money and fame, and his dreams stuck to his skin and made him shimmer, so that even grown women who should have known better found their heads turning as he passed them by on the street. Why, his mother's friends couldn't keep their eyes off him when they came to the house to play cards. *He's trouble,* they said, their tongues practically hanging out, no matter that he was years younger than many of their own sons. *Have pity for the woman who wins this prize,* that's what these women warned one another, and as it turned out, they were right.

It was Marie Bennett he wound up with, a pretty forty-year-old who should have known better. When his own mother kicked him out, Bryon moved in with Marie and stayed in her house overlooking the shore for the next two years. Marie gave him too much money and she didn't reprimand him for his selfish deeds, not even when she knew he was meeting young girls down at the dock. She bought him a leather coat, fine boots that would last a lifetime, a gold chain that he quickly traded for cash at a pawnshop. She could give him every gift money could buy, but Marie understood he would never be true.

She never said a word when he didn't come home until two or three in the morning, and then, when he stopped coming home altogether, except to eat or to get clean clothes or to demand a loan to tide him over. Bryon stayed with Marie until two weeks after his nineteenth birthday, and when he couldn't bring himself to go to bed with her one more time, he forged her name, then went down to the First National Bank and withdrew ten thousand dollars. After he'd gone, Marie didn't tell anyone what he'd done to her for months; when she finally admitted what had happened and that her life's savings had vanished along with Bryon, the other women in town told her she was lucky. *Good riddance to bad rubbish,* they said. Bryon Bell had only taken her money, they reminded her, but from the look on Marie's face they knew this wasn't the case, and no one was surprised when she had that accident out by Cove Road. By then, she was drinking too much, and to her most intimate friends she'd already confided that she had nothing to live for now that Bryon Bell had left town; everyone knew it was only a matter of time before Marie crashed in one way or another.

With Marie Bennett's money in his pocket, Bryon knew he had a chance for something better than Neptune, so he drove to Baltimore, hoping for a chance at the minor leagues. He rolled down the windows of his truck, relieved to no longer smell the sea, happy to be on a road that led to a city where no one knew him and he'd be free to spend Marie's money however he liked. But when he tried to sign up for the tryouts, the manager just laughed at him. There were boys there from college, stars of their university teams who had practiced for up to six hours each day. There were young men who had traveled all the way from the Dominican Republic and Puerto Rico, individuals so serious and focused, they didn't move a muscle until their names were called, and then they hit ball after ball out of the park, so that the blue sky above was filled with blinding white circles, until each one fell into the grass, where they sat smoldering, like stars.

As it turned out, the manager didn't care what people in Neptune, Maryland, thought of Bryon Bell or how highly he regarded himself. Bryon was nothing here in Baltimore; he didn't stand a chance. By accident or by design, the old man spat upon the ground as he dismissed Bryon, dripping spittle on the dirt and on Bryon's boots. Bryon had a bad temper when things turned against him; he liked things easy, and he could get downright evil when the least difficulty arose. It had happened when that pregnant girl begged him to marry her; he'd just lifted her up and tossed her out the door—pregnant or not, pleading or weeping, he most assuredly did not care. He didn't stop to think at such times; the adrenaline ran through him, like poison that had been heated up to a feverish temperature. Facing a man who laughed at him, who reduced him to dust the way he had always turned others to ashes, he picked up the bat closest to him and he slammed the hell out of that big-shot manager. Down on the ground, the manager had spit up bile like anyone else. His blood was just as red as the next man's, and although there was a certain savage satisfaction in that, there was a steep price to pay as well.

Bryon Bell served eighteen months for assault, enough time for him to harden into the sort of man that no one would wish to cross. He no longer saw faces when he looked at people; he thought only about how they might serve his interests. When they let him out of jail, he wasn't a boy anymore, but a full-grown, spite-filled man who was so handsome doves toppled out of the sky to light on his shoulders and women dropped the keys to their front doors into his lap. His eyes were so dark a woman could drown in them; she could fall so deeply and so fast she'd never know she had stumbled until she was gone.

As for Bryon, there was something unquenchable inside him, and an emptiness too infinite to ever be satisfied. As he walked through the world, all he could hear was the word *mine.* There was so much he wanted, so much he needed to have. It was hard for him to stay in one place after spending a year and a half in a cell, so he took to the winding roads of Maryland. In the spring, when the fruit trees began to flower, so many peach and quince, almond and plum, that the air itself seemed scented with perfume, he worked as a roofer. In the winter, he cleaned chimneys and plowed snow. Throughout the year, he hired himself out to contractors as a day laborer, happy to tear down walls or raze buildings, as if destruction had been bred in his blood.

Years passed this way, and in this time he became so embittered about his place in the world that he cared not a damn for the human race. For amusement, he'd taken to setting fire to farmers' fields. He'd start a blaze in the foxtail grass that grew at the edge of cornfields; he'd throw lit matches at the leaves of the sweet gums and the myrtles, making certain to leave a black and burning trail behind. Although such senseless acts gave him a jolt of gratification, happiness was further and further away every day. He had started to feel as though he were drying up inside, the way a man does when he's walking across the desert. One summer day he came to a town he had never been to before and found he was thirsty. He was so thirsty, as a matter of fact, that he thought he might die if he didn't have a drink, and that was how he came to the general store where he bought a six-pack of beer and noticed a beautiful girl at the register. As she rang up his purchases, he could tell by the way this girl looked at him that he could have her if he wanted her, and a gorgeous, slow smile spread across his face.

Bryon had been working outdoors for more than a month, helping to build fences and backyard decks, and he'd turned a golden color.

In all that gold, there was that dark gaze a person could drown in if they failed to look away. The girl behind the register stared at him blankly with her pretty green eyes. Bryon figured her to be eighteen, a hometown girl who had a lot to learn. She had long red hair that he wanted to get his hands on. She wore shorts and a little shirt that he wanted to tear right off of her, so he smiled more deeply, the smile he knew women loved. Not exactly sincere, but full of possibility and promise and pleasure.

"What time do you get off work?" he asked. He figured the smile on his face told the rest of the story about everything he was looking for, which was a good time and something to make him forget his thirst.

"Not till nine," the girl said. "I'm trapped until closing."

"Kind of like being in jail. That is some bad luck." Bryon Bell lifted a pack of cigarettes and ripped open the cellophane; he was pleased to note the girl behind the register didn't ask him to pay. "Not that luck can't be changed."

The girl laughed, a sweet, musical sound. She was too tall and freckled for boys her age to notice she was beautiful, but Bryon Bell had an eye for such things.

"Let's take off," he said. "Let's have some fun."

"Now?" The girl laughed again. She had an itchy *I've got to get out of here* look that allowed Bryon to gauge what would happen next. He knew that she was coming with him long before she knew it herself.

"There must be someplace to go swimming," he said. It was a blistering hot day, and the store wasn't air-conditioned. One fan hummed in the window and pushed the heat around.

"Hell's Pond," the girl said.

Bryon laughed at that, and liked it fine. "Hell?"

"It's spring-fed, almost like a hot spring, but at high tide it's half salt water."

"It is much too nice outside to be working." Bryon gave her a look and held up the cold six-pack of beer he'd grabbed to ease his thirst. One more peal of laughter and he had her. She left her boss a note—*Gone swimming*—and locked up the store.

"They're going to fire me." The girl hesitated before she got into his truck. It was early August and the wild rice was turning yellow all over town, as pretty as sunlight. "They're going to kill me," she said.

"For swimming? I don't think so. That's not a federal offense. And take a good look around." The girl eyed the empty road, the fields of millet and wheat, the red-winged blackbirds on the telephone lines. "I really don't think you're going to miss many customers today," Bryon told her.

And so she got into his truck, eyes closed, as if she were taking the plunge into cold water instead of directing a stranger toward the warm and brackish shore of Hell's Pond. He promised not to look when they took off their clothes and dived in. But of course he did, and he'd been right, she was gorgeous, so tall and pale, turning green in the murky water of the pond. Unfortunately, every time he tried to get near, the most he could manage was a kiss. Later on she ran behind some pine trees to get dressed, then came back to drink beer with him, their feet in the water that had begun to seem warmer than the air. Little shadowy fish came to nibble at their toes, and Bryon told his companion he knew why that was: even the fish could tell how delicious she was, good enough to eat.

When the day was done, Bryon still hadn't gotten what he wanted, but that didn't mean he was giving up. He drove her home through the dusk. A scrim of pollen was floating through the air. She gave him directions, and as soon as he pulled off the road, he kissed her deeply, leaving her breathless.

"This isn't enough," he told her. "I want to see you some more."

"What difference does it make?" The girl shook her head sadly. "You're just going to leave town."

The sun had burned her cheeks, and she looked hot and flushed. This girl had probably fallen in love with Bryon Bell at the moment when he first walked into the store, if not before. She had been daydreaming about a mysterious stranger when the bells above the door jingled, someone with eyes as dark as the feathers of the blackbirds that now cut across the sky.

"Well, I might leave," Bryon teased her. "Or

I might not. I'll come back for you later, and we'll ride around awhile, and then we'll see."

The girl looked across the field. The lights in her house were on. It was a white farmhouse, miles from anywhere.

"After midnight. I'll blink the headlights, and you come on out."

"I can't," the girl said, but she kissed him once more.

"Don't disappoint me," he told her right before she got out of the truck and ran to the house.

Bryon went back the way he had come. He was maybe forty miles from home as the crow flies, but people in Neptune never went anywhere, and he felt sure he wouldn't run into anyone he knew. As it turned out, the town he was in was called Holden, and it had a decent bar called Holden's Corner, and Bryon sat there for a good couple of hours, getting drunk and trying to extinguish the anger he always had boiling inside him, hoping to somehow quench the desperate thirst he felt within. Afterward, he drove around on the back roads for a while, thinking maybe he'd head for the interstate and go on up to Philly, where there would certainly be jobs. But he'd had quite a lot to drink, and he started thinking about that red-haired girl from the general store, and before long he found himself on the dirt road that led to the farmhouse where he'd brought her earlier. Instead of drifting up to Philadelphia, the way he'd intended, he went there instead, out past the dark fields, guided by starlight and his own drunken sense of direction.

He pulled his truck over and turned off the engine. He blinked the headlights, but the girl didn't appear. He blinked them again; a tunnel of white light illuminated the stand of bald cypress by the house, but again nothing happened. He got out of the truck, already starting to feel the heat of his anger. He had parked in a field of strawberries, but he didn't notice as he walked over the plants. He started once, when he glimpsed someone lurking between rows of berries, but it was only a scarecrow, set there to frighten the blackbirds away. So he went past the lettuce and the corn and the trough filled with water for the two sheep that slept in the barn, then headed up to the house. He looked in the windows, and he figured out pretty quickly which was hers, the one with the sheer organdy curtains. He climbed in the window, just like that, good and drunk, and more than a little pissed off.

She was in her bed, under a white blanket. He got in with her, fast, pulling the covers over them, disregarding the mud his boots would leave on the sheets. She almost screamed, but he put his hand over her mouth.

"I told you I'd be back," he said.

The room was like a child's room, with dolls and stuffed animals and pink wallpaper patterned with daisies. Bryon figured some women never grew up. Some women liked to act like little girls, when it suited them. Sure enough, this girl looked terrified, even though they'd been together all day, and for some reason Bryon liked that. Maybe she thought she was too good for him, but when he was done with her, she'd be mooning over him for weeks. She'd wish on every star for him to return, but he'd be in Philadelphia by then; he'd have already forgotten her and moved on to the next girl, and maybe the one after that.

"Where were you?" he whispered. "You were supposed to come out when I flashed the lights. That wasn't very nice of you."

She was wearing lightweight pajamas and as soon as he moved his hand to cover her breast, she panicked. One touch and she started to fight him, arching her back, using her nails, as though she hadn't spent the afternoon kissing him at the pond, swimming without any clothes on. She tried her best to get away, until he slammed her up against the wall; then she fell backward, like one of those rag dolls on her bed. Her long red hair swept across her face, and at last he did what he'd been wanting to do all day. She was tight, as though she were a virgin, and she smelled good after the sort of girls he'd gotten used to, girls he picked up in bars who begged for him to go home with them and wept when he left them, long before morning.

He didn't even know he'd hurt her until he was done. He whispered in her ear, "I'll bet I'm your first," which, in fact, he was since she was fifteen years old, not eighteen as he'd assumed, and had never even kissed a boy before this afternoon at the pond. She had indeed been a virgin, and maybe that was why there was blood all over him.

"Hey, you," he said. "Answer me."

It was then that he saw blood on her face. He had hit her head against the wall too hard, and it had split open, just like that. He scrambled onto his knees. For some reason, every breath was stabbing through him like a knife. There was blood on his hands and his legs and his cock, and he grabbed the sheet and wiped himself clean. He was hysterical, but he knew enough to be careful. If he didn't calm down, it would be over for him. Something had happened that he'd never expected, but it had happened all the same.

Shit, shit, shit, he said to himself, until the words became nothing but a chain of breath. He hadn't even thought to ask her name, but now he saw a plaque on her bookshelf. She was a dancer and had won first prize at a competition. Her name was Rachel Morris, and she had just finished tenth grade. He saw her diary, there beside her bed, and the key, which was strung on a blue ribbon. By now, he could hear her blood falling onto the carpet. He got down on his knees right then and there, and as he did, he felt himself leave his own body. The responsibility of his deeds descended upon him like a mountain of murderous stones, and for the first time in his life, he cried.

It was the rain that made him snap out of it; rain had begun to fall in buckets, and it hit against the windows as it poured down, drenching fields and roads alike. Bryon forced himself to move; he grabbed his clothes and used a pink sweater he found on the dresser to clean his fingerprints off the window glass and the ledge. He slipped into the night, naked as the day he'd been born, with nothing in his hands but his own bloody clothes and the key to Rachel Morris's diary, which he'd grasped so tightly, he couldn't seem to let go. He went into the strawberry field, where he'd seen the scarecrow, and quickly reached for whatever he could find—a white shirt, black slacks, old, worn shoes—leaving his own clothes behind, shirt, jeans, and boots, blood-stained and burning hot, there beside the scarecrow. Still, he could taste blood, and to wash it away he grabbed a handful of strawberries. As he swallowed the sweet fruit he felt how alive he was. His mouth, his eyes, his ears, all alive in the dark rain-drenched night.

He could feel his old self sink into the field as he walked away, and the person he was about to become rose up to enter into the same blood and bones. He got into his truck and drove to Hell's Pond, the place where she'd taken him when the world seemed so splendid and he was certain he'd have whatever he wanted. He got out, but he left the engine running; he wedged a rock against the gas pedal, then leapt away as the truck lurched into the waters. Already, the rain was nothing more than a drizzle, gray and heartless and cold. He stood there in a bank of pickerelweed and wool grass, breathing hard as everything he'd ever been disappeared. His wallet and identification were stowed in the glove compartment, and thinking about the way he'd lost himself, he was as sober as he'd ever been in his life.

He was shivering, though the night air had turned mild and sweet as tears. The truck splashed and strained like a big fish, and then the waters closed over it. Bryon watched, but not for too long. He would need identification, a new name and a new history, but that wouldn't be difficult. He was the sort of man who could compartmentalize the different sections of his mind, and the segment that held all that was selfish and cruel, that small, evil section, was floating beneath the green water. Under the cover of the night, he washed his hands and prayed for guidance before setting off on his travels. As far as he was concerned, Bryon Bell was gone.

Fair or Foul

THE HEARING IS BRIEF, held on a muggy day, when the sticky heat and the rain boil the dispositions of just about everyone in Monroe, including the most even-tempered citizens. Four years from now, when the referendum to overhaul the town offices and the courthouse comes up once again, people will remember this stifling day, they'll fan themselves and think of how they longed for air-conditioning and peace of mind. No one is fully prepared for what is to come, save Jorie, who sits behind Ethan with her head bowed, and Barney Stark, who has taken his place beside Jorie, his heavy, serious face showing nothing, though he is on alert, ready to pick up the pieces when they begin to fall. Collie, too, knows what is about to happen, but he is nowhere to be seen; he's off by himself, watching the steady rainfall from what was once the parlor of the abandoned house where he feels so comfortable, at the far end of King George's Road, just three miles as the crow flies from the courthouse steps, but a world away as well.

Mark Derry sits in the last row to watch the proceedings. He has worn a tie and a jacket for the occasion and is sweltering for his troubles. This morning he phoned Dana Stark to inform her he wouldn't be back till the end of the week to finish up their new bathroom. He waited for her to take him to task, more than ready to quit the whole damned project if she did, which would leave her without a commode or a sink, but Dana had surprised him and said there was no hurry. Mark had other things on his mind. Anyone could understand that. The Howards over on Sherwood Street haven't made a fuss either; they already know their kitchen won't be completed until well into the fall, despite the efforts of the handyman, Swift, hired to finish installing the

cabinets and lay the floor. There are, indeed, more important issues to deal with, that much is true. There are circumstances that can't be put on hold, to be set aside and forgotten for a better day to come.

On the afternoon after Ethan was arrested, Mark had a fight in the hardware store with that harebrained Steve Messenger, who'd started mouthing off about burning the Fords' house to the ground. They'd had to pull Mark off Steve in the paint-and-fixtures aisle, but now Mark feels confused about his loyalty. Sitting in the courtroom, hearing Ethan referred to as Bryon Bell, Mark can't quite believe what is happening. Perhaps it's all a joke, a scene filmed for a TV show; perhaps at the end of the afternoon, the actors—Ethan and the judge and the lawyers included—will rise to their feet and take their bows, thanking the clutch of reporters and the Fords' neighbors and friends for being in attendance.

For haven't these two men, friends for the past thirteen years, been there for each other no matter what the circumstances? Haven't they cried together over the death of Mark's father and rejoiced at Collie's birth, making themselves queasy with scotch and cigars? Ethan coached Mark's son Brendan, back when Brendan was in Little League, and is the godfather to Mark and Trisha's daughter, April. These things are real; they happened, there's no denying that. But are they as real as the moment when Ethan stands up to enter his plea, announcing his guilt with an open, untroubled

expression? Mark Derry feels a shudder pass through him as he sits there in the courthouse. He is reminded of a magician he had once seen as a child who had terrified him by bringing forth scarves and birds out of the most unexpected places, shirtsleeves and tabletops and the upswept hair of the birthday girl's mother. After that illusion, he'd gone home and hid beneath his bed and refused to come out for supper; for months following the party, he had half-expected to find doves on his bureau or trip over silk scarves snaking through the floorboards of his room.

Now Mark looks over at Jorie, seated beside Barney Stark. She's motionless, wearing a dark blue dress that makes her seem plainer and older. Mark is flooded by a memory of working with Ethan on one of those big new houses that went up on the far side of the high school a few years back; they had gone into the field at lunchtime, and after sharing the picnic Jorie had carefully packed, stuffing themselves with hard-boiled eggs and ham sandwiches, with apples and chocolate cupcakes and cold bottles of beer, they had stretched out to gaze at the sky.

I'm the luckiest man on earth, Mark remembers Ethan saying. *That is a fact.*

Mark slips out the back door immediately after Ethan states his plea, and goes directly to the Safehouse, where he orders a draft, which he drinks alone at a rear table. It's always dark in the Safehouse, but with the rain falling so hard, it's even gloomier than usual,

thick with the damp smell of failure and alcohol. One night when they sat here, Ethan had said something that, looking back, Mark thinks, should have given him a clue. *Nobody ever really knows another person,* Ethan had declared as the wind rattled around the roof of the Safehouse and a sprinkling of snow began to fall. They'd had a few, and Mark remembers saying something on the order of, *Bullshit. If you think I don't know you, you're wrong, buddy. Hell, I'd trust you with my life.* Ethan had clapped Mark on the back, and as he thanked him he'd gotten kind of emotional. Now Mark feels cheated; he wonders if he's been conned. He has another beer; then he goes home, and before Trisha can stop him he takes out the piles of photograph albums she's worked so hard to put together and begins to rip up the pages.

"Stop that right now," Trisha demands when she comes in from the kitchen to see the shredded paper on the floor and her husband down on his knees, searching for a pair of scissors in the bottom drawer of the bureau they inherited from his grandmother. Trisha grabs the album away. For a second she has a shivery feeling. Who is this man she's married to, who has already torn up a dozen or more photographs? And then Mark does the most unexpected thing of all—he starts to cry. Trisha sits beside him on the floor. Her face is mottled and red; she has the sense that some things will never be the same, that just knowing Ethan has somehow placed them in jeopardy.

"He had everybody fooled," Trisha says, "including his own wife. There's nothing for you to feel bad about."

Still Mark Derry knows that a man may have good reason to mislead his wife, but never his best friend. Mark decides he needs to think over what has happened, he needs to sort things out, and all the rest of that week he takes to staying late at the Safehouse. Most nights, he closes the place down, getting a ride home from Warren Peck, let out on the corner to stumble the rest of the way down his own driveway. Mark no longer shows up for his jobs, and the three Derry boys, Sam, Christopher, and Brendan, hardly see their father these days. Even April, the Derrys' eight-year-old daughter, notices the change, and she's started to mouth off to her mother, refusing to bathe or to go to bed on time, when in the past she's always been an angelic child.

It isn't as if Mark Derry had never had a drink in his life—he likes a good time as much as the next man—but now he's settled into drinking, as though he were falling into a soft netting that was swallowing him whole. Every time he thinks about Ethan, he has another drink, meant to clear his mind, but managing to do the opposite instead, leaving him fuzzy and far more confused. By the end of July, when Mark has lost ten pounds off his already thin frame and hasn't been home before midnight for eight nights straight, Trisha Derry goes to see Kat Williams's grandmother to ask what

Katya might suggest to bring a wayward husband home. Katya is an unlikely friend for a woman as young as Trisha, but Trisha lost her own mother at a tender age and she'd always felt she needed some maternal counsel. When Brendan and Rosarie first started dating, Rosarie's mother didn't seem the least bit interested in the children's future, but Katya always welcomed Trisha to stop in for coffee whenever she was trying to track Brendan down.

Now Trisha goes to Katya in need of good advice, the sort her mother might have given if only she'd lived longer. She lets April play in the Williamses' yard, where nothing much grows aside from the feathery black mimosas, and she watches through the window as her daughter makes pies out of handfuls of weeds. In a surprisingly calm voice, Trisha tells Katya how her marriage has gone wrong. She has not been here since Rosarie broke Brendan's heart, and perhaps she would feel uncomfortable returning if Katya were not so understanding. A man who drinks is a man who's afraid of the truth in some way, and in Katya's opinion, it is Trisha's task to figure out what her husband is afraid of, then help him face whatever it might be straight on, with no alcohol inside him.

But how can Trisha help Mark when he barely spoke to her anymore? When he fell into bed beside her at the first light of morning, stinking of alcohol and shrinking from her touch?

"Wherever he goes, you go," Katya says as they stand beside the window, watching April search for butterflies in the desolate yard. "Then you'll know what he's running from."

Trisha decides to follow Mark the very next day, to take the same path he is now on, and in so doing, understand why he's running so fast. It's a splendid morning when she sets out after him in her Honda. It's already eight o'clock, two hours later than the time Mark used to leave the house, back when their lives were normal. Trisha knows he has a job to finish at Barney Stark's, and Josh Howard had tentatively phoned that morning to report that the handyman, Swift had recently disappeared, leaving the Howards' kitchen in ruins. But work is clearly not on Mark's mind, for he heads to Kite's Bakery, on Front Street.

Trisha sits in her parked car, engine running, watching her husband get a black coffee, which he certainly could have had at home. She can see through the window that Charlotte Kite is back to work after the surgery people said she'd had over in Hamilton. Charlotte's parents had built the place up from nothing into a chain that crisscrossed the Commonwealth, and the bakery must have felt like home to Charlotte, because another woman might not have returned to work so fast.

Trisha had heard through the grapevine that there was some sort of cancer involved, and she'd brought over flowers earlier in the week, even though she and Charlotte had never been friends. Charlotte had accepted the zinnias and lilies, cut from the Derrys' own garden, but she hadn't invited Trisha in. She'd insisted she was doing just fine, the same cheerful speech she gave to everyone, including Jorie, who still didn't know the extent of her friend's illness. But Trisha Derry was not so easy to fool. She saw how gaunt Charlotte was as she stood in the doorway of her huge house, dressed in her bathrobe with some sort of bulky pump attached under her arm. They had been a year apart in high school, and Trisha had always thought Charlotte was too sophisticated for her, as her family was among the wealthiest in town. Trisha had often whispered that Charlotte was stuck-up and full of herself, a real ice princess. She'd made jokes at Charlotte's expense, but as she peered at Charlotte through the meshing of the screen door, Trisha thought maybe she'd been the cold one, and that's why they'd never been friends. Perhaps she'd been the one to reject Charlotte, because Charlotte lived over in Hillcrest, just as she'd avoided Jorie because of her beauty, a singular gift that had always seemed so unfair. She'd been jealous, and jealousy always curdles. Trisha can't help but wonder if she wasn't paying a price for her lack of understanding and if that wasn't the reason her loyal, dependable husband was drifting away from her.

When Mark leaves the bakery on the morning he's being followed, he gets into his truck and drives around town in what seems to be an aimless pattern. Trailing at a safe distance behind, Trisha quickly finds herself confused, although she grew up in Monroe and knows every turn. It takes a while before she realizes that he's heading for Maple Street. Mark stops across from the Fords' house and sits there for so long Trisha grows concerned that he's fallen asleep or become suddenly ill. She herself has pulled over beside a hedge of lilacs on the corner of Maple and Sherwood, a spot where the rangy shrubs protect her from sight, but after close to half an hour has passed, Trisha is growing restless. She's wondering how long she can wait here like this, when at last Mark opens the door of his truck. Trisha gets out of her Honda as well; she edges along the lilacs, hidden by their dusty heart-shaped leaves. Her breathing is ragged, and it's such a hot day she's begun to sweat. In order to keep out of sight, she has no choice but to go through Mrs. Gage's yard, even though Betty Gage, always so fanatical about her perennial beds, has been known to scare people off her property from the time Trisha herself was a little girl.

From the rear of Mrs. Gage's yard, Trisha can see through the fence. Jorie is out in her garden, trying to make the place more presentable, as Liz Howard, who runs Monroe Realty, suggested when she came by to appraise the property. Two months without Ethan working and it will be hard for Jorie to make the mortgage payments. Three, and it will be impossible. So there she is, attacking tall bunches of Queen Anne's lace, pulling out the heads of lettuce that have gone to seed. Jorie is wearing shorts and one of her son's tee-shirts, and from a distance she looks as beautiful as she did in high school, when Trisha had thought her too high and mighty to ever approach.

Though she's not one to trespass, Trisha continues on through Mrs. Gage's yard to where her husband is standing, gazing into the Fords' garden. He has such a puzzled look on his face, and yet he doesn't seem surprised to see Trisha step out from Mrs. Gage's carefully weeded flower bed where the phlox are doing so well, banks of purple and fuchsia and white.

"I keep thinking that I'll figure it out," Mark says. "If I just keep at it, it's got to make some sense."

All that morning, at the bakery, as he drove through town, and now again as he stands here observing Jorie, he's been counting the times he and Ethan had gone fishing together, the number of beers they'd enjoyed, the nights they'd spent at the Safehouse playing pool, the times they'd rushed from the fire station on emergency calls together, hoping that the blaze they hurried to didn't affect anyone they loved. More than once, Mark had told Ethan he didn't know if he'd done the right thing in marrying Trish. They'd been dating since they were fifteen, and she was the one and only woman he'd ever been with, and Mark had the feeling he'd missed out on something most other men had experienced.

True love comes once in a lifetime, Ethan had told him. *And that's if you're lucky.*

They had been over at the fire station the last time they talked about this. The other guys had been in the front room, watching baseball on the big-screen TV Warren Peck had donated. The day had been hot, but when Ethan started talking about love, Mark had been aware of an icy sensation across his chest. He wished he could be as sure of himself as Ethan was, and now here he stood, watching Ethan's house nearly every day, trying to understand what had happened and thinking about his own life and the course it had taken.

He doesn't step away when Trisha comes through Mrs. Gage's yard to stand beside him. "Not everything makes sense," she says, thinking about Charlotte Kite, the girl she'd always been so jealous of, how pitiful she'd looked in her bathrobe, leaning her weight against the screen door. Who would have guessed that out of all the girls at school, Trisha would be the one to find true happiness? She gets on tiptoe and leans close to her husband. The acrid smell of the soil in Jorie's yard is in the air. "I'm so glad I have you," Trisha whispers to Mark.

On the day when Ethan and Mark talked about love, Mark had begun to cry. He told Ethan that he had a wife and three boys and a beautiful little daughter, and still he hadn't a clue as to what real love was.

Don't think about what you don't have, Ethan had told him. *Enjoy what you have right now.*

There has not been a day since when that thought hasn't run across Mark Derry's mind. These words have brought him comfort on the days when he's felt like getting in his truck and driving north along the highway to look for another life, one where he didn't have to be as responsible, one in which he loved his wife the way Ethan loved Jorie. It is only on this hot summer afternoon that Mark figures it out as he follows Trisha home. He's started smoking again, and the cab of his truck smells like sulfur. A man could change, that's what he decides as they drive down Sherwood Street, and Miller Avenue, and Front Street. He thinks of himself at fifteen, how he'd pledged his love to Trisha, how he'd made a life plan when he knew absolutely nothing about life. If he'd had the boy he'd once been in the truck with him right now, he'd tell him a thing or two. He'd advise him to go on the road, to live out in the world before he made commitments that would tie him up until he was an old man. *People make mistakes,* that's what he thinks as he pulls up behind his wife's car in the driveway, that's what he decides.

That evening, Mark Derry phones Kip Louis, president of the town council, as well as Hal Jordan, the county commissioner of Little League, and Warren Peck, the most senior member of the volunteer fire department. In this way the defense fund for Ethan is begun, and why shouldn't these good people rally around him? He is their neighbor, the same man he'd been last month when they'd trusted him with their children, when he'd carried the keys to their houses in his pocket and was considered by one and all to be the most honest man in town. Mark sits in the dining room for hours on the night the defense fund is born, with the Monroe phone book open before him, and a growing list of donations. Trisha gives the children dinner, and hushes them when they're too rowdy, sending them out to play in the fading blue dusk.

As the light grows dim, Trisha stands in the kitchen doorway, in order to watch her husband. Katya was right, and Trisha has been wise to heed her counsel. Following Mark has helped her understand the road he's been on. In fact, she is truly impressed. As well as she knows him, she had no idea that he could string so many words together; she's never heard him talk as much or be as passionate about anything. Already, there are plans for a rally and talk about approaching town businesses for pledges. Mark has come up with every bit of this strategy on his own. While he works, Trisha fixes him a sandwich, roast beef on rye, and places it on the table. It's done the way he likes it, with horseradish sauce and sour pickles. Mark smiles up at her and nods his thanks as he speaks to their minister, Dr. Hardwick, about a particular Bible passage that might be the source of a suitable sermon for their congregation on the Sunday to come, given the circumstances and the fact that Ethan never walked away from a man in need.

"You see what a person can do when he sets

his mind to it," Trisha says to Brendan, who is mooning around the kitchen, in a bad humor ever since Rosarie Williams dumped him. "You get on your computer right now and make up a flier for your father's rally. Get your mind on something important."

Startled by his mother's harsh assessment of his lovesick ways, Brendan goes up to his room. The rest of the Derry children are playing kickball in the street with the Howard kids from over on the next block, and Trisha can hear them through the open window. The sky outside is tinted pink and a breeze trickles in, ruffling the curtains. Everything seems different to her on this evening, hopeful somehow. Trisha tells herself she will have to remember to bring dear Katya the lemon-poppyseed coffee cake that is her favorite, in gratitude for what is certainly some excellent advice.

At the end of this long day, when the children have all bathed and gone to bed, Trisha peeks her head into the dining room. The house is quiet, aside from the click of Brendan working at his computer upstairs and the low rumble of Mark's voice as he calls neighbor after neighbor.

"How about some coffee?" Trisha suggests to her husband between phone calls. She is proud of the fact that instead of sprawling on the couch or taking up space at the Safehouse, wallowing in the sorrow of the situation, Mark has the character to do something to rectify the mess Ethan Ford is in. Her heart is full of love. "It won't take me a minute," she says, and looking up at her, nodding as he dials the next number on his list, Mark Derry wonders if contrary to what he's thought all along, perhaps he is indeed a lucky man.

Those fliers Brendan Derry printed up can be found everywhere in the next few days; black print on orange paper, they flutter around town like orange lilies, planted on lampposts and shop owners' bulletin boards, stuck in mailboxes and on car windshields. This is the week when Jorie and Collie move over to her mother's home on Smithfield Lane, driven off by the reporters stationed in the driveway of the Gleasons' house across the street. The same week when Charlotte's doctor informs her that her course of treatment will take ten full months of radiation and chemotherapy. On this day, Charlotte finds a stack of fliers left outside the bakery door and, disturbed by Ethan's confession, she tosses them in the trash. But when Rosarie Williams sees the orange paper tucked into the mailbox, she sits on the porch and studies it carefully. She calls Kelly Stark, and the girls head to the firehouse on the night of the first rally. At least it's something to do, and there will probably be reporters there, interested in taking their photograph. The girls stand at the edge of the surprisingly large gathering and listen to Mark Derry speak about forgiveness and compassion and before long they find themselves cheering with the rest of the crowd.

Jorie is supposed to be there as well; in a way, she's the guest of honor whose presence will surely elicit compassion and large donations, but when Mark stops by to pick her up at her mother's house, Jorie's not ready to leave. It's a quarter to eight, and people have begun to gather on Front Street; Jorie should already be seated on the center chair of the dais behind the podium, but she can't find Collie anywhere.

"I'm sure he'll show up," Mark assures her, but Jorie's not listening. She hasn't seen Collie for the better part of the day; the later the hour has grown, the more distressed she's become. She actually sent her niece Gigi out to look for him, scouting the field beyond the high school and the park over on Center Street, with no success. Jorie has no idea where her boy might have gone, for it isn't like Collie to disappear without leaving a note. He's reliable and careful, or at least he had been until now. With Mark Derry there urging her to come with him, Jorie finally understands. It's the rally. Collie doesn't want to know about it or think about it. He doesn't want to be in the same universe as his father.

Jorie assures Mark that she'll be down to the firehouse before long, and there's nothing he can say to stop her from getting into Ethan's truck and going off to search for Collie. She drives through the quiet streets of the old section of Monroe, looking down lanes and into backyards the way she might search for a lost dog. The sky has faded into darkness and Jorie feels cold pinpricks of worry up and down her arms. She circles around Lantern Lake, terrified she might spy something floating in the shallow waters, which thankfully are empty and glassy green. She crosses the highway, looking for a lone hitchhiker, but sights nothing except bramble bushes and row after row of those orange lilies she's never liked. She knows that lights have been set up outside the firehouse for they crisscross the sky, but there's no one on the streets of Monroe. People are either at home or attending the rally, depending upon their allegiance.

It isn't until after nine that Jorie thinks of going to their house, and when she pulls into the driveway, she can tell he's been there. The garage door is ajar, and when Jorie goes to investigate she sees someone has been through Ethan's tool shop. Screwdrivers and wrenches are scattered on the floor, and one of the saws is missing. Jorie has a tight feeling in her chest. She closes and locks the garage, then cuts across Mrs. Gage's lawn. By the time she knocks on the Williamses' door, she's in a panic.

"I need to talk to your granddaughter," she says to Katya when at last the door opens. "Right now."

Kat is standing behind her grandmother. She's gotten tall this summer, as tall as a woman, though she's dressed like a little girl. Her hair is in scraggly braids, and she's wearing jeans and a white blouse that's a hand-me-down from her sister.

"Is something wrong?" Katya, the grandmother, asks.

"I just need to talk to her." Jorie is speaking to the girl's grandmother, but it's Kat she's staring at. She nods for Kat to come outside.

"Well, it's late," Katya begins. She doesn't like the expression on Jorie's face. A desperate woman, that's what Jorie looks like. One with very little to lose.

"It's okay." Kat Williams slips out from behind her grandmother and steps onto the porch. "It's fine," she says as she closes the door behind her.

"Where's Collie?" Beneath the porch light, Jorie notices that Kat is wearing lipstick. Isn't she too young for such things? Shouldn't there be a few years more before she starts trying to look older than her age? "Don't tell me you don't know, because I can tell from your note that you seem to know everything."

Kat feels the heat of an accusation and she raises her chin the way she always does when she's cornered. "I said I was sorry."

"Right. That fixes everything." Jorie sounds more spiteful than she intends. "Well, you turned my husband in, so do me a favor and do the same for my son. Where is he?"

Kat stares back at Jorie. They are nearly the same height, which surprises them both. "How would I know? He's hardly talking to me."

The lights from the fire station are like streaks of lightning in the sky. On the other side of town, Mark Derry is making an appeal to the crowd, and the cheers in response to his pleas ricochet over rooftops and chimneys.

"You know." Jorie's voice is quiet, but it's sharp. "Tell me."

"Go left on Front Street, then head to King George's."

Jorie is surprised. "To the jail?"

"Way past. But the thing is," Kat informs her, "you won't find the place without me."

And so they walk across Mrs. Gage's lawn together and get into Ethan's truck. On the way through town, Jorie avoids Worthington Street and the rally and goes around on Miller Avenue. When they pass Liberty Street, Kat understands what Collie's been up to. There, in front of the library, is the fallen apple tree, the boughs and bark tumbled across the lawn and onto the sidewalk. The sight of it fills Kat's eyes with tears, and she has to blink hard. She cannot believe he did this without telling her.

They turn onto King George's Road and travel beyond the county buildings, past the courthouse and the jail, until the road becomes more rural, unlit by street lamps, and lined by old stone fences that are crumbling into dust. The night is dreamy and dark. Along the side of the road, there are banks of daylilies; the flowers look like birds that have settled down to sleep among the leaves.

"Right here," Kat says suddenly. "Turn."

Kat knows that Collie may not forgive her for leading his mother here, but what choice does she have? Sitting in the passenger seat, holding on tight while Jorie makes a wide, wild turn onto the dirt road, Kat knows that she will always feel the way she feels about Collie right now. No matter what happens, even if she gets married and has a dozen kids, even if she never says it aloud. It will always be him.

"How did you know this was here?" Jorie wonders when the old Monroe house comes into view. She and Anne came here several times when they were kids, but she never could have found it again. She cuts the headlights and lets the truck roll closer to the house. Something flutters in the trees up above, bird or bat, it's impossible to tell.

"He comes here to get away from everyone," Kat says. "Including me."

Jorie looks at Kat and thinks to herself, *She's only twelve.* She tells Kat to stay where she is, then goes out into the warm, hazy night. As Jorie makes her way up to the house, she breathes deeply. The air carries the scent of apples and ashes, and when she goes in through what she supposes was once the side door, she picks up the scent of another human being. She can feel someone watching her.

"Collie," she calls. Her heart is beating too fast, perhaps because it's even darker inside the house than it is outside among the overgrown shrubbery. There's no response, and Jorie finds herself wishing she'd brought along a flashlight. She can't force her son to come to her; she can't pull him by a leash or a string. If he flatly refuses to come home, Jorie's not sure what she'll do, but then out of the emptiness he calls back, "Go away." Just hearing his voice makes everything bearable. She can see more clearly through the dust and the dampness of this old house.

"I'm not mad or anything," Jorie says. "I just came to take you home." There are crumbly things under her feet, rotting floorboards, most probably, and she makes certain to walk toward the sound of his voice carefully, arms outstretched to catch herself in case she should fall. They haven't talked about Ethan's confession; they've avoided it thoroughly, going so far around it, all they've managed is to get stuck right in the middle of it.

"Oh, yeah?" Collie says. "Where's that?"

He's sitting on an old timber in what was the parlor, a large, gracious room where cider soup was served to guests on cool, crisp days. The scent of apples here is strongest. Perhaps the wooden fireplace was carved from one of the hundreds of Christmas apple trees that once grew on the property. Jorie finds herself imagining what it would have been like to live in this house. What it would have felt like to look out your window and know you owned everything as far as the eye could see, trees and land, hillsides and fields.

"And here's another question." Collie's tone is harsh. "What's my name supposed to be?"

The moldings around the ceiling of the room have retained some of their gold leaf, so that there is a gleaming through the darkness, even in the places where the plaster has become little more than powder.

"If our real name isn't Ford, and I don't want to take a murderer's name, who am I?"

Jorie sees the saw then, one of Ethan's best, ruined and sticky with sap, tossed into a dim corner. The odor of the apple tree Collie cut down clings to the saw, and to his hands, and to his clothing. He is staring at his mother, desperate for an answer. He barely looks like himself in the dark, but she knows him, perhaps better than she knows anyone in this world.

"You're still the same person." Jorie is surprised to find she continues to have faith in someone. She still believes in who her son is and who he will be. "Even if he's not."

Collie thinks this over as he follows her out of the old house. They go through the front door without bothering to collect Ethan's saw. Instead, they leave it in the parlor, where the wood is so rotted one heavy footstep can cause an individual to fall right through.

"I'm not going to use his name," Collie says once they're outside.

"You might want to think about it." It's warm outside, but Jorie wraps her arms around herself as though she's cold.

"I already have."

Collie sounds too old, and Jorie wonders how this has happened so suddenly. Her boy nearly a man, with opinions of his own. But perhaps this transformation would have occurred anyway; certainly it is happening to Kat Williams as well. The little girl next door who's now as tall as Jorie is sitting on the bumper of the truck with a lit cigarette in hand.

"That's how you found me." Collie nods to Kat. The cigarette she smokes is one swiped from Rosarie, lit in Kat's attempt to try to calm her nerves. As soon as she spies Jorie and Collie coming toward her in the dark, Kat drops the cigarette and stomps it out beneath her sneaker. Red sparks fly up, and she crushes them, too.

Ever since Collie took *King Arthur* from the library, Kat has been stealing books. She's taken at least one a day and on some brave and crazy afternoons, she's filled up a whole backpack. She now has novels and biographies under her mattress and in her underwear drawer. Not that she reads any of them. She doesn't even open the covers. Still, these books make her think of her father. In his last year, Aaron Williams often checked out twenty or more books at a time, huge piles that Kat helped to carry home. This, of course, was expressly against the rules—there was a six-book limit—but anyone could look at Aaron Williams and know he was dying. He'd been a big, robust man before he'd taken ill, and although he was soon puffed up from steroids and chemo, it was clear that underneath it he'd become a rail of a man. No matter. If he'd wanted a hundred books, the librarian would have checked them out for him. If he'd wanted a thousand, Grace Henley would have plucked the wheelbarrow from the library's garden shed and carted the editions along to his house.

"You cut down the tree," Kat whispers as Collie comes near. Jorie has gone around to the driver's side of the truck, and they only have a moment out of her sight.

"You told her where I was." Collie looks straight at her and Kat feels dizzy, probably from the cigarette, although she didn't inhale. Maybe being light-headed is what allows her to be bold, or maybe it's the notion that the time for this may never come again; whatever the reason, when Collie moves back so Kat can step into the truck, Kat leans toward him and kisses him. She does it so quickly that they both think they have imagined what just happened as they ride home, sitting close together, pretending to listen to the radio as Jorie drives toward town.

In the morning, blue jays perch on the fallen apple tree. The trunk has been chopped in half, the ragged bark hacked through unevenly but thoroughly. Green leaves and petals drift over sidewalks and lawns. Grace Henley is the first to see what's happened. She arrives early, woken by the stifling heat of the day and her own internal alarm clock, set to five-fifteen for the past twenty years. The morning is still dark when she briskly turns onto Front Street. Grace's eyesight is failing, so at first she imagines that what she spies is a dragon on the library lawn, coiled and fallen under the sword, and that there are pale sweet-scented scales floating above the grass, onto the roof, dusting windows and doorways and gutters alike.

When the librarian realizes what has been felled, the hateful fruit tree that has been the bane of her existence each autumn with its bushels of rotten fruit and its pools of deep shade, she decides that some prayers are indeed answered in ways no one ever would have begun to imagine. Grace takes off her shoes and climbs skyward, and she's still there, comfortable as a jay herself, when the first of the children arrive to practice for the yearly talent show scheduled to take place after supper. Grace allows the children to climb to their hearts' content, never mind that their hands will be tacky with sap and that the bits of bark are sure to give them splinters. She insists that the town crew wait on the sidewalk with their saws and all their stern warnings that someone could easily break a leg, leaving the town open to a negligence suit. Grace Henley lets the children play until every petal has been shaken loose and the grass has turned white as snow.

People who disdain Grace Henley as a bookworm who desires nothing more than peace and quiet and a good cup of tea are doing her a disservice and fooling themselves as well. Books should never be judged by their covers, and Grace happens to know quite a lot about the people in this town. She knows, for instance, that Collie is the one who chopped down the tree, not that she would ever let on. Just last summer, Ethan Ford had been hired to replace the rickety steps leading to the stacks on the second floor, and Collie had often come to assist him. Grace had enjoyed watching them work together, and had been delighted to find that rather than running over to the Dairy Queen at lunch time, the way most people would have, they sat and had their noon break beneath the apple tree. They brought along thermoses of lemonade, and sandwiches wrapped in foil, and thick wedges of angel food cake.

Grace Henley recalls how the boy had held planks of wood steady as Ethan sawed through them; how serious his expression had been, how much it meant to him to be of use to his father, whom he clearly admired. Hearing of Ethan's past, Grace feels betrayed, not for her own sake, but for the sake of the children in town, and most especially for Collie. She doesn't blame him one bit for needing to cut something down. She's observed the look on his face when he sits in the reading room, half-hidden behind the fish tank. She's noticed the hurt and the frustration there. Although Grace has refused to discuss Ethan Ford's guilt or innocence with any library patrons wishing to gossip, privately she feels quite pleased that during the last town referendum, she voted against air-conditioning the jail. She thinks it's just fine for Ethan Ford to sit in his cell and sweat.

Grace Henley is not the only one who's pleased with the current turn of events. Jorie's sister, Anne Solomon Lyle, is somewhat surprised to find herself back home at the age of forty, but even more amazed to discover she's not unhappy with her situation. After more than twenty years of moving around from town to town, following her husband across most of New England and half the Southwest, she has a settled feeling at last. As it turns out, everything she was running away from is a comfort to her now. Most people in Monroe would guess Anne must consider herself to be a failure coming home at this stage, divorced with no man in sight, dragging Gigi back to the house she herself couldn't wait to escape when she eloped with Trent right after their senior year in high school, two smitten fools who didn't know the first thing about real life.

Regardless of other people's judgments, the concerned *How are you?* that always seems to greet her in the market and at the bank, Anne actually feels better than she has in ages. The truth is, she's never lived anywhere where the summer air is as sweet as it is in Monroe. It's only recently that she's realized the reason for this scent is that her mother keeps flowering jasmine in the yard. Because jasmine cannot tolerate a Massachusetts winter, Ruth always brings the pots inside at the first sign of a chill, ensuring that the glassed-in porch is always fragrant, no matter what the weather outside.

Anne's daughter, Gigi, will be going into her junior year at the high school in September, and thankfully she's not in with the crowd that includes Rosarie Williams. How Anne ever wound up with a daughter like Gigi is proof that there are indeed miracles on earth.

Whereas Anne was lazy and self-centered as a teenager, Gigi is thoughtful and a hard worker; she helps her grandmother around the house, made honor roll last spring even though they moved to Monroe midyear, and is currently a volunteer counselor at the library summer program. This evening, Gigi is responsible for organizing the talent show. Although her grandmother has gone to root her on, Anne worked all day at the country club up in Hillcrest, where she has recently begun a position as part-time hostess in the restaurant, and she's opted out. Her feet are killing her, and she doesn't have the patience for a bunch of kids singing songs and juggling.

Anne has to be pleasant at work, no matter how rude a customer might be, and maybe that's the reason she likes to be alone in the evenings. She had thought she'd miss Trent like crazy, but as it turns out, she loves being by herself. She would like Trent to see her for one single instant. If only her happy face would bubble up in a bowl of chili as he ate lunch, or reveal itself in a glass of beer the way fortunes appear in crystal balls, just so he'd know how wrong he'd been. She's doing just fine without him, thank you very much. For the first time ever, she's at peace with the world.

The one recent development that really gets to Anne, as selfish a sentiment as it may be, is the fact that Jorie has moved home. Naturally, Anne feels bad for her sister, but they had settled down to such a perfect routine before Jorie came back, and now that's all shot to hell. Although Anne would not admit this to anyone, she's enjoyed being at the center of her mother's world. It's true she's never been especially generous, never had any big-sister urges to protect or to guide. She wouldn't know how to help Jorie if she tried, and thankfully she's never been asked to.

Tonight, Anne pours herself a glass of white wine and grabs a bag of potato chips. She has decided she will tie one on, all by herself. She'll celebrate being alive without Trent around to tell her what a mess she's making of everything and how inconsequential a human being she is. Anne is on the lawn, stretched out on a chaise, the open bottle of wine beside her, a mild buzz just beginning, when she spies her sister coming down the street. Earlier, Jorie had gone to her house on Maple Street; she really had no choice. A couple relocating from Framingham have put a bid in on the house, and it's a fair one, more than generous considering that the address has recently been in the news, which often turns buyers away.

Liz Howard had phoned to inform Jorie that offers like this weren't made every day, not for the house of a self-confessed murderer. Liz had gone so far as to come and pick her up, and Jorie, who'd been napping, had thrown a light raincoat on over her pajamas. She'd stood there in her own backyard while Liz and the couple from Framingham went over the house's flaws and its strong points. In the end, Jorie had told them she needed to think things over, and she'd left Liz there in the garden and set off on her way back to her mother's house.

Anne is startled to see her sister walking down the middle of the road, following the white line that glows in the dark, her concentration as focused as if she were on a balance beam. Anne had assumed that Jorie, always better at everything, would also be a better mother; she took for granted that Jorie's absence here suggested she had gone to the library talent show along with Collie and Gigi and Ruth. But instead, here she is, barefoot, hair streaming silver.

"Hey," Anne calls. "Come get a drink. I've got white wine."

Jorie starts up the herringbone path that Ethan put down for her mother last spring. Lining the bricks are several moody hosta plants which send out tendrils that often catch visitors by the ankle if they aren't careful, and should be trimmed back before someone gets hurt.

"I thought you'd be at the talent show." Anne refills her wineglass and hands it to her sister. After all this time, she figures she might as well share.

"Damn. I forgot."

"Hey, you're only human."

It's something of a joke, and Jorie winces. She knows what Anne thinks of her, Miss Goody-Two-Shoes, far from human in her estimation.

"I didn't think you noticed," Jorie says.

Anne watches as Jorie sinks down to the grass.

She sees that beneath the light coat, Jorie is wearing her pajamas. "Do you realize you're not dressed?"

Jorie has, indeed, been spending more and more time in bed. She failed to go to the jail today because she was sleeping and then she neglected to attend a meeting at Mark Derry's house to discuss the direction the defense fund should take, dozing dreamlessly, not realizing her mistake until Mark called, concerned. Lately, she's been remembering that as a child she'd been afraid of the dark. She had to leave every light on in her room at night and had been especially frightened of the spaces in the closet and beneath the bed. Before she goes to sleep she once again checks those places with a flashlight, just to reassure herself that she's safe, at least for the time being.

It's unusual for the sisters to be sitting outside together, for them to be talking at all. Jorie and Anne have always been at odds, vying for their mother's affections; they've been so distant that Jorie hadn't even known anything was wrong with Anne's marriage until Anne and Gigi arrived with their suitcases in March. Funny how they enjoy being out on the lawn together on this evening; they don't have to speak to each other if they don't want to, they don't have to pretend to be polite. No traffic goes by. No dogs bark in the distance, out where there are still orchards and fields.

"Charlotte is sick," Jorie says.

"So I've heard. News travels fast."

"I need someone to talk to, and I can't talk

to her. I can't burden her with my problems on top of everything she's going through."

Anne snickers. "Oh, sure, but you can burden me."

The sisters laugh, but Jorie's laughter veers off course and she covers her mouth with her hand, the way she always used to when they were children and she was trying to hold back tears.

"Don't do it," Anne warns. "I'm a terrible shoulder to cry on. You know that. I'm the worst. I have no sympathy for anyone, and I always say the wrong thing. Even Gigi confides in Mom instead of me."

"I have to decide whether or not to sell the house. I've never made a decision like that on my own."

"Welcome to the real world." Anne takes back the glass of Chardonnay and raises it in a toast. "Herein is the place where no one can tell you whether or not you've done the right thing. But actually, I never did like that house. Too perfect."

"Did you ever think there was something wrong with him? Did you know something I didn't know?"

"About Ethan? No. He seemed totally normal to me. Frankly, he seemed great. But look at who I was married to. Do you know Trent has seen Gigi exactly twice since we moved out here, and if I hadn't taken her down to Boston when he was in town on business, he probably wouldn't have even done that much."

"That's not a crime," Jorie reminds her.

"Yeah, well, it is in my book. But I guess you're right. It's not the same. If it makes any difference, Mom still thinks the world of Ethan. She'll stand by him, do or die. She's ready to back him all the way, guilty or not. Poor deluded creature."

"I don't know. She seems better off than we do." Jorie stretches out in the hot, dark night, her head resting on the grass. Her pajamas are shimmery, and her hair is white as snow. "I want to go back in time. That's what I want."

Both sisters can hear mosquitoes drifting past, as well as the echo of traffic from the highway. With four years between them, they were never close; Anne was already gone by the time Jorie was in high school, and they've been as good as strangers ever since. Now they look at the stars. Jorie can spy Orion, the only constellation she knows for certain, those three bright, beautiful stars. She thinks about devotion and betrayal and about how young she had been on the night when she met him. Had she been happy all this time, or had she been fooling herself? Inside the house, their mother's dog, Mister, howls when a siren begins to wail on the other side of town, and the sound raises goose bumps on Jorie's arms. She knows this signal, long and low, a summons to each volunteer firefighter: *Call in, come home.*

"Has he tried to explain what happened?" Anne asks. "Can you make any sense of the reasons behind it?"

"He told me he didn't mean to do it. He never would have hurt anyone."

"Ah." Anne grabs some chips from the bag. "But he did."

"He says he prayed for forgiveness, and forgiveness came to him, and that's when he knew he had to admit what happened."

They stare at each other, and Anne shakes her head. "Easy as that?"

There are so many stars in the sky, but neither sister has ever bothered to try to learn what they are. Tonight, they regret not knowing their names. A car turns the corner and through the dark Jorie and Anne recognize their mother's Toyota, ten years old and badly in need of an oil change, as Anne well knows because the last time she borrowed it, the car had huffed and puffed its way up Horsetail Hill to the country club.

"Do you think you can do that?" Anne asks quickly, before the children are near.

"Do what?"

Anne looks at her sister straight on. "Forgive him."

"I don't know." Jorie closes her eyes; still she can see those bright nameless stars. "I think I must be dreaming."

Once the Toyota has parked, Collie is the first to get out. He goes around and opens Gigi's door, since she has the leftover sheet cake in her lap from the party that followed the talent show. He's a gentleman even at twelve; with his whole world falling in around him, he still remembers what he's been taught.

"How'd it go?" Anne calls.

"You should have been there." Ruth Solomon approaches; her face is somewhat pinched, the way she always looks when she feels someone hasn't lived up to her responsibilities.

"One more thing I've done wrong," Anne says under her breath.

Collie goes by without a word, hightailing it into the house, where the dog is waiting for him. In the past, Collie always loved to play with Mister, for the pug will dance on its toes if offered pretzels or chips, but tonight Collie slinks into the living room and switches on the TV. Ruth perches on the arm of a chaise. From here they can see shadows in the living room and a blue, flickering light.

"Collie and Kat Williams disappeared halfway through the show. Rude as can be. Nobody knew where they were."

Gigi hands Anne the sheet cake and sits down beside her mother in the grass.

"Yum," Anne says, as she picks at stray bits of yellow cake.

"Three people got stage fright, and Noah Peck told some jokes that were in such bad taste his grandmother pulled him off the stage." Gigi sighs. She's something of a perfectionist, although she's already learning that perfection isn't one bit easier to find in Monroe than it was in any of the other towns where they've lived. "Collie just didn't want to be there. It's not like anyone said anything mean to him, but I guess he knew what everyone was thinking."

"What are they thinking?" Jorie turns to her niece.

Gigi looks over at her grandmother for assistance.

"What?" Jorie demands to know.

"They're thinking his father killed somebody, dear." Ruth slips off her shoes, which always raise bunions on her toes. "Not that I believe in judging Ethan."

"Me either." Gigi is quick to agree. Gigi wears no makeup and her face, if not pretty, is fresh and sweet.

"There are often circumstances that none of us understand." Ruth sits with her hands folded in her lap. She is well aware that people were staring at her tonight in the library, and every time she caught someone's eye, she made certain to smile. "You just have to have faith," she says gently.

Anne lets out a laugh. "Oh, come on, Mom. He admitted his guilt. What are we supposed to have faith in?"

"He also said he'd repented," her mother reminds her.

When they head for the house, Jorie's gait is unsteady. Maybe it's the Chardonnay that makes her woozy, or the conversation at hand.

"What would you do?" Jorie whispers to her niece as they reach the front steps. She wants the opinion of the most innocent among them, someone as young as Gigi, a girl who might still believe in possibilities and true love and forgiveness.

"Well, first of all, I wouldn't wear pajamas

outside," Gigi whispers back as they go through the door. "You'll never get those grass stains out now."

Inside, Jorie finds Collie watching TV in the dark with Mister curled up beside him on the couch. Funny how the entire time the girls were growing up, Ruth refused to let them get a dog, but since Anne and Jorie moved out, she's had a series of pugs, the most recent of which is her beloved Mister, who sleeps in Ruth's bed and dines on boiled chicken and rice on Sunday afternoons.

Jorie sits down on the other side of Mister, and the dog wags its whole body in a greeting. Collie, however, doesn't bother to acknowledge her presence. He stares straight ahead, watching the flickering cartoons.

"You and Kat took off?" Their bad behavior was probably her fault for not being there. She hopes they weren't out in the bushes smoking or getting into any more trouble than they've already been in.

Collie shrugs. "The whole thing was stupid. We didn't want to sit there and watch a bunch of kids make fools out of themselves."

"Look at Mister—he really is crazy about you." The dog has rested its head on Collie's knee, but as soon as Jorie brings it to his attention, Collie moves his leg. "Maybe we should get a dog," Jorie suggests. She has the desperate edge of a parent who wants her child to be a child once more. "Maybe we should go look for one this weekend."

"We're not living anywhere, so we can't

have a dog." Collie has become a rationalist, matter-of-fact and cynical and impossible to win over.

"We'll be living somewhere soon enough. We'll get a place with a yard."

Even in the blue tint of the darkened room, she can see Collie roll his eyes. He doesn't believe anything anymore. These days, if you told him it was raining he'd probably have to go stick his hand out the window and feel the drops himself before he could be convinced.

"Until we settle down somewhere, we're living here. Mister could help us train the new dog," Jorie prattles, but she stops when she sees the way Collie is looking at her. He wants to know the truth, and he doesn't want to know anything. He's tied up in knots, and those knots are only going to get tighter. Already, it's changed him; Jorie can see it in the way he holds himself, by the way his hands are curled into fists and by his hooded expression.

"You could have told me you were putting the house up for sale. I heard about it from Kat."

"You're right." Jorie could throttle Kat Williams. "I should have talked to you first."

"Kat said most people can't pay the mortgage after two months with nobody working."

Jorie tries her best to reassure him. "I don't see any reason why I can't start teaching again, so we don't have to worry about money." *That Kat Williams is far too smart for her own good,* Jorie thinks. *She's trouble for sure.* "It's late. I'm going to make up the couch for you."

Jorie goes to the linen closet in the front hall for a blanket and sheets, and meets up with her mother in the hallway. Ruth has just tidied the kitchen and she stops to peer into what had been her living room until Collie took up residence. She shakes her head. "I don't like what's going on here," she says. Collie has fallen asleep in his clothes, with Mister there beside him. "A boy that age should have his own room. Maybe you put the house on the market too quickly. You still don't have all the facts. You've got to just wait and see."

In the dim light, Jorie notices that her mother looks older. Ruth Solomon is dealing with this, too; it's her son-in-law sitting in the jail, not two miles from here. Every time Ruth ventures out to the market or the bakery, every time she walks out to get her mail or retrieve her newspaper, she invariably meets one or another of her neighbors, asking her how she feels about the charges against Ethan. Tonight at the library, for instance, Margaret Peck had leaned over during the finale, while the younger children, including her grandson Noah, were singing "All You Need Is Love," to ask if Ruth had heard a defense fund had been started for Ethan. For a minute, Ruth was relieved. Defense funds were started for innocent men. But then Margaret had said, *Guilty or not, I guess you plan to stand by him.* Well, that was no comfort to Ruth. *Judge not lest you be judged,* she'd said to Margaret, but by then the children were taking their bows and Margaret Peck had turned away to applaud.

The details of what happened in Maryland so many years ago have been printed up not just in the *Globe* and the *Herald*, but in the *Monroe Gazette* as well, there for anyone to read. All Ruth can hope for is that Collie hasn't seen any of it, especially the part about the girl only being fifteen. That's the part Ruth has to put out of her own mind, each and every day.

"It will be easier than you think to stand by him." Ruth has lowered her voice so it is nearly all breath. She's thinking about her husband, the way she felt when he walked out and the way she felt when he came back home, sick and ashamed of himself. "You'll do it because you have to. You'll do it for Collie."

But this is exactly the reason Jorie has been so uncertain and angry, on behalf of Collie. "I'm different than you are. I don't know what I feel."

"Well, you had better decide," Ruth tells her. She takes her daughter's hand for a brief moment. "Otherwise, honey, you will surely drown."

Jorie looks at her mother, surprised; it's precisely what she's been feeling, that sense of being pulled down into the coldest and deepest of waters, bottomless and deep, a thousand times darker than Lantern Lake ever was even on the shortest, most miserable day of the year.

Ruth hushes Gigi and Anne as they come by,

on their way upstairs. Jorie waits, then turns off the lights when everyone else has gone up. She leans against the wall. She knows every inch of this house, even in the dark. She'd been standing in this very hallway when she told her mother she'd met the man she planned to marry. It was here that her mother threw her arms around her and wished her only happiness from that day forward. Jorie goes into the living room, unhampered by the dark. She eases Collie into lying down and covers him with a light quilt. He has decided to take the last name of Solomon, her family name, and if the truth be told, Jorie, too, has been thinking of herself that way, as the person she was before she was Jorie Ford.

Ordinarily, she would have shooed Mister off the couch, but tonight she lets the dog stay beside Collie. She goes on, to the sun porch where her father slept when he was ill, after he came home with his tail between his legs. Ruth has made up a cot, but she didn't have time to hang the curtains she'd sewn when the porch was last used as a bedroom. Moonlight falls into the room and spills across the wooden floorboards. Dan Solomon had left Ruth for another woman, but in the end, he found his way back; he asked to be taken in after an absence of more than ten years, and Ruth couldn't deny him, even though her daughters thought she was crazy.

He was my husband, Ruth said, and there was no arguing that. She nursed him through his cancer as though he'd never hurt her, and if she's ever regretted the choices she's made, she's never mentioned it aloud. Jorie, however, had been far more wary when her father returned. The first time she saw him again after so many years apart, she thought she'd want to strike him, that's how angry she was at what he'd done to their family. But he was so very changed, by illness and regret, that she'd hugged him instead, although what she feels about him she still can't quite make out.

Jorie sits cross-legged on the cot where her father slept during his illness. It seems as though a lifetime has passed since she's last lived in this house. She thinks of Ethan, who would be lying on his cot at this very moment, staring at the ceiling of his cell, a bumpy plaster that was painted pale green. He always told her he couldn't sleep right without her, and on those few occasions when they'd been separated—a fishing trip for him, a three-day weekend in Puerto Rico for her when Charlotte's marriage was in its final last-gasp stages—Ethan told her he'd slept in a chair. A bed without her was not worth getting into, that's what he'd said, and sleep was a foreign country without her hand to hold.

Well, she can't sleep either, and it isn't because they're apart. She's kept awake by moonlight, and perhaps it's the glint of that silver light that makes Jorie go to what had long ago been her father's bookshelf. She takes down a leather-bound atlas and props up the book on her father's old desk, where he had faithfully paid the bills each month when she and Anne were little, before he went away. Now there are pots of begonias and curly ferns on the desk, but still there is room enough to open to the map of Maryland and trace the route she plans to take. She wants to see for herself what sort of place can make a man turn and run so fast and so hard that he'd lose himself as he traveled, with pieces of his history falling like leaves, until he was empty enough to be brand-new, like a man dropped to earth from the farthest reaches of the moon, with silver light running through his veins, where there should have been blood.

Three

Dreamland

FIFTEEN YEARS AGO, THE fields in this part of Maryland were yellow, burned and discolored by a season of unusual heat, but now, in the first week of August, they are sweet and green, rich with corn and soybeans and millet. Out here on the Eastern Shore, two hours from Baltimore and half an hour past the Bay Bridge, the old roads buckle in the summertime. Late in the afternoon, when the air becomes cooler, a person can smell the tide upon approaching the marshes past Blackwater. When Jorie stops for gas, she stands beside the rented car in the fading light and tries to get her bearings. The landscape is one she's not accustomed to, with bits of extreme beauty peeking out from between asphalt and billboards. Beyond the gas station, for instance, lies a stretch of wild rice, golden and blooming riotously in the damp, brackish soil.

I could move to this place right now and nobody would know who I was and what I was leaving behind, Jorie thinks to herself as she pays the attendant and gets a Pepsi from the soda machine. She holds the ice-cold can to her forehead and blinks in the sharp light. *I could tell people anything I wanted to, and whatever I told them, that would be the truth as far as they were concerned. Whoever I said I was, well then, that's who I'd be.*

Jorie gets directions and heads out. It's been a long while since she's been anywhere on her own, and she has a nervous, prickly sensation up and down her spine. What would happen if she never returned? Anne is the only one who knows where she is, a necessity in case of an emergency. But Anne is disorganized and may already have lost the sheet of paper with the vitals written down—time of departure, time of arrival, the name of the town that is Jorie's destination. With no husband and no child to accompany her, Jorie feels oddly light, as if she could float away through the open car windows; the breeze catches her pale hair so that it flies everywhere and is quickly tangled into knots. She thinks warmly of the vacations she and Charlotte used to take when they were young, always staying at third-rate motels, whether on the shore in Rhode Island or up in Maine, weeks when they ate fast food, and stayed up all night, and had a ridiculously wonderful time. It astonishes Jorie to think of how young they were, how hopeful and free. Amazing where your life can deposit you before you know it. One, two, three, and you're on a completely different road than the one you'd always expected to be on at this point in your life. There is no compass when such things happen, no rules and no maps to guide you, and no one who cares if the sun is glaring or if the asphalt is melting beneath your tires.

As Jorie drives on, loblolly pines edge the road and cast shadows across the thickening air. She turns on the radio for company, but the southern twang of the voices and the chords of a sorrowful country song only serve to sharpen her loneliness. At the turnoff to Holden there's a stretch of cordgrass that is nearly eight feet tall, and Jorie can hear the call of birds from within the reeds. As she gets closer to town, she can't help but wonder if Ethan had driven down this very same road fifteen years ago, and if, as he'd passed by the marshes, he'd noticed the wild cherry and sweet gum trees.

Although she's exhausted from traveling, Jorie finds the Black Horse Hotel easily enough; it's the only hotel in town, far less busy than the Econo Lodge she passed before she stopped for gas. The building is framed by tall white pillars and there is a set of gray stone steps, swept clean every morning. Inside, the lobby is cool without benefit of air-conditioning. There's a restaurant that looks decent, and a bar called the Horseshoe. The woman behind the desk is pretty and lively, the sort of woman Ethan might have dated if he'd stayed in this town instead of traveling north to New England, instead of running as fast as he could.

"You look like you need a good night's rest," the desk clerk says cheerfully as Jorie signs in.

Jorie feels a little guilty about using Anne's credit card, but with Ethan no longer working and so many bills to pay, she is frighteningly low on funds. With unexpected generosity, Anne had shoved the MasterCard into Jorie's hands. *Go on and enjoy it,* Anne had told her as she left for the airport. *Trent will be the one paying the bill, so honey, live large.* They'd laughed as they'd imagined Trent's distress upon seeing the charges, but as Jorie signs her sister's name on the register, she wonders if she isn't committing some punishable offense. Perhaps this simple act would be considered forgery or grand larceny; still, it's the only way she can pay the bill, so from now on she is Anne Lyle. In truth, she's more comfortable under the cloak of her sister's identity. It's as though she has discarded herself somewhere between Baltimore and the Bay Bridge, and has become the sort of woman who uses falsified ID and spends nights alone in a hotel, the sort of woman whose husband is sitting in a jail cell hundreds of miles away with no idea of where she is and when she'll be home.

Her room is nice and clean, with a down quilt on the bed and a hand-hooked rug ringed with flowers which covers most of the wide, pine floorboards. Sheer curtains frame a view of town hall across the street, a brick building fronted by glossy magnolias. There's air-conditioning up here, but Jorie doesn't bother with it. She opens the window and breathes deeply; she wants to know what it feels like to be in Holden in the summertime. The damp scent of evening falling, the heavy August air, the song of the red-winged blackbirds, alighting in the fields around town by the thousands, to feed on wild rice and fight for their territory.

After she's settled in, Jorie orders room service, choosing a house salad with vinaigrette dressing along with a steak sandwich and fries. Once the food arrives, she finds she's ravenous. And she's equally tired; soon after she's eaten, she falls asleep on the bed in her clothes, shoes still on, desperate for rest, even though the sky is still light in the farthest corners and the hour isn't much later than nine. On this night, Jorie dreams that Ethan is with her, beside her in the hotel bed, his face close to hers. He is so handsome that she is blinded, and for an instant she's unable to make out her own husband's features. He leans closer, and although she cannot really see him, she can feel his warm breath, as well as the catch in her stomach as her desire for him rises, the way it always does when he's near.

Who did you think I was? he whispers to Jorie in her dream.

He gets out of bed and walks to the window. He moves the filmy curtains aside, then turns back to smile at her. She wants him so completely she's tied up in knots, yet when she tries to speak, she finds she cannot say one word, nor can she leave her bed and go to him. She can only watch as he steps beyond the curtains and casts himself out the window, like a bird who has longed to be free, disappearing from view so quickly that when Jorie finally struggles from the tangled bedsheets to look for him, there is nothing to see in the hot, pallid air. Anything a man might leave behind, footprints and fingerprints alike, have vanished, and the clothes he wore have unraveled into a pile of white cotton thread.

Jorie awakens the following morning with a terrible headache. Her feet hurt from sleeping in her shoes, her mouth is parched, and she rises from bed with her dream still around her, a foggy halo that nags at her. She showers and dresses, then phones her mother's house, as she'd told Anne she would, to check in on Collie. Collie's fine, or so Anne says, and Jorie will just have to take her sister's word for it, since Collie himself won't come to the phone. He's too tired, he's still half asleep, he has nothing to say. No matter how Anne tries, he cannot be convinced or cajoled into speaking to his mother, and this isn't like Collie.

"He's so angry," Jorie says.

"So is every twelve-year-old boy," Anne tells her. "At least yours has a right to be angry. Stop worrying about Collie. Gigi's going to take him and that strange little girlfriend of his down to the lake. They can cool off and eat the picnic lunch I'm sending along with them—peanut butter, pickles, and pink lemonade. Remember? We used to think it was a sure cure for just about everything."

Jorie does indeed recall that she and Anne used to fix that exact picnic nearly every day after their father left them. It was the only summer when they spent any amount of time together, and now it comes back to her, how they used to walk to Lantern Lake, the long way around, past the old orchards that grew spicy russets and buttery Keepsake apples, along with McIntoshes and Macouns. It was the only time they had ever felt close to each other, gorging on that wretched menu no one else would have cared to eat, wanting only what was salty and sour to ease their pain.

Jorie knows Anne is taking good care of Collie, yet for what is perhaps the thousandth time, she wonders if she's done the wrong thing in leaving her boy. She cannot imagine he will understand that this trip was hardly a matter of choice for her. How could she ever be sure this place existed if she hadn't flown to Baltimore, and rented a midsize car, and followed her map of the Eastern Shore? She needed to do these things, just as she needed to sleep in this hotel bed and dream her terrible dream, and wake on this sunny morning in Holden, Maryland.

Most people look inside to know what they feel, but Jorie has nothing left inside anymore. The truths by which she has lived her life have evaporated, leaving her empty of everything except the faint blue static of her own skepticism. She has never been a person to question herself; now she questions everything. Yes, she is looking out the window at town hall as she sips the coffee room service has brought her, but mightn't that vista— the knobby gray stone building, the lustrous trees and wrought-iron benches—just as easily be a moonscape? Magnolias don't grow on the moon and red-winged blackbirds don't fly there, or so she has always been told. Yet how does she know that for sure? Where are the documents, the photographs, the hard and fast proof? In a matter of weeks, Jorie has become a disbeliever in just about everything, including herself. She, who took people at their word and always trusted her own instincts, is now a woman who wants only facts, black ink on paper, eyewitness accounts.

As soon as the clock on the night table is at nine on the dot, Jorie leaves the hotel to go across the street. It's another hot day, and she's already overheated by the time she finds her way to the department of records. The woman behind the desk, busy with some mail and muttering to herself, ignores Jorie, until Jorie asks to see a death certificate. The clerk, a local woman named Nancy Kerr, who's never lived anyplace but Holden and has never wanted to, is suddenly interested. Nancy is a few years younger than Jorie, with dark curly hair and a no-nonsense demeanor. She's the person folks in Holden come to when they want to complain about something, and after a few years at the job, most of the soft edges she once had have been eradicated.

"Whose death in particular?" When Nancy hears the name Rachel Morris, she shakes her head. "Poor thing." For an instant, Nancy almost seems like the girl she once was, vulnerable and easily wounded, long before she

222

got divorced and took on this job in order to raise her daughter. But that reverie doesn't last. Nancy gives Jorie the once-over, and as she does, her face takes on a clouded cast. "You're not a reporter, are you?"

"I'm just interested in the case. I'm trying to figure out what happened."

"I can tell you exactly what happened. Somebody killed Rachel fifteen years ago, and now they caught the fellow, up in Massachusetts. You can read all about it in the papers."

"Well, I thought I'd start by taking a look at whatever files you had."

"And the reason I should do this for you would be?"

"It's a personal matter."

"Really."

They look at each other and Jorie realizes Nancy Kerr had probably gone to school with Rachel Morris. She'd probably grown up right alongside her.

"You sound like you're from Massachusetts, so I'm guessing it's pretty damned personal." Nancy is smart and she's not afraid to speak her mind, but she's had a rough week, with her daughter in bed with a stomach virus. All the same, she finds herself being won over by the fact that Jorie's eyes are glassy, the sure sign of a woman who's a stranger to a good night's sleep, much as Nancy is herself. Perhaps this is the reason Nancy Kerr goes to a file cabinet and comes back with a folder. "Well, now I know I'm crazy. I just hope I'm not going to regret this as much as I do every-thing else in my life," she says as she hands over the information.

When Jorie opens the file and sees the death certificate, she feels dazed, almost as though she's been blinded somehow. She has to sit down, quickly folding herself into one of the hard plastic chairs, each of which has a desktop conveniently attached. Here are the papers, right in front of her. Here is a photograph that doesn't even seem like a human form. Well, this is what she wanted, isn't it? She had to know the official cause of death, had to see it in black and white, and now she has the coroner's report in her hands. She forces her-self to go over how the internal bleeding was caused by trauma, how the skull was cracked, leaving fragments of bone lodged in the brain. What she finds hardest to read are the simplest of facts: the color of the deceased's eyes, green, and of her hair, red as roses, and the grievous information offered by a crude sketch of the birthmark at the base of the girl's spine, a plum-colored blemish in the shape of a but-terfly.

When Nancy Kerr sees how pale Jorie is, her skin turning to ice on this summer day, she comes over and pulls up a chair. Nancy hadn't planned to be helpful, but the mention of Rachel Morris's name has opened her heart. Up close, she notices that Jorie has written down the address of the Morris farm.

"He won't talk to you, if that's what you're planning," Nancy tells Jorie.

"He?" Luckily, Jorie has her trusty map in the car, for the address is a rural route east of town, out past a series of inlets and ponds. She thinks of butterflies and birthmarks, and of a sorrow so deep a person would have to dig with a shovel and a spade all night long just to reach its outermost edges.

"Rachel's brother, James. You can forget about it. He won't see you if you go out to the house. There were a lot of reporters hanging around when it happened, and some awful people with their own agendas, psychics who didn't have a clue and such. Everybody was looking to get their names in the papers. It wasn't more than a few years before Joe and Irene, Rachel's parents, both died, one after the other, the way people do when they don't want to live anymore. After that, James stopped talking to people. Especially reporters and lawyers. Now they're back, like flies. And even if that's not what you are, there's no way he's going to see you. Unless you give me one good reason to try and talk him into it."

"I know the person who's been accused." Jorie's face tilts upward, as if she half-expects to be slapped. "So I'm involved, whether I like it or not."

"And you don't like it."

"No." Jorie closes the file on the Morris girl. She has already memorized most of the words within. "I hate it."

Some people say Nancy Kerr is too soft-hearted for her own good once you get past her tough exterior. Certainly, it's not easy for her to turn down someone in trouble. Nancy takes a hard look at Jorie, then heads over to the phone and dials; she speaks in a hushed tone for a few moments, then signals to Jorie.

"It's James. He'll hear what you have to say."

Jorie takes the phone. She feels cold standing in the middle of this strange office, in a town she never knew existed before this summer.

"Go ahead. He'll talk," Nancy urges.

"Hello," Jorie says uncertainly.

There is deep silence on the other end of the line. Jorie can almost feel how conflicted James Morris is and how close he is to hanging up on her. Why shouldn't he greet this call with mistrust? Who in this town, or any other, can assure him that people are worthy of a moment of his time? It's the hour when the town offices are growing busier. The motor vehicle department is at the end of the hall and already a line of customers has gathered. Several people call out a greeting to Nancy as they walk past the office of records.

"I know you don't know me," Jorie forces herself to go on, "but I'm related to someone who was involved in your sister's case."

Silence again, and then after what seems like forever, a man speaks. "Are you referring to the murderer?" James Morris has a raspy voice, and he speaks so softly Jorie has to jam her ear up to the receiver in order to hear. "You think I should talk to you because you know my sister's murderer? Let me guess— you want to tell me what a good man he is. You want to tell me I should forgive what I don't

226

understand. But the way I see it, if I listen to you, I'll have everyone who ever knew him in Massachusetts knocking on my door to plead his case. So, no, I don't think so."

"You won't have everyone. You'll just have me." Jorie can hear James Morris breathing. "He's my husband."

There, she has said it, the nightmare sentence she's been dreading so, and with these words released she is melting, like green ice in the shallows of a pond, like crystals evaporating into flame. Before long, little blisters will rise on her tongue, the price, perhaps, for speaking the truth; she'll have to stop at the water fountain in the hallway for a long, cold drink.

"Your husband?" James Morris says. "And you want to come out here and talk to me?"

Nancy Kerr pretends to be busy with some files, but Jorie can tell she's listening in to Jorie's part of the conversation. How could a woman who's been raised in this town not be interested in this turn of events? When a second phone line rings, Nancy doesn't bother to answer. Instead, she lets the machine pick up.

"I very much want to talk to you," Jorie tells him. "Please."

She has actually broken into a sweat talking to this man, James Morris, and it doesn't help that town hall isn't air-conditioned. She's close to begging for something she's not even certain she wants. All the same, she knows if she misses this opportunity to go out to the Morris farm, she'll never be sure of what she feels. If she doesn't walk along the same roads, breathe the same air, how can she ever understand what happened that night?

She has come hundreds of miles not to look for a way to pardon Ethan or to condone what he's done, but to see if she can find a way to live with what's happened. That's what James Morris doesn't understand; it's not so much his forgiveness she's searching for, it's her own.

"I won't take up much of your time. I promise."

James Morris surprises her when he responds. "Sure, you can come out here." Maybe he wants to get a good look at her: the woman who's spent all these years with the man who killed his sister. He must be standing near a window or out on a porch as he speaks to her, for Jorie can hear the chirrup of birdsong through the receiver. It's a mesmerizing sound, a chorus from heaven, sweetness from the skies up above. "But just so you know, you're not going to like what you find."

Jorie takes down the directions, and when she hands the phone to Nancy Kerr, she's shaking. "Thank you. He never would have agreed to see me if you hadn't called him."

"Don't be so quick to thank me," Nancy warns. "And don't think just because he's going to see you he'll be nice to you, because James Morris isn't especially nice. Not anymore. And especially not to you."

Jorie heads out to her parked rental car, left in the sunshine and hot as blazes, the steering wheel burning her fingertips as soon as it's touched. She opens the windows, then follows James Morris's directions, west on Main Street until the turnoff at Greenway Road and then left on Route 12. On her way out of town, she passes a block of stores and then a more residential section of the village, lanes of pretty brick homes surrounded by hedges of azaleas. As she drives along, Jorie is thinking about Rachel Morris and the birthmark at the base of her spine. Rachel must have taken this same road a thousand times or more; she must have ridden her bike through the leafy shadows cast by the sweet gum trees and stopped to grab handfuls of fruit from the stands of wild cherries that grow here in such abundance. Surely, she bought her shampoo in the pharmacy on Main Street and ordered vanilla Cokes and French fries with vinegar at Duke's Diner on Greenway Road, where the crullers are fresh every morning and the menu hasn't changed for the past fifteen years.

Once again, Jorie has the feeling of having dropped off the face of the earth as she's known it, only to surface in another time, as if this deserted road is a tunnel leading back through the years. She is engulfed in the heat, dizzy with it. She has always thought herself to be a compassionate person, as sure of right and wrong as she is of herself, but now she's not so certain. The person she's always assumed she was would not be driving on this road in Maryland all alone, passing huge osprey nests balanced on telephone poles, heading farther into the countryside as scores of fish crows soar through the sky. After she passes a wrecking shop and a market and a tiny post office, she spies the turnoff James Morris has told her about—a swampy stretch of pickerelweed and brackish water that was once a swimming hole with exceedingly warm temperatures. Now, the shallows are clogged with water parsnip and mallow; some mallow roses are blooming, pink and sweet as they manage to grow through the wool grass. No one goes swimming here anymore, and they haven't for years; these days, people worry about bacteria and leeches, they take into account factors no one used to even consider when diving into the murky depths of a natural pool that was so hot steam rose from the surface of the water and clouds formed only inches above the ground.

Jorie takes the turnoff and rides along until she finds the dirt road leading to the farm. The strain of her engine startles a covey of woodcocks in the thickets of dogwood and sweet pepper bush when she passes by. As the birds flap into the sky, prattling, Jorie feels a chill go through her, even though the temperature is hovering above ninety. Her heart is like one of those birds, easily startled, too quick for her own blood. She can see the white house, unpainted for the past several years, the black shutters sagging at odd angles. All she wants is the tiniest shred of information that will allow her to believe in her husband. At first, she'd been convinced that Ethan's confession was intended to cover up someone else's crime. Surely he must have a brother on a chain gang, or a cousin gone wrong, perhaps a best friend he'd vowed to protect on that August night so long ago.

Now that he's given testimony and recounted facts no one save the guilty party could know, she's still convinced there's an answer. There must be an explanation for what happened, some strange set of circumstances that led him astray. Drugs, perhaps, or alcohol; a dire phase of the moon, the drought-scarred season, the rising temperatures, any of these factors might have been at play. Or perhaps it was the girl who was at fault; she may have egged him on, tricked him, teased him until he had no other choice but to respond. This girl may have possessed a violent nature. She may have spat in his face, tried to scratch his eyes out, left him no choice. Such things happened, didn't they? Good men were trapped when they least expected it, they were ambushed and set upon, with end results they never could have imagined.

There is a reason for what has happened, there must at least be that, and that is why Jorie has come here and why she brings the rental car to a stop in this red dirt driveway, hundreds of miles from home. James Morris is waiting for her on the porch. He doesn't get up when she parks and steps out, not even when his dog, a lanky cross between a bulldog and a shepherd, comes racing up, barking and showing its teeth. For a minute Jorie truly thinks she might faint. It's the heat, the sunlight, the growling dog; it's the look on James Morris's face and the last several weeks of her life, rewinding in her head like a movie she's been forced to watch too many times. Jorie places one hand on the burning hood of the car to steady herself. The air out here is thick, salt-laced from the marshes that surround the farm.

"Mr. Morris?" Jorie calls.

James Morris whistles, and the dog goes trotting to him. Morris stands then; he pats his dog as he watches Jorie approach. He is younger than Jorie had expected him to be, and Jorie is surprised when she understands: he was Rachel's younger brother, not much more than ten when it happened. Not so very far from Collie's age.

"Nancy must have told you I don't like visitors," James Morris says. "Well, she was right about that. I don't."

"I appreciate you taking the time to see me." Jorie holds one hand over her eyes. Although she can't quite make out his expression, she can see he's a good-looking man in his twenties, blond and tall, with a narrow thoughtful face. He wears old jeans and a gray tee-shirt stained with sweat. He'd been working outside when the phone rang, cutting down some of the foxtail grass that always encroaches upon his fields. Jorie suddenly understands why she'd heard birdsong through the telephone wires when she'd called earlier from town hall. Though they are usually territorial, there are hundreds of red-winged blackbirds perched in the cypress trees, and hundreds more swoop across the cornfield beyond the house. James Morris had been working with a scythe earlier, and when clouds of mosquitoes rose from the shorn grass, huge flocks of birds had come to dine upon them. Even now, the sky is aflutter with black wings; the birds are unsettled and feeding wildly, as if they might never again be offered a meal such as the one set before them in the white-hot air of the morning.

"This probably isn't very smart of you." James Morris is looking at Jorie closely. He has pale eyes, like Collie's, and like Collie he's not easily read. "What if I wanted the man who killed Rachel to know what it felt like to lose somebody? What if I shot you right now?"

Morris comes down the porch steps. He might have a gun with him at this very moment, but Jorie doesn't turn and run. She looks right back at him. He's a big man. Close up, he's even taller than Jorie would have guessed when she first got out of her rental car, maybe six two, but on the night when it happened, he probably wouldn't have come up to Jorie's shoulder. Perhaps she should be afraid of him, but she's afraid of something else entirely. She's afraid of the way it might be possible for her to feel inside if she doesn't find the answers she needs.

"I don't think you're going to shoot me," she says calmly.

"Oh?" James Morris almost smiles. "But we

already know you're a bad judge of character. I'm guessing you didn't know about what happened here when you married your husband."

"I still don't know what I need to. That's why I came to talk to you."

They stare at each other across the heat waves that separate them. James Morris hasn't trusted anyone since the time he was ten, but Jorie is new to this, and there's an innocence about her that makes Morris want to shake her and wake her up. *Come on, girl,* he wants to say. *What does it mean to you that you trust a complete stranger more than you do the man you're married to?*

"You want to see where they found the truck?" he asks instead. "You know, without that truck we never would have found your husband. His ID was left in the glove compartment, and they took the photo off his license. Want to see the place?"

Jorie nods. She has been prepared for James Morris to tell her to get off his property, to turn tail and run back to Massachusetts as fast as she can. Instead, he's opening up to her and Jorie has already decided she will agree to see anything he offers to show her, no matter where it might lead. She follows James through the cornfield with the dog racing ahead, cutting a path through the green husks. She could be anywhere on this earth, lost to everyone who's ever known her, so far from home she might never again find her way back. It's so hot out beyond the shadows of the sweet gum trees that a person could easily confuse what is real and what's imagined, thrown off by the floating scrim of heat waves and the sea of green. For an instant, Jorie isn't sure of what's in front of her eyes—a black angel, a man tied to a tree—but as they grow closer she realizes it's only an old pole once used for a scarecrow. The pole has a metal whirligig attached, set out to scare away grackles and swamp sparrows and crows. James stops and the shadow of the pole slides across his face in a single dark bar. His dog leans against his leg and looks up at its master, anxious to walk on.

"After that night, kids around here said the scarecrow had done it. They said he'd come alive in the middle of the night and walked through this field and climbed in through Rachel's window. And then he'd done all those horrible things. You know why they thought that?"

Jorie shakes her head. She doesn't want to look at him, but she forces herself to meet his eyes. He's an extremely handsome man, she sees that now, one who hasn't had any life to speak of. He lived here with his parents until they'd died, and after that he never for a moment thought of going anywhere else.

"They thought it was the scarecrow because no one could believe anyone human could do the things that had been done to Rachel."

James Morris's life might have taken him anywhere, to a place where the well water didn't taste like salt, a town where no one even knew

235

what a blackbird looked like. The women in Holden have given up on him, and they shake their heads when they think of what might have been. They used to bring him suppers of baked ham and beans, they'd stop in on Saturday nights with homemade pies or six-packs of beer, but even though James Morris was always polite, he clearly had no interest in any of them. Something had stopped for him a long time ago. Their lives had gone forward, but his had come to a halt, in shades of gray, as if he were living in a snapshot, frozen in place. He didn't even notice the blackbirds swooping above them; they ate crumbs from his hands, they rode on his shoulders, pecking at bits of grain caught in the seams of his clothes, and still he pays them no mind.

James Morris has spent years trying not to think, and that's the way he's managed to rise from his bed every day. He's a man who stays clear of town, unless he needs provisions; he goes to the bank and the post office once a month, more than enough as far as he's concerned. A few summers ago he sold a parcel of land to a neighbor, so he has some money in reserve, and he does well enough with his cornfields to pay the taxes and the utility bills. When it comes right down to it, there wasn't much he wanted. Unless you count going backward in time. Oh, if only he could wake up and be ten years old all over again on a splendid summer morning. If only the most unusual thing that was about to happen was that he'd finally manage to dive into Hell's Pond from the highest branch of the big sweet gum tree that grew on the shore until lightning struck a few years back, cleaving the giant trunk in two.

James Morris is looking into the distance, and from the expression on his face, Jorie can picture the boy he once was. Keeping himself away from other people the way he has, James Morris has maintained a sort of purity of spirit, despite everything that happened that night.

"There was another reason folks around here said the scarecrow had done it. Its clothes were gone. Of course, someone had stolen them and left his own bloody clothes behind, but no one could convince anyone around here of that. Not for quite a while. It got so most people who grew up in this county wouldn't go out at night, especially the ones living on farms. A week or so after the funeral, my father burned the scarecrow. He doused it with so much gasoline, he nearly set fire to all our fields, but he didn't care."

After that, James confides, there wasn't a farm anywhere near Holden where scarecrows were set out in the fields, and that's true today. Fifteen years after it happened, some people still swear that scarecrows can walk on hot summer nights, they can slip into houses while people are sleeping, they wait by the roadside in order to trap children and turn them into blackbirds. Maybe that's the reason this area seems overrun by birds; there, in the distance, Jorie watches as clouds of blackbirds form a dark horizon, whirling back and forth across the white heat.

"They've still got those bloody clothes down at the district attorney's office," James Morris says, "and something tells me when they finish running the tests they're doing now, the DNA is not going to belong to any scarecrow. But when I was a kid, I really believed it. I couldn't sleep until my father burnt the damned thing, and even then I kept dreaming about it. Every night it was walking through the fields, coming for Rachel." He turns to Jorie, his face wary, as it has been for all these years. "Is that what you came here to hear? You want to see firsthand how our lives were ruined? You want to hear how he raped her and killed her and left the clothes on the ground for any ten-year-old boy to find?"

Jorie can feel how dry her throat is, like paper or parchment, aflame with grief and guilt. James Morris is being cruel, he wants to hurt her, but so what? He has a right to do so. He had been the first one up that next morning; he'd gone into the field with his old dog Cobalt, who's been dead twelve years now. He didn't know what the pile of clothes was covered with until he'd already stopped to pick up the shirt, and by then it was too late. He had blood on his hands, and it burned him, it stained him right through his fingertips, through his flesh, and he knew that no matter what he did, it would never wash away.

He should have called for his father. He should have screamed until the neighbors on the other side of Route 12 could hear him. Instead, he ran in the opposite direction, and he sat in the woods crying, until Cobalt found him. By then, Rachel had been taken away. In a matter of hours, on a perfect summer day, the house where they lived had become completely empty, even though there were still three people living inside.

"I want to hear whatever you want to tell me," Jorie tells James Morris. "I'm trying to understand."

He laughs at the notion. It's not so much that he doesn't believe her, it's that he knows what she wants is impossible. All the same, he leads her down to the place where Hell's Pond used to be, the mucky inlet Jorie spied on her drive in. This is where the truck had been found when the water was drained as a way to stop the spread of mosquitoes.

"He must have parked down here, and afterward he decided to roll the truck into the pond so no one could find a trace of him."

Jorie crouches down. The shallows are thick with smartweed and needle rush. King rails nest here, along with mallards and those swamp sparrows that always sound like women crying when they call to each other. It's cool in the shadows at the edge of the water and everything smells like earth and salt. The air is tinged green, and little fish swim through the few pools that are left, each one drying up in the heat of the day, evaporating by the second.

"Those were her favorite flowers." James

239

Morris nods to a ring of rose mallow, luminous and pink in the brackish water. "She used to put on my father's high boots and tromp through the mud and get a whole basket of them, and our house would be full of them. I told her there were rice rats out there, but that didn't stop her. She was the kind of girl who was always better at everything than everyone else was. Dancing, climbing trees, even using my father's shotgun. She had twenty-twenty vision. She could see things nobody else could."

When they turn back, they don't speak as they follow the path their footprints have made. Jorie is thinking of baskets of mallows. She is thinking of a girl pulling on her father's old green boots. The more she imagines this, the more her head hurts, until it is pounding. At the turnoff, they leave the path through the woods and head back through the field. As they make their way through the tall grass, the dog flushes some woodcocks out from the reeds and runs off barking. James whistles through his teeth. "Hey, Fergus," he calls, and the dog comes racing back, its tongue lolling out of its mouth. James Morris reaches down and pats the dog's head, and in that moment Jorie sees the man in all his loneliness. Right then she knows that she is walking beside a shattered individual who has never gotten beyond that terrible day. James Morris might as well still be ten years old for all the good being a man will do him. For an instant, as they traverse the cornfield, Jorie feels like holding his hand.

"I'm thinking of getting my boy a dog," she says as they near the house.

James Morris looks at her, hard. "You've got a son with him?"

"I've been married to him for thirteen years. We've had a regular life. Just like other people's."

The heat is crackly, a sure sign of rain later in the evening. But for now the sky is still ablaze with light, azure above them. "It used to be like other people's, but that was before you knew what he was. Now it sounds like you had nothing." It's taken years for such a sweet boy to turn ill-tempered, but he's managed it, almost. "Isn't that right?"

The red dust that had risen as they tramped through the fields has begun to settle on Jorie's skin so that she looks slightly sunburned. "All this time I've loved him, and now what am I supposed to do? Am I supposed to walk away? Just like that? Chalk every day we had together up to one big lie?"

"You want to see who you married?" James Morris's tone is soft, but it's also growly, like his dog's, like that of any man who's kept things inside until they've simmered into a stew of fury and regret. "Because if you want to see, I'll show you."

It's a threat, and James's voice breaks, but allowing her into the house is also a gift of sorts, Jorie understands that. As he opens the screen door, it's an invitation into his pain. It's not often that a closed-up man like James Morris makes an offer such as this, so Jorie nods. She looks back at him, straight into his beautiful face with its lines of sorrow and hard work.

"Don't say I didn't warn you," James Morris says as she steps inside. "Don't say I didn't tell you to get into your car and drive away."

He takes her inside, where the rooms are dusty and cool. There are photographs on the mantel—James Morris's parents in happier days, aunts and uncles from Annapolis and Virginia that he hasn't seen for more than a decade, the old dog Cobalt, and the next dog as well, a sweet-tempered Doberman, mistakenly taken for a deer and shot a few years back. In the center of the mantel are the photographs of Rachel. Jorie approaches for a closer look, though she feels even dizzier inside this darkened house than she did out in the hot fields.

"May I?" Jorie says, and when James Morris shrugs, she picks up a photo of Rachel at five, front teeth missing, red hair cut in bangs. The silver frame is shockingly cool in Jorie's hands, like stones in a river or hail from above. She replaces that photograph and turns to the next, Rachel on horseback, her smile gorgeous, and then the next, Rachel in a party dress, her hair carefully curled, and then one that James tells her was taken two weeks before she died, Rachel and her mother at the shore, arms around each other, mouths wide with laughter.

Rachel was beautiful, Jorie can see that even in the half-light of the living room. She was a real live girl with hopes and dreams who loved the beach at Ocean City and collected stray cats, dozens of which she kept in the barn. She was a girl who walked into the swamp searching for rose mallows, and who had once raced her horse, Sugar, all the way to the pharmacy in the center of town, where she yodeled at the top of her lungs, then galloped her way home through the woods, all for a dollar bet made with her brother.

"She looks like someone I would have liked," Jorie says.

"Oh, yeah. Everyone liked her, even Nancy Kerr, who was the shyest girl you'd ever met back then. Rachel had more best friends than most people had acquaintances. That was Rachel."

When James signals, Jorie follows him down the hall, past the kitchen, past his own bedroom, to a closed door. Jorie can feel her head pounding again. Her legs feel heavy; if they hadn't turned to lead, surely she would have run, back into the burnished light of the field, the red light of the road, the blue-black light of her hotel room.

James Morris eyes her carefully to see if she's changed her mind.

"Go on," Jorie tells him. This is what she came here for. She knows whose room this was.

James opens the door into a fifteen-year-old-girl's bedroom where everything has remained the same—there are her stuffed animals, the white curtains and the pink wallpaper patterned with flowers, a design that's nearly unrecognizable, faded from the constant stream of sunlight. There is the dressing table on which there are barrettes, and bracelets, and bottles of cologne that have evaporated within their glass stoppers. Her books are piled upon her desk, and across one wall are ribbons from the horse shows she'd entered, along with awards from dancing school.

Jorie goes to the dressing table and picks up the hairbrush. Three strands of red hair are still caught there, twisted like gold. It's colder in this room than it was in the rest of the house; it's icy, as a matter of fact, and the air, trapped for so many years, is difficult to breathe. Jorie forces herself to look at the single bed, up against the wall.

"My mother spent two weeks scrubbing the blood, and later on she replastered and painted, but it never went away. Maybe you can't see it anymore, but I know it's there."

Jorie narrows her eyes and sees a shape not unlike the coroner's sketch of Rachel's birth-mark.

"It's a butterfly," Jorie says.

"It's blood," James Morris informs her. "You never get rid of it."

James opens the closet and all at once the room smells sweet. *Sachet,* Jorie thinks, *lily of the valley,* the same scent she herself had loved as a girl. Rachel's dresses are still there, fifteen years out of date, but still pretty. There are her blouses and her shoes, her winter boots with the laces threadbare. There are her mittens, her winter parka, her Easter coat with its gold buttons. There are her blue jeans, neatly folded over hangers. On the shelf along one wall are piles of sweaters and of underwear; as she peers through the dim light, Jorie notices that the socks are a far smaller size than the ones Collie wears.

James Morris can hardly talk. He never comes into this room anymore, and this is why.

"This is what we lost," he tells Jorie.

Jorie walks the perimeter of the room. She wants to remember how the sunlight falls in through the gauzy curtains, how wide the pine floorboards are, how the silver barrettes on the dressing table are placed in a pink glass dish. She stops in front of the night table. There is a diary, pale blue leatherette trimmed in gold.

"We found this, but the key was missing. My mother thought it was disrespectful to read the private thoughts of the dead, but the investigators insisted. They broke it open, but I had them lock it again before they gave it back to us. I figured somebody should respect the person that she was."

Jorie goes into the hallway, where she hides her face in her hands. She has no right to cry, but she does so anyway. She can't stop herself. James stays in his sister's room awhile longer. He knows when women cry, they'll eventually stop, or at least that was true for his mother. He waits, and sure enough when he comes out and closes Rachel's door, Jorie has gotten herself back under control.

"Sorry," she says. "I didn't mean to do that."

"I'll make coffee," James offers with surprising generosity.

He shows her to the bathroom, which is uncommonly clean for a man living alone, where Jorie washes her face. The scent of the water is nasty, rusty and filled with salt, but it's cold, and Jorie's burning eyes are refreshed. Afterward, she finds her way to the kitchen, and while James Morris fixes coffee, she stands by the back door. It's so peaceful here, watching the blackbirds swoop across the open sky. It's easier to breathe if she thinks about blackbirds.

"Thanks," Jorie says when James hands her a mug of hot coffee.

"I don't have milk or sugar." James Morris has not had anyone in his kitchen since last Christmas, and even then it was only his nearest neighbors, the ones he sold his land to, good people who insist on bringing him platters of turkey and mashed potatoes and sausage stuffing on the holidays, though he's told them they needn't bother. But even his neighbors didn't come in much past the back door, and he has never offered them anything in return, not even a glass of cloudy water.

"Black is fine," Jorie assures him. She looks down the driveway as a truck passes by on the road. It's the kindhearted neighbor, off to the post office, a trip he makes every morning at this time. It's somebody with an ordinary life of the sort Jorie once had, only weeks ago. "My husband says he wants to take responsibility now. He says he's a different man."

246

James Morris studies Jorie and sips his coffee. He has absolutely no expression in his eyes. It's the way Collie has been looking lately, as if he's taken three giant steps back inside himself.

"It was a horrible accident, that's what he's said. He knows he should have called the authorities, but his mind shut down. It was a terrible mistake, but he swears he's not that person anymore." Jorie hasn't touched her coffee. In fact, she's nauseated. It's all she can do to keep down the breakfast she ordered earlier from room service, just some tea, along with toast and jam. "I wouldn't have married that person," she says.

Jorie is not sure why she is defending her husband instead of watching the blackbirds in the trees. She's seen the room where it happened, she's seen the girl's diary, and the brush, and the window he climbed through on that rainy night when the air was sweet and the future was right there before him, his for the taking. She's seen it all and she's standing here making excuses. "You can see who I am. I wouldn't marry the kind of person who killed your sister."

"But you did." James Morris slams his coffee cup down on the counter. It's good china, and the force of hitting it against the counter causes a chip that will, before long, crack the cup in two. "I know why you really came here. You want me to tell you it's all right, but I'm not going to do that. Because it's not all right and it never will be. Your husband came

247

here and he killed my sister and she never had the chance to be a different woman the way he's had the opportunity to be a different man. So what do you say to that? She never got to be a woman at all. She was fifteen, and that's what she'll always be. There are no second chances for her."

If there was a time for Jorie to be frightened of this man, it would be now. It's been years since James has spoken to anyone about this subject, and the words come pouring out; they're savage and painful, and if they ever could have been forgiving, the years spent unspoken have turned every syllable into burning ash.

The dog, Fergus, sits on the back porch and whines, concerned for its master, who is usually such a silent, gentle man.

"I see what you're telling yourself." James gives a broken laugh. "He's different. He's not the same. Well, he's made up of the same flesh and blood as the thing that crawled in here. I feel about him the same way my mother would have felt. She was a woman who wouldn't even tolerate anyone shooting a squirrel. She said every creature had a soul, but she changed her mind after what happened. She told me straight out how wrong she'd been. Not every creature has a soul. That's what she said. Not whoever did this."

He's going on in the manner of a man who's lost control, and even Fergus, loyal as can be, is shivering out on the porch, the way the dog always does before a storm. Jorie should be frightened, she should be wondering if she'll get out of this in one piece, but all she can think about is that she's watching a grown man cry. He doesn't even seem to notice, he just goes on shouting at her, but she can see who he is, the boy who raced into the field one fine morning, thinking the whole wide world was his home, sweet as new corn, sweet as summer can be.

"Now your husband wants to say it was just a big mistake? Well, nobody forced him to come onto our property. Nobody made him sneak into our house. He did it on his own. When they do bring him down here for trial, I'm going to sit in that courtroom every day, and when they convict him, I'll be thinking about my mother and how pleased she would have been that at last he had to pay the price."

The dog is pawing at the screen door, whining low down in its throat. Jorie thinks of Collie, sleeping on the couch with her mother's dog, Mister. She thinks about how it would be to spend her life without him, to have him snatched by moonlight, wrung out and left like a husk on her doorstep, to find him in her garden on a summer's day between the rows of sweet peas and strawberries.

"Why do you care what I think, anyway?" James Morris looks exhausted. He's wishing he hadn't bothered to answer the phone or allowed Nancy to convince him to talk to a stranger or opened up his door. He wipes his eyes with his large hands. "I'm nothing to you."

Jorie sets her coffee cup on the counter. She hasn't taken a sip, all the same, she can tell it's far too strong, undrinkable at best. She has come here with a puzzle that cannot be solved, she sees that now. For if Ethan is the man who murdered Rachel Morris, then who is she? If he is that, what is the life they've been living?

Gazing out the back door, wondering herself why she cares so much about what James Morris thinks, Jorie notices that the tallest cypress outside is filled with red-winged blackbirds. Why, they're everywhere; if you looked quickly you might think there were black flowers growing on that tree, each one streaked with crimson, as though cut and bleeding still.

"The blackbirds came when Rachel died." James is looking outside, too. "At first my father thought it was because he burned the scarecrow. He thought the birds would take over the cornfields, but they haven't. My father's been gone for eleven years, and my mother for almost that long, but it's Rachel who seems like she was here yesterday."

James walks past Jorie and goes out to the porch, where his dog is waiting. He sits in one of the old wooden chairs on the porch, then pets Fergus, who quivers with delight just to be noticed, clearly grateful that the quiet man the dog is accustomed to, that kind and generous master, has returned. Jorie follows James and stands with her back against the same door Rachel walked through every day of her life, off to school and back again, off to work at the general store, off on that last morning of her life. James's sorrow is there in the set of his shoulders, in the way he looks out at the bald cypress trees, as if there were answers in those dark leaves, to be found somewhere between the blackbirds and the branches. Jorie has the urge to put her hand on his shoulder, but she doesn't.

"Did you ever think it would be better for you to sell this place and move away? Start up someplace new?"

James Morris lets go of what amounts to a laugh. "Not in my lifetime. I'm here for good. I'm not fit company for people out there in the world."

"You didn't have to be nice to me," Jorie says. "But you were."

"No, I wasn't," James tells her. "I was honest."

He walks her to her rented car and shakes her hand, but then he doesn't let go. His loneliness has come up and ambushed him because of the talking he's been doing. It's far easier for him not to see people at all, but then, he knew that long before Jorie arrived.

"Did you get what you wanted?" he asks.

His blue eyes are narrowed. He hasn't trusted anyone for so many years, he certainly isn't about to trust Jorie; and yet he's curious.

"I don't feel like I have anything I want." Jorie can feel the calluses on his fingers, formed from years of working this land. She thinks of home, and smiles. "Except my son," she amends.

"Well, then, there you go. You have something." James Morris lets go of her hand. "I understand you didn't know. But that doesn't change what happened. He's the same man who came here that night. I know that for a fact." James nods in the direction he once ran from, far from here, into the woods. "He's the one."

Jorie drives back the way she's come, past the fields, past the pond where the shallow water used to be so warm it turned to steam, out onto the two-lane road that will lead her to Main Street. Blackbirds follow her into town, swooping and chattering above her, casting shadows on the asphalt. After she parks at the hotel, Jorie walks back to Duke's Diner. Although the lunch hour has come and gone, she sits at the counter and orders a chicken salad sandwich on whole wheat toast and an iced tea. She's starving, but when the sandwich arrives, she can't eat. She keeps thinking about the brush left on the bureau, the diary without a key. She sips at her iced tea, and as she does she notices Nancy, the clerk from town hall, picking up a Greek salad to go.

"Did he talk to you?" Nancy asks.

Jorie nods and takes a bite of her sandwich to ensure she won't get involved in a conversation, not that such tactics will thwart a woman like Nancy Kerr, who approaches and sits on the stool next to Jorie's.

"Well, that's a surprise." Nancy lights a cigarette and pulls over the plastic ashtray on the counter. "I didn't think he'd say more than two words to you." Some people truly love to talk, and Nancy is clearly one of them. "What a waste of a man. I could personally name five women who would have jumped at the chance of settling down with James Morris, myself included, but he wasn't interested. It's like it happened yesterday as far as he's concerned, and you can understand why." Nancy's face seems crumpled as she speaks about the past. "I was at school with Rachel, you know."

"He said you were one of her best friends."

"He said that?" Nancy looks pleased. "A lot of the girls in town weren't very nice to me back then, but Rachel wasn't like that. She didn't care how much money you had or what you wore." At last Nancy pauses. "I happened to overhear you talking about your husband when you were on the phone with him." She glances around Duke's, not particularly crowded, except for two police officers bolting down a late lunch, and a table of elderly women ordering decaf coffee and peach pie. "You might want to keep his involvement to yourself," Nancy advises. "People around here still have strong feelings about what happened back then."

"It was an accident. He never meant for it to happen."

"Yeah, right." Nancy blows out a stream of smoke. "Maybe it was accidental rape, too. I've heard that one before. His dick just climbed through the bedroom window, and he had no choice but to follow along."

Stung, and more than a little exhausted, Jorie leaves some money on the counter, along with her barely touched sandwich, and quickly rises from her seat.

"Thanks for helping me out," she tells Nancy before she walks out of the diner. What Jorie wants is to get to her hotel room and slip into bed, but there's no escape; the town clerk follows her out, clutching her take-out order, calling for Jorie to wait up.

"I shouldn't have said that," Nancy apologizes.

"Why? You seemed to enjoy letting me have it. I'm simply trying to understand what happened."

"Well, I can show you exactly what happened." Nancy's boss, Arnold Darby, will probably dock her for the extra time she's about to take, but Nancy isn't too concerned about getting back to work. She never takes a proper lunch hour; she's entitled to this one. "Come on."

It's hot as they walk up the hill leading to the oldest section of town. The cemetery has been in this part of the village since 1790 and is ringed with hedges of sweet pepperbush and dogwoods that bloom pink and white in the spring. Rachel Morris is buried between her parents on the far side of the second hill. It's a shady spot, one that is damp enough for the rose mallows someone has planted to thrive.

"This is what happened. Somebody died." Nancy's mouth is set. She has her salad-to-go under her arm, wilted long before this trek, and the paper bag rustles. Just standing here causes a catch in her throat. She was one of those girls who would have waited for

James Morris forever, if he'd even looked at her twice. She could have made him forget some of his pain, if only he'd let her, if only he'd tried, but some things aren't destined to be, no matter how you might want them, and so she gave up and married Lonnie Kerr, who, even though they're divorced, is a good father and a good man, despite the fact that he's not James Morris.

There are red-winged blackbirds here, too, and because they defend their territory by song, the sky is filled with a riotous band of trilling. Jorie goes to the stone, then bends to run her fingers over the carvings. Beneath Rachel's name, a message from her parents has been engraved: *You are with us every day.*

Jorie can feel something cold settle around her. She is coming to a conclusion here on this hillock where the grass was so recently mowed the fresh scent brings tears to her eyes.

"One weekend she was sleeping over at my house, and by the next week she was dead, and there wasn't anything anyone could do about it or any story they could tell themselves to make it all right." Nancy doesn't seem like a stranger. She seems like the kind of woman who would be a good friend. "Sometimes I think no one in this town ever felt safe again, not the way we used to."

They stand at the gravesite for a while longer, then walk back along the cemetery path to the main road beneath the azure-colored sky. This was the same sky Rachel had seen every day. These blackbirds had woken her each morning with song. What happened then feels so real here, whether it was yesterday or fifteen years ago or this morning. Jorie's history is fading under the weight of the Morrises' sorrow, disintegrating strand by strand, year by year.

"I've got a boy with him." They have gone past the black cemetery gates and have turned toward town. "Twelve years old."

"Well, then, you have my sympathies." Nancy is sincere. "I don't envy you."

The street they walk along is shady and cool and there's the odor of sweet gum in the air.

"It must be nice to live down here. There's still so much country around."

"It was nicer back then. People felt so safe they used to sleep out on their lawns in the summertime. They used to leave their doors wide open, and their cars running with the keys left in the ignition. Then we wised up."

When they pass a cottage with a "for rent" sign in the window, Jorie stops to gaze through the small-paned windows. All the place needs are the hedges trimmed and a new coat of paint.

"I hear the heating system is terrible," Nancy Kerr informs Jorie. "The last tenant nearly froze to death last winter. He packed up and drove south to North Carolina with icicles in his beard." She peeks into the bag to see if Duke remembered to put in a roll with her salad order, which, of course, he never does. "Some things look a whole lot better from a distance, and this town is probably one of them."

"Do you ever feel like running away?" Jorie asks.

The full heat of the afternoon is upon them now, so they walk slowly. Surely, they'll never see each other again, so it doesn't hurt to be honest.

"I don't have anything to run from, honey. That's the difference between me and you."

They shake hands when they reach the Black Horse Hotel. Under different circumstances they might have become friends, or perhaps they would have passed each other by entirely; now they will always have this walk they've shared, under the blue sky, up to the second hill, where Rachel Morris is buried. When Jorie goes to her room in the hotel, she takes off her clothes and lies on the bed, between the clean sheets. At last, she can cry in peace. The room is glassy with heat, and by the time Jorie is done weeping, her face is splotchy, her eyes red. She used to cry over foolish things, movies and books, stubbed toes, stories of children rescued by their mothers, suddenly strong beyond human limitations in the face of danger. Now she cries for herself, and she's shocked by how much salt water there is contained within her. She could collect buckets of it, wash her clothes in it, boil a sour teary tea that could bring grief to the drinker with a single sip. She goes into the bathroom, naked, then steps into the shower and runs cold water over herself, streams of it hitting her hot, dusty skin, grateful that the racket of the faucet stops her from thinking, at least for now.

Some things, however, are true no matter how hard you might try to block them out, and a lie is always a lie, no matter how prettily told. Jorie thinks about Rachel Morris's bedroom; some doors, once they're opened, can never be closed again, just as some trust, once it's been lost, can never be won back. The past thirteen years feel less real to Jorie than do the last twenty-four hours. She sleeps with dreams of blackbirds and rose mallows, and when she wakes, she notices that her pillow is faintly red, as though she's been crying blood and not tears. It's the dust that collected on her skin, granules that remain even though she's washed carefully.

Jorie has slept so deeply she hadn't heard anyone outside her room in the hallway of the Black Horse Hotel. She doesn't find the package James Morris leaves for her until she's about to go down for breakfast before driving back to the airport in Baltimore. By then, Jorie has nearly made up her mind; she has the bellman carry her bag downstairs, then goes back to sit on the edge of the bed. She opens the envelope neatly tied with brown string and brings forth Rachel's diary. It's still locked; Rachel's privacy has been preserved since the summer when she died. She would have been a junior in high school that next year if Bryon Bell had never come to town, if he'd just kept driving north, if he hadn't been so damn thirsty and the heat hadn't been so brutal, if he hadn't seen her red hair through the window of the market.

Jorie looks at the bottom of the envelope and finds the note James Morris scrawled on the back of a hardware store receipt last night as he stood in the hallway while she dreamed of blackbirds.

Take this with you. So you'll remember who she was.

James placed the package so gently against the door, Jorie hadn't heard a thing. On this, her last morning in Maryland, she feels the tenderness of his message, as well as the strength. People pity James Morris, but Jorie finds she respects him. He is one man who knows exactly what's inside his heart, and he refuses to pretend otherwise. What he told her was true. He will never move forward, and he'll never forgive. He's honest, simple as that, and this has become the trait that Jorie finds most admirable.

When she leaves the hotel, Jorie stands out in the parking lot to take a last look at Holden. Although it's not yet nine, the heat is already rising off the blacktop in transparent waves. Jorie can feel the sun on her back as she packs Rachel's diary into her suitcase before driving back to the airport. She has the suitcase right under her seat as the plane taxis out across the runway, for as it turns out, the flight to Massachusetts isn't the least bit crowded. Jorie leans against the headrest and closes her eyes during takeoff. As they hurtle into the milky blue air, awash with cloud and sun, she can no longer tell the difference between east and west. But there's one direction of which she has no doubt, and one thing she knows for certain: she is not about to forget.

Nightshade

MY GRANDMOTHER TOLD ME that on the day my sister was born, two blackbirds arrived at her bedroom window, and there was nothing my grandmother could do to chase them off, not even when Rosarie came home from the hospital, bundled in blankets and wailing like crazy. Some people thought the birds were an omen, of good luck or bad fortune to come, no one was certain. But my father didn't wait to find out; he took a hose from the yard and sprayed those blackbirds until they had no choice but to fly away, dripping water and feathers all the way down our street.

It is certainly bad luck that has struck Brendan Derry after his association with Rosarie. He comes by our house every day, even though my sister has told him in no uncertain terms not to bother her anymore. Brendan was working like a madman on Ethan Ford's defense fund, but anyone could tell it wasn't Mr. Ford he cared about, he just wanted to stay close to my sister, who was hanging around the firehouse every afternoon, stuffing envelopes and raising money and eating the free pizza Mark Derry provided for the volunteer staff.

"I don't get it," Brendan confided in me. "I don't know what I did wrong."

Nothing, you big idiot, I wanted to say. *She's just moved on, the way she always does. You were never important to her, you were nothing more than a speck of dust, good-looking dust, but dust all the same. Why, by now,* I wanted to tell him, *she barely remembers what it was like to kiss you. Can't you see just by looking at her that she's managed to stop feeling? Didn't you notice the burn marks on her arms all those times you held her tight?* But when he rambles on, I nod and listen and keep my mouth shut. I even let him take me down to the bakery and buy me a plate of pie and ask me questions about my sister, but that doesn't mean I ever tell him the truth. I surely don't mention the fact that Collie and I have taken most of the fliers Brendan had posted on trees. That's what we did when we went on a picnic with Gigi. We tore those fliers to pieces, and we didn't go back to where Gigi was waiting until we were finished destroying Brendan's hard work, only taking time out to practice our kissing, which was getting better by the day. By then we couldn't look at Gigi any more than we could face each other.

For her part, Rosarie never took the time to notice Brendan mooning around our property; she was far too caught up in Ethan Ford's defense fund to pay attention to some pathetic heart she'd carelessly broken. But the real question was, why this sudden interest in Ethan's case? Why was she doing something when there was no foreseeable payback? That wasn't the Rosarie I knew, and I knew her better than anyone. She wouldn't scratch anybody's back if they didn't scratch hers twice as hard, and for twice as long a time, too. I knew something was up when Rosarie started to come out to the yard whenever Collie was around. Usually, we were too far beneath her for her to bother saying hello. Now she brought out a cold glass of lemonade for Collie, and that just wasn't like Rosarie, to think of anyone else's needs.

"What about me?" I said, but there was nothing she wanted from me, so I was ignored and left thirsty. She smiled at Collie so brightly that he looked a little stunned in the glare of her attentions.

"I think what they're doing to your father is awful," Rosarie told him. She had a frown on her face that made a little line right between her eyes. Collie seemed unable to look away from that line or from her dark eyes. He opened his mouth, but nothing came out. "After everything he's done for this town, he should be considered a hero."

Collie finally broke away from her gaze and stared at me, panicked, like a fish on a hook.

"It's late," I said. I knew how he felt about his father and I wished Rosarie would just leave him alone, but she wasn't about to do that, so I had to save him. "Your mother will be worried about you if you're not home soon."

Collie nodded gratefully and took off for his grandmother's house. It was awful that he didn't live on our block anymore. I hated to see the real estate agent showing the house to prospective buyers, and there was one couple in particular who kept coming back. I wanted our neighborhood to look bad and scare them away, so when my grandmother hired Warren Peck's nephew, Kyle, to clean up our yard, I told him that we couldn't afford his services and sent him on his way before he could cut down the hedge of black thorns on our property line that was such an eyesore. In our backyard there was one of the first apple trees in town, a Baldwin that some people say was planted by Colonel Baldwin as he rode through town in the year 1749. Every fall my father would make something called mole-cider from these apples, mixing cider and milk with eggs, but this summer the tree was failing, and I couldn't care less. I hoped when people came to look at Collie's house they'd peer past the fence in Mrs. Gage's yard and when they saw the half-dead apple tree and the hedge of thorns and the black mimosas they'd decide to live somewhere else.

After Collie went home, my sister began to confide in me, which took me completely by surprise. I didn't want to hear the things she told me, but I'd been waiting so long for her to treat me like a human being, I didn't tell her to shut up. As it turned out, she'd done such a good job for the defense fund, stuffing envelopes and going door to door, spending countless hours on the hot line, that Mr. Hart, the attorney in charge of the case, and Mark Derry, who'd started the whole fund-raising process, had brought her down to the jail to let Ethan Ford thank her in person. If my grandmother had known about this she would have surely grounded Rosarie for the rest of the summer, not that it would have done any good to try to discipline her. Something in Rosarie had changed, and it wasn't just the way she looked that was different. She had personally raised twenty-eight thousand dollars for the cause. When she asked for help, people couldn't seem to refuse her, despite the dark clothes she'd taken to wearing, and the fact that her face was clean of makeup. No more shorts for her, no gobby mascara and red lips. But if anything, she was more beautiful this way, with her long dark hair pulled back, leaving her heart-shaped face so exposed. People wrote out checks and then they thanked her, as if they were grateful for her presence, and her guidance, and her charity.

In some ways, though, she was the same old Rosarie, still thinking about herself. She had gotten to the part she was most excited about, the thing that made her swoon. She told me that when she went to see Ethan in jail, he'd gotten down on his knees and kissed her feet, first one and then the other. She was wearing sandals, and she'd polished her toenails a pale shell pink, and she had almost fainted, except that the jailhouse floor was probably filthy, so she'd forced herself to stay conscious. She willed it with all her might. As she spoke of what had happened, she was trembling. She had a strange look on her face, the way people do when they know a tornado is about to hit, but out of loyalty or stupidity they just stay put, right there in the eye of the storm.

"Who kisses someone's foot?" I wanted to know.

It was time for a defense fund meeting, but I wanted to hear the rest of the story, so I tagged along when she headed toward the center of town. This was the only activity Rosarie bothered with these days; she wouldn't go to keg parties at the lake, she wouldn't shop at the mall in Hamilton. Money could be better spent, she told me, than on clothes that would be out of fashion before you could turn around twice.

"I don't believe you've stopped shopping," I said. "You love buying clothes."

"That just goes to show how little you know," Rosarie said to me as we turned onto Front Street. There were banks of black-eyed Susans on the median that ran down the center of the street, and the linden trees we passed by outside the post office smelled like allspice. It was all the same as it was every summer. It just felt different. My sister was wearing a white dress, and her black hair streamed down her back the way night spills across yards and lawns.

"I know one thing," I told her. "He's a murderer."

Rosarie reached into her pocket and handed me a note. "Read this. Maybe then you'll understand."

Inside every guilty man is an innocent one. Thank you from the bottom of my heart. Ethan Ford

"That is such bullshit." I handed back the note. Frankly, I had the urge to wash my hands after touching something that had belonged to him. "That's not even his real name, you know."

On the day we'd been avoiding Gigi at the lake, Collie had informed me he had decided to use his mother's family name, Solomon. He was going to have it officially changed and everything. He told me he didn't even want to hear the name Ford; whenever he did, he felt sick to his stomach. It seemed especially unfair that Rosarie would be so quick to forgive Collie's father when she still was so furious at our father for getting sick and dying. I wondered if she wasn't as smart as I'd always thought she was, and right then and there I started to worry about her, in spite of the fact that I didn't even like her.

Rosarie was meeting Kelly Stark at the corner of Front Street and Worthington

Avenue. Kelly had the longest hair of any of the Stark girls, so long she could sit on her own braid. I had often wished Kelly was my sister. She was extremely brilliant, and had won a National Merit award, and sometimes I wondered why she hung around with Rosarie instead of the group of smart girls like Gigi Lyle, who were taking summer study courses in order to be prepared for the SATs in the fall. I guess Kelly was rebelling in some way, if going to rallies for a murderer could be counted as such, or maybe she was like me and simply couldn't say no to Rosarie.

"Hey there." Kelly grinned when she saw us. She looped one arm through Rosarie's and the other through mine. Kelly Stark was much more tolerant than Rosarie. She had a kind heart that would probably get her into trouble, unlike Rosarie and me. I had to believe that being mean would save us both; it was our protection and our armor, or at least it had been until Rosarie started getting involved with Ethan Ford.

"Uh-oh. Brendan with the broken heart is here," Kelly whispered when we turned the corner.

They both laughed when they saw him moping around outside the firehouse, hoping for a glimpse of Rosarie.

"I don't think it's funny," I said.

"He's just a child."

Although she was busy putting Brendan down, Rosarie had the look that she always had whenever she was falling in love with somebody. Her face was flushed and her eyes were blacker than ink, the sure signs of her devotion. I watched Kelly and Rosarie walk right past Brendan Derry, and then I knew who my sister had fallen for. It turned my stomach to realize she was thinking about Ethan Ford that way, after what he'd done. I should have known Rosarie wouldn't have given up so much of her time for a civic cause. There was always self-interest when it came to Rosarie, the selfish beat of her own cold heart.

The sheriff and two of his men had agreed to bring Ethan Ford, or whatever he was calling himself, to speak at tonight's meeting. When he came walking along the sidewalk flanked by the officers, no one had to tell me what Rosarie was doing here or why she was wearing her favorite dress. I saw him wave to Rosarie, and I saw the expression on her face when she waved back, and even I could understand how somebody could make a mistake and think she was in love with him. Mr. Ford's dark hair had been cropped close and he'd lost weight, but he was still the handsomest man in town. You could tell just by looking at him that he'd been caged and that he wanted his freedom. One look and it was obvious that there would always be women ready to fall in love with him. They'd believe in his innocence because he believed in it. His faith would give him power over them, and those women wouldn't know what hit them. His smile would run them down just as surely as if he were a freight train, and it didn't matter how smart Rosarie thought she was, she'd probably give up whatever he asked just to be near him.

For days afterward I tried to think of what I could do to show Rosarie that she was making a mistake. I was spending most of my time in the backyard, wearing my old bathing suit and running the hose over my head when I got too hot. By that time, I had stolen thirty-seven books from the library, thirty-eight including the one Collie had taken. It was like I was addicted to stealing, or to not getting caught, or something. I was getting good at it; I could do it in a roomful of people and they'd never even know I'd slipped the history of the Nile under my shirt or that I'd dropped a volume of poems into my backpack. But for some reason, all those books made me sad, too.

When Collie came up to my room and saw how many books I'd stolen, he looked worried. He looked the way he did whenever we sat close together, troubled in some way that made him seem older than he was.

I don't want anything bad to happen to you, he told me when he saw the piles of stolen books in my room, and just the way he said it made me feel like I'd never be able to let him go.

I thought I'd have to beg Rosarie to listen to me, but on Saturday morning my sister put on her bathing suit and came to lie out in the sun beside me. She was going to the jail that afternoon, so I guess she wanted to look good, as if she didn't look great no matter what she did.

"You're surprisingly stupid," I told her. I was reading a book of Russian fairy tales that I'd stolen from the children's reading room the day before and wishing I was more like Baba Yaga, the old woman whose house ran around on chicken's legs. You could bet that Baba Yaga didn't care what anyone thought of her. She might have been mean, she might have been hideous, but she didn't cry herself to sleep at night.

"Well, one of us had to be stupid and one had to be ugly, and I guess I got the better deal." Rosarie piled her hair on top of her head. She was in extremely good humor as she slapped lotion on her dusky skin. Even though she was my sister, I wanted to kill her.

"Stupid as a mule," I said.

"Ugly as one," Rosarie shot back. She handed me the lotion and suggested I use some. "You're burning," she told me.

I had freckled skin that didn't do anything right. I shrugged and told Rosarie it was pointless, but when she closed her eyes, I used some of the lotion. It smelled like coconut candy.

"Ethan Ford is old enough to be your father," I said.

"If he was my father he'd be dead." Rosarie had an answer for everything. There was a little smile on her lips.

"And he's married," I reminded her.

"Really? Well, his wife didn't even come to the rally. She hardly ever visits him in jail." Rosarie turned to me then; she smelled sweeter than usual, and I wondered if she'd given up smoking. I wondered if she was still burning herself to try to feel something, or if Ethan Ford was like a match. "A person in his situation needs someone who will stand by him and see him every single day."

"My God. You're more of an idiot than I would have guessed." Although the sun was strong, I had goose bumps on my arms and legs. For the first time in my life, I felt sorry for my sister.

"It's not the way you think." Rosarie's cheeks were pink with the heat. "He doesn't look at me the way other men do. He respects me."

If Ethan Ford didn't want her, then he was the only man in town who didn't, and maybe that's what interested Rosarie most.

"It's because he kissed your feet. It made you crazy."

"Oh, shut up," Rosarie said, but she was smiling. She was thinking all sorts of things, but I was pretty sure the one thing she wasn't thinking about was how Ethan Ford had taken the life of some girl in Maryland.

"I'll bet he used his tongue."

"I said, shut up!" Rosarie pulled my hair, but she didn't deny it. "You think you're so smart," she went on, "but you don't know anything. You think Dad was so high and mighty because he killed himself and supposedly spared us so much pain, but he was just taking the easy way out. Ethan Ford has lived a perfect life, he's actually saved people. And he's not the only one in this world who ever made a mistake."

I looked at my sister and thought of how she must have felt the night she found our father. She had begged my mother to take her to the mall in Hamilton, she'd had a fit if you really want to know, and because of that our father had gotten the chance to be alone when my grandmother and I went up to unpack in the attic. I supposed you could see that as a mistake if you looked at it in a certain way. You might think you have to pay for such an oversight for the rest of your life.

That night, when everyone was asleep, I went into the garage and lit a candle and begged my father to forgive Rosarie for her unkind words. *She knows not what she says,* I told him. *Or what she does, either, when it comes right down to it.* Our father was the sort of man who thought things over carefully and weighed his words before he spoke. He must have measured the length of the days he had left against the sorrow he would have caused us with each of those days. It didn't really matter what Rosarie thought. Everything our father did, he did out of love. I'm sure of that. I didn't need anyone to tell me that he would have showed true conviction if he'd forced himself to go on living. That might be true for somebody else, but it wasn't true for him.

Some people needed saving, and I was beginning to realize that Rosarie was among them. That night I stayed awake, thinking of how I could set things right. Before I fell

272

asleep I made a vow that I would complete three good deeds. I would choose the tasks that were the hardest for me, the way people always do before setting off on a quest. If it was easy, it was worthless, even I knew that. There were so many things that were hard for me, I could have had a ten-page list, but it came down to this: I would return the stolen books to the library; I would see to it that a stone was put up at my father's grave; and I would make certain to protect Rosarie, even if that meant protecting her from herself.

There was no law against taking care of the easiest task first, so I brought the books out to the garage, a few at a time, and piled them into an old wagon. I waited until dark before going down to the library, dragging the wagon behind me. It was the time in August when the crickets start going crazy, and in spite of the heat and how many sprinklers were switched on, anyone could tell it was the end of the summer. I started thinking about the things Collie and I had done together, and how I'd never felt like I needed another friend when he was around, and how Rosarie had said it would all change. I'd probably gone ahead and brought that change on myself when I kissed him out at the old house. He looked at me in a different way now, like he was trying to figure me out and having no luck whatsoever.

As I walked through town, I was worried about what excuse I could give if somebody stopped me and questioned me about the wagon of books, but a bomb might as well have dropped for all the people I ran into. Even though I've lived in Monroe my whole life long, I started thinking maybe someday I should move somewhere where there are people on the street after nine o'clock. It was so quiet you could hear the air make a pinging sound, and the linden leaves rustled like paper.

I went past Hannah's without anyone seeing me; even Brendan Derry, who was at a window seat, sorrowfully drinking coffee and writing some sappy poetry for Rosarie, failed to notice when I went by. Kite's Bakery was closing early these days, and there were no rallies going on at the firehouse, and the stores on Front Street were shut down for the night. I figured I was in luck. I felt so sure of myself I started to whistle, or maybe it was fear that made me do that, I don't know. All I know is that when I turned onto Liberty and saw the library, I got a shaky feeling. Maybe I was thinking about my father, and how nice Grace Henley had been to let him take out so many books when he was sick, or maybe I just didn't like the dark. I left the wagon beside some honeysuckle vines, but when I took the first bunch of books up to the library, I felt kind of exposed without the old apple tree to hide behind.

I slipped every book through the return slot, even though the edition of King Arthur was so thick I had to push, hard, until it fell with a clump on top of the others, just inside the door. That was when I glanced up and saw Miss Henley watching through the window.

We looked at each other, and I felt like crying because instead of opening the door and screaming at me, she smiled. She'd known all along that I was stealing those books, she just never said anything.

I turned and ran. I grabbed the wagon and pulled it behind me so that it banged into my legs and left bruises. I ran so fast I thought my lungs would break apart, but I kept going long after I was past Front Street. I thought about the people in my life who were good, people who weren't the least bit like me, the kind of individuals who never accused you of anything, even when they were well aware of all you'd done. I had overheard Grace Henley talking to Margaret Peck, who volunteered at the library, when Mrs. Peck brought up the subject of the books that seemed to be disappearing from the shelves. As it turned out, Grace Henley hadn't been worried. I heard her say that in her experience, missing books often returned, sometimes after weeks or months, occasionally, after years; sooner or later, they usually came back, as if they'd returned of their own accord, drawn back to the library like sheep to the barn.

When I got home, I stood outside, trying to catch my breath. At this hour, everyone I loved was sleeping or already gone. I stood there for a long time and thought about my father and how no matter where I lived or how far I went, I would always think about him. I hadn't known that before, not really, but I knew it now. It would be harder to get to sleep tonight without all those books hidden around my room, but as far as I could tell, it wouldn't be impossible.

Mercy

THE LAST WEEKS OF August are always a time for family reunions and blueberry pie, the season when goldenrod appears along roadsides and the lilies that bloom in daylight lose their short-lived petals as soon as moonlight begins to spill from the sky. The process is so rapid that by morning there is often nothing left of these flowers but green stalks and the yellowing tendrils of leaves, as though summer were already ending while most people were safely in bed. Charlotte Kite, however, notices what happens to the lilies at night, because she can't sleep. She is victim to her own racing thoughts, incessant, surging terrors that keep her up at odd hours, at two and at four, so that she is awake to hear the fluttering of the sparrows when they first stir in the bushes; she listens to the quiet cooing of doves. She is already at her window when the first radiant bands of light break open the leaden blue sky of morning, a witness to the hour when the fallen petals of the lilies are curling up in the grass like bits of paper, too thin and delicate to last.

For five years or more, unbeknownst to her, renegade cells have been finding a place in Charlotte's body. Now that she's had the tumor removed, along with several lymph nodes, her treatment will devour the next ten months of her life. Already, she knows that win, lose, or draw, nothing will ever be the same. There is a scar under her arm that aches, and her left breast is half the size of her right, but what keeps her up at night is the realization that everything she has at this moment can be lost in an instant. She doesn't want to waste precious time with something as prosaic as sleep. Every second is a second that belongs to her, one she understands could well be her last.

The illness and the intricacies of dealing with treatment are actually far easier to handle without Jay around. Everyone knows Jay has never been the sort of man to see anyone through hard times, though he has the best intentions. He's called several times, which is sweet of him, always with the tentative greeting of someone who can't stand to be around illness. Charlotte remembers that Jay often found excuses not to visit his own father at the nursing home; he has always turned away from the scene of an accident. He wants to hear good news, or nothing at all. She can't picture Jay walking through the doors of the hospital in Hamilton, let alone being there waiting for her to snap out of the anesthesia or holding her hand while she suffers through treatment.

Charlotte has no second thoughts when

she hires Barney Stark to act on her behalf in her divorce proceedings. Although she's more than willing to give Jay whatever he asks for, Barney gently lets her know it will most probably take the best part of a year to complete the divorce, considering the complicated financial arrangements of the bakery. Well, what does that matter to Charlotte? Her treatment will take nearly as long, with radiation sandwiched between the cruel months of chemotherapy; she might as well throw in the divorce proceedings along with the rest of the mess.

"I know this is bad timing," Barney said before she left his office. Clearly, there wasn't a soul in the village who hadn't learned of her illness, Barney among them. He had an apologetic look, as though he was the one who had failed her.

"The marriage was bad timing," Charlotte informed him. "The breakup is perfect. I hear you're in a similar marital situation," she'd added then, which was perhaps less than thoughtful. But how could she not know? People tend to talk in a town the size of Monroe; it's impossible to make a move without everyone being apprised of an individual's new address weeks before the furniture is delivered. In Barney's case, the new address is the conference room of his office, where he's set up a cot, and a hot plate, and one of those little refrigerators kids in college dorms fill with cans of soda and beer.

"It should have happened a while ago."

Charlotte had gotten into her car and Barney was leaning down to talk to her through the open window. He could feel his heart pounding, or maybe it was just the heat of the day that was affecting him so, and all the stress and exertion of packing up and leaving home, no matter how right the decision might be. "We just kept pretending everything was okay."

He backed off and waved to Charlotte as she drove away. His marriage would have failed sooner or later, and he would have moved out of his house even if Charlotte Kite had never existed. True, he might have waited a while longer, but that would have been a disservice to everyone involved. When it came right down to it, the worst part about the whole thing was having to tell his girls. It was a measure of how well they loved him that all three of his daughters ran off to their rooms, slamming their doors behind them, even Kelly, who was usually so even-tempered and understanding. Barney went to speak to each one individually, and assured Kelly, and then Josie, and lastly and most difficult his dear Sophie, that his love would remain constant. Though none of the girls was speaking to him, they adored him in return, and so they did him the service of listening to him as they tried to hold back their tears.

On the day he packed up his car with his belongings, Barney kissed his wife good-bye and thanked her for all that they'd been to each other, then went off to coach Little League, as he always did on Saturdays. Sophie still wasn't speaking to him, but she accepted a ride to the field beyond the high school with an angry nod. It was a bright day, and the early evening promised to be perfect. In the distance, sunlight threaded through cumulus clouds, and the windows of the high school flashed with streaks of iridescence, now blue, now pink, now lavender. Barney's suitcases and boxes rattled around in the back of the car, and Sophie looked over her shoulder.

"You're not a very good packer," she observed. "You're disorganized."

"Maybe you can help me unpack later." They pulled into the lot at the edge of the field to park. Barney had the team's equipment in his overstuffed trunk, and while Sophie helped him unload the bases, he said as lightly as he could, "No matter what changes, my feelings for you never will. You'll always be my daughter, and I'll always love you."

Sophie grimaced as though she'd heard it before. "I thought you loved Mom, too."

"Well, I do, but this is something different."

"She told us there's probably another woman, that's why you're leaving so suddenly."

Horns honked as parents dropped off their children—the game was against the team from Essex, their fiercest opponents, and many of the parents would be staying to watch. Frankly, the Bluebirds didn't stand a chance of winning, especially now that Collie Ford had quit the team; he had such a fine, strong arm, they could always depend on him to be consistent.

"To be honest, there is someone I've always cared about, but I don't think she knows I'm alive, so she can't really count as another woman."

"Puppy love," Sophie said. "That's what that is."

"Except that I'm about to hit forty, and I still feel the same way."

Sophie thought this over. "Then you're just stupid." She looked at her father closely; she'd wanted to hurt him, but once she did it hadn't felt as good as she'd imagined it would. Sophie looked away, but she took her father's hand.

"You think we have a chance at winning?" Barney said, grateful beyond words that his daughter had reached for him. The bus from Essex had pulled into the lot, and they could hear the rival team chanting, gearing up for the game.

"Nope." Sophie was a sweet, honest girl. She dropped her guard; standing there beside her father; she seemed far too young to understand why happiness could be so difficult to find. "Do you think I could move in with you?"

"I think you can spend as much time as your mother allows."

They did lose the game against Essex, and that evening Sophie came back to Barney's office, where she fell asleep on the conference room floor, curled up in a blanket, her head resting on pillows taken from the waiting room couch. Barney went into his office to phone home.

"She's asleep and I don't have the heart to wake her," he whispered to Dana.

Dana would be the first to admit how they'd grown apart; why they hadn't even slept in the same room for over a year, but now she seemed regretful. "If you want to come back, it's fine. For the girls' sake," she added.

"You told her there was another woman."

"Well, isn't there? Come clean, Mr. Detecto, you know there is."

That particular woman, however, was not interested in finding another man now that Jay was gone. Charlotte certainly didn't mind living alone, especially with Jorie bringing over dinner every night. Jorie has been cooking for Charlotte ever since her return from Maryland; as the days have passed, she's brought over apple cobbler and pots of noodle soup and enormous pans of vegetarian lasagna until at last Charlotte's refrigerator, large as it is, is full. When Kat Williams's grandmother, Katya comes calling with her goulash-and-rice dish, Charlotte thanks her, but she has to turn the food away.

"I think I went crazy," Jorie says, staring into the huge Sub-Zero fridge when she visits her friend on a gorgeous August evening, toting a roast chicken that is still warm. "Did I really cook all this?"

"You definitely went crazy." Charlotte is at the counter, sipping from a large, steamy cup of green tea.

"What was I thinking?"

"You weren't. That's why you've been

282

cooking so much. You wanted to forget. It happens to me at the bakery. I get involved with lemon-poppyseed muffins, and before I know it they're my whole world and my biggest problem is getting them out of the oven before the edges turn brown. To hell with divorce, disease, despair. Give me the perfect lemon-poppyseed muffin, and I'll be fine."

"Is that why I did this?"

"You know it is. It's so you don't have to think about whatever you found in Maryland. Have you talked to Ethan about what it was like?"

Jorie has been thinking about James Morris more than she should, perhaps because she carries the blue diary wherever she goes. She tells herself it's so Collie won't discover the little book, but the diary is locked, and Jorie could manage to hide it in the cellar of her mother's house, perhaps, or out in the garden shed. Or does she keep the diary with her simply because every glance at the blue binding returns her to the place where there are blackbirds and endless fields? Each time she sees it, she is reminded of how some things are never over; they stay with you until they're a part of you, like it or not.

Jorie has been to the jail only once since her return, and she didn't mention her trip to Holden. Maryland is a secret that might easily scald her tongue if she spoke the name of her destination aloud. Ethan had held her tight when she went to see him, so tight she could barely breathe, and he'd said, *Where have you been?* in a hurt voice. She'd laughed and pulled away and told him it had only been a few days since she'd last been to visit. Hadn't she the house to get ready for sale, and Collie to take care of, and her mother to help out?

I don't give a damn about any of that, Ethan had said, and when she'd looked at him she'd understood it was true. *I just want you,* he'd told her, words that might have brought her pleasure before, but which now caused her not the least bit of happiness.

She had brought the diary with her to this visit; it was there, in her purse, and she wondered what Ethan would do if he noticed it. What if he searched for the papers she'd brought along from his lawyer, Fred Hart, instead of waiting for her to hand them over? Would he recognize the blue leatherette and the gold clasp? Would he drop it as though it were poison, or perhaps not even recall to whom the diary belonged? As it turned out, Ethan had waited, rather than look through her purse. He'd sat down on the edge of his cot until she handed him the papers, and he read them over carefully, which was more than Jorie had done.

He's looking for a place for you and Collie, Ethan had said.

Jorie hadn't understood. *But we're at my mother's house,* she reminded him.

In Maryland, he'd said to her then. *So you can be with me during the trial.*

The very idea of Maryland, of that deserted cottage she'd seen, perhaps, furnished with bits and pieces, of walking down the road with Collie as local people jeered, had made her recoil. Even now, when Charlotte questions her, she has a burning sensation on the tip of her tongue. Has she ever told a lie before? She doesn't think so, but she's party to one now; she's kept silent, she's hidden her trip to Holden from Ethan and that surely makes her as false as any liar.

"I don't want to talk to him about Maryland," Jorie tells Charlotte.

"Then talk to me."

"Absolutely not. You don't need to know what it was like there."

Charlotte smiles. "I already know how bad it was just by looking at you."

"You always know everything." Jorie's tone is more mournful than she intends. "What would I do without you?"

"You'd live."

"That's a terrible thing to say." Jorie shivers at the very thought, and she turns away so that Charlotte can't read how much she fears the possibility of this loss.

"Well, you would." Charlotte is as stubborn as she is honest. "People go on."

"It would never be the same without you. I don't even want any friends if they're not you."

"I always was the one with the good ideas," Charlotte allows.

Jorie laughs and reminds her of the results of some of those good ideas, including dying their hair black one Halloween, back when they weren't more than thirteen. Their hair had been

285

so damaged, Ruth Solomon had been forced to take them to a salon in Boston, for they knew that Chantel's over in Hamilton couldn't deal with a problem of such enormous proportions. The girls came back to town with coifs so outrageously short, they were certain they'd be laughed at by one and all, but as it turned out, the haircuts had suited them, showing off their fresh young faces. Still, that was more than twenty years ago, when they would have looked good no matter what.

"Well, it's going to be short again," Charlotte says. "I'm probably going to lose it. And even if I don't, it will be thin. They said it will break every time I use a brush."

Sunlight is falling through the window, crisscrossing Charlotte's pale skin with a brocade of pink and gold. Her hair is a deeper, wilder red than the strands in Rachel Morris's brush. It's blood-red, heartbeat-red, as close to scarlet as a natural color can be.

"Let's just do it," Jorie says. "Let's cut it really short. Like it used to be."

"Now?"

They look at each other and each knows the other has her own reason to feel there is only the present moment, this single instant when they are here together. Why wait for anything when the world is so cockeyed and dangerous? Why sit and stare into the mirror, too fearful of what may come to pass to make a move? Jorie gets the scissors from the kitchen and a big bath towel to drape around Charlotte's shoulders and they traipse out to the backyard patio. The day is filled with birdsong at this hour, and Jorie is reminded of Maryland. Although no one in town knows where she went, people are well aware of how many days passed when she didn't visit Ethan. They know she hasn't been to the rallies supporting him, and has refused to speak with even the more sympathetic reporters, although Mark Derry has tried to set up several interviews.

The reporters who are still hanging around town have given up on Jorie as a newsworthy subject, focusing their attentions elsewhere, setting up outside the courthouse. Friends and neighbors are the ones who are watching her. There are actually some people, the sort who are easily amused and start drinking at the Safehouse at an early hour, who have begun to take bets on whether or not the Fords' marriage will last. A few weeks ago, most everyone in town would have guessed that Jorie would stand by her husband, but currently the odds are only sixty-forty, and that just goes to show nothing's a sure thing. These people would not understand that Jorie has set out to see Ethan on most days since her return from Maryland. She had fully intended to get there again, but she continually ends up turning off onto the road to the lake instead. She has spent countless hours watching dragonflies hover over the water. She has thrown smooth gray stones until her arms ache. On each of these days, she has carried Rachel Morris's diary with her. Every time she reaches for her car keys or her comb, it's there to remind her of all she observed when James let her into the house, when he walked with her across the fields, when he held his head in his hands and cried.

This is the reason why every night, after the household is asleep, Jorie goes to her mother's kitchen. She stands over pots of boiling water in the half-light, she has patience for sauces that take hours to concoct and doesn't turn away from peach pies, with their tricky lattice crust. Charlotte is right; Jorie never thinks when she's at work, but she can't spend her whole life in front of a stove, and whenever she does allow her mind to wander, it's James Morris who comes to her, James counting out the days of his life all alone. When this happens, Jorie feels a cold, white anger for the man who's done this to him, who's stolen both his future and his past, and because that someone is her husband, she is trapped in the strange, high province of grief, a most hazardous and empty location, a place she never in her life expected to be.

"Are we really going to do this?" Charlotte asks once they've gone outside with the towel and the scissors and an extremely radical haircut in mind. Charlotte has always been the fearless one, the one who dragged Jorie along on vacations or made her hike through the woods, who had insisted they learn how to ski and to skate, who acted on impulse, who had daring to spare, but today Charlotte's voice wavers. She washed her hair earlier that morning; the shampoo she used was scented with vanilla, and the aroma saddens her. She hadn't known she had so much vanity about something as unessential as hair. She hadn't expected to take it so hard.

Jorie sets up a lawn chair and dusts off the seat with a towel. "Madame," she says to Charlotte, "sit your ass down."

There is honeysuckle planted in tubs out here, and the hollyhocks are in full bloom, huge saucerlike flowers weighing down their stalks. As soon as the sparrows perching upon the wooden fence notice the hair that begins to pile up on the patio after Jorie's clipping begins in earnest, they flutter near, chirping and waiting for a chance to dart closer still, and steal a strand or two.

"If we're going to do it, let's do it right," Charlotte says once her hair begins to fall. It's only hair, after all. It's not her soul that's being shorn, not her heart ripped out from within, not her blood, her bones, her even white teeth. "Make it short."

"I am making it short."

"Shorter," Charlotte demands.

Jorie puts her hands on her hips and laughs. "Who's doing this? You or me?"

"Me," Charlotte says simply, and Jorie knows she's not talking about the haircut. She's talking about driving herself over to the hospital in Hamilton at the end of the week, taking the elevator up to the second floor and making polite conversation while the nurse hooks up the IV that will fill her with the poison intended to make her well. She's talking about her life on the line, with hair or without it, with luck or without it, with hope or with none at all.

Jorie puts the scissors down, then kneels to embrace her friend.

"I'm sorry," she says.

The sparrows take this opportunity to light on the patio while Charlotte Kite cries in her friend's arms.

"God, no, I'm sorry." Charlotte wipes her eyes with the back of her hand. "Ugh. I hate making a scene." Charlotte is not the sort of person who breaks down easily, and her chances for recovery are quite good. The real problem is that the strategy she has previously used to get through her life is being blown to pieces, minute by minute, day by day. Denial has always served her well; it's gotten her through her parents' death and an extremely unsatisfying marriage, but here, in her own yard, a veil has suddenly been lifted. It's as if Charlotte has never seen anything before. She's been blindfolded, and now all the glory and the sorrow before her is blinding. She blinks back tears, but that doesn't help. Her eyes are still burning.

"I have half your head done," Jorie says. "You'd better let me finish."

It's true that Charlotte has always been identified with her auburn hair, but it's hardly her best feature, which, in point of fact, is her dark, intelligent eyes. She went through surgery with no complaints, and yet Charlotte Kite, who has always prided herself on her tough, resilient nature, cries throughout her haircut.

"Keep cutting," she insists when Jorie hesitates, scissors held aloft. "Don't pay any attention to me."

When Jorie is done, she gently towels away stray snippets and runs a soft brush through what's left. The length is the same as Collie's, boyish and sweet, but before long, Charlotte may have to take a razor to get rid of even that. In the yellow August light Jorie realizes they both look much older. What did she think? That they'd be girls forever? That nothing truly bad would ever befall them if they just kept to the right path?

"Tell me it's not over," Charlotte says to her friend.

Above them, the clouds are clotted and the sky is feverish with mosquitoes and heat. They have both already lived more than twice the time Rachel Morris had on earth. In that regard, they are lucky.

"It's not over." The words are sweet in Jorie's mouth, they taste like apples as she speaks. "It will never be over between me and you."

As the sky deepens and the clouds begin to blush with mauve shadows, Jorie goes to fetch a pitcher of warm water and some shampoo. When she comes back, she washes Charlotte's hair there on the patio, beneath the pink sky, while dozens of sparrows gratefully wind bits of red hair into their nests. Afterward, Jorie gets them dinner, which she brings outside so they can picnic on the grass. There's the roast chicken she's brought today, along with some eggplant casserole Trisha Derry delivered earlier in the week. Once the chemo treatments begin, Charlotte won't be able to keep anything down other than bread and butter and applesauce, but at the moment, she's ravenous. She eats until she feels she will burst. There is no one to try to impress anymore, not even herself. She has already decided she will not look at her own reflection, at least not for a while. If she's alive and well next summer, then she'll buy a full-length mirror to hang in the hallway. She'll stare at herself night and day.

"What do you know." Jorie grins as she peers at the street where a car has come to park. They're finishing supper, which is delicious, and drinking tall glasses of lemonade sweetened with cherry juice, exactly the way they used to like it when they were girls. "Is that Barney Stark?"

Sure enough, it's Barney's Lexus, with all the windows rolled down and Barney himself behind the wheel, staring into the hot, glassy air.

"I heard he's moved out of his house. He's living in his office on Front Street."

"What is wrong with that man?" Charlotte asks. "Every time I turn around, there he is."

Jorie laughs. "Did you ever think he might be interested in you?"

"Oh, don't be ridiculous. Take a look at me. On second thought, don't." Charlotte gets up and heads for the gate. "Hey, Barney." She waves. "Don't just sit there. Come on over and have some supper."

Sitting in his parked car, Barney looks startled. For a moment it seems as though he may bolt, turn the key in the ignition and drive out of Hillcrest as fast as he can, back to the safety of his office and the haze of indecision he's been living in these past years. Instead, he gets out of his car and comes around the path.

"I didn't want to interrupt you if you had company," he says as he hands Charlotte the box he has with him, a pink bakery box she instantly recognizes as one of her own. "I guess this is like carrying coals to Newcastle."

"Isn't that nice, to be compared to a hill of coal," Charlotte counters. All the same, she's oddly moved. Since she owns the bakery, no one has ever thought to bring her dessert before. "Ah," she says upon opening the box. "Chocolate confession cake. My favorite."

Charlotte goes inside to fix a plate of chicken and vegetables for Barney, leaving Jorie and Barney together,

"Tell her some good news," Charlotte calls to Barney as she goes inside. "She could use it."

Barney sits down in the grass. He's sweating too much, so he takes off his jacket, then loosens his tie. He's somewhat embarrassed in Jorie's presence, for there's a part of him that feels he's let the Fords down by not handling Ethan's case personally. In order to tell her anything even slightly resembling good news, he'd have to lie to her, and that's not within Barney's capabilities.

"Fred Hart seems to be doing a great job," he says instead, hoping this opinion will comfort Jorie. "He thinks he can prove Ethan is a changed man, and he's got half the town willing to vouch for him. They've already raised close to fifty thousand dollars, and that's certainly a vote of confidence."

"You never would have taken the case." Jorie seems quite certain of this. "You couldn't defend a guilty man."

When Charlotte comes back with a plate piled high with chicken and eggplant, along with some dessert dishes and silverware, Jorie takes the opportunity to say her good-byes. She tells them she's tired, she jokes that since she's moved back home, her mother has taken to staying up, waiting by the window until Jorie is safely through the front door, but they both know she's exhausted from keeping up a facade of good cheer. Cover up grief and it grinds away at you, from the inside out. It makes you run for dark corners and empty rooms, heartsick and mute, despising your own company.

"She doesn't know what to do," Charlotte says after Jorie has left. "She doesn't even know what to think."

"She knows, all right. That's the whole problem."

It's time for dessert, so Barney takes the serving knife Charlotte's brought him and cuts two large slices of cake. People say this rich concoction can force a person to admit almost anything, if he eats enough of it. Well, Barney's never been afraid of the truth. Truth is his business, he's not going to turn away from it now, no matter how high the price. Dana was not especially surprised when he told her he was moving out; if anything, she seemed relieved, particularly when Barney assured her that she and the girls wouldn't have to change their lifestyle even though he would no longer be living in the house on Evergreen. Since then, he's been keeping up with the girls, spending as much time with them as he can. He's come for dinner the last two nights, much more pleasant events than what they'd all come to expect, and he knows exactly where his daughters are this evening. Kelly is out with Rosarie Williams, at one of those damned fund-raisers for Ethan, held in Hamilton this time. Josie is at her dance class, and Sophie, his dearest, his baby, is up in her room, writing in her journal, trying her best to deal with how angry she is.

And so Barney thinks about the truth, now that he has the time and opportunity to do so. He is glad to be in Charlotte Kite's backyard, that is the truth. Glad to be watching the dusk settle in between the twisted apple trees on the hillside behind her house, to be here eating chocolate cake with the scent of strong coffee and honeysuckle in the air.

And what does Charlotte make of this large, quiet man in her backyard? When he gazes at her, she can tell he hasn't noticed that her hair is different. He is looking at something else entirely. He's looking inside her. That's when Charlotte realizes what's going on here. Jorie was right. Charlotte is surprised it's taken her so long to figure out why Barney Stark is always around.

"I'm not in the market for a boyfriend if that's why you've been following me," she says matter-of-factly, between bites of cake. In two weeks, chocolate will make her queasy, but right now she can't get enough of it. People say that eating chocolate can bring on a rush much like falling in love. It makes a heart beat too fast and stimulates far-fetched ideas. "And even if I was interested, I have cancer, you know."

"So I hear." In point of fact, Barney knows quite a bit about her medical status. He called the hospital so often when Charlotte was there for her surgery that the nurse on duty came to recognize his voice.

"Let's be honest," Charlotte says, which makes him admire her all the more. The shape of her head seems perfectly defined to him tonight, even more beautiful than usual. "I could be dying."

"Well, we're all dying of something, aren't we?" Barney responds, cheerfully.

"That's true, Barney, but some of us may be doing it sooner than others."

Barney cuts himself another piece of cake. In his line of business, he has learned that there were no guaranteed outcomes and no certainties, good, bad, or indifferent, that a man could depend upon. At seventeen, he never would have been able to imagine having chocolate cake with Charlotte Kite in her backyard. He wouldn't have dared to dream such a thing. Now he puts his feet up on a chair and gazes up at the sky.

"There's Orion," he says.

Charlotte gazes up as well. She can feel pinpricks of starlight in her eyes. She shakes her head and blinks, then gives her attention back to her half-eaten slice of chocolate cake because what seems to be occurring is too crazy for her to contemplate. "Does your wife know where you are?" she asks.

"We're not living together, so why should she? Anyway, she doesn't even know who I am."

They both laugh at what is clearly not a joke, and then, awkward with the sudden intimacy between them, fall silent.

"I don't think Dana much cares where I am." Barney narrows his eyes, and the stars above are circled with halos. "She's a good person, don't get me wrong. She just doesn't happen to be the one I want."

"You would have to be out of your mind to do what I think you're doing," Charlotte says.

"And what's that?" Barney looks young in the dark.

"Asking me out. Or whatever they call it nowadays."

"That's what I'm doing. Although we don't have to actually go out. We can just sit here."

Charlotte laughs; that makes twice in one evening, something of a record for her of late. "Is this because I never would have gone out with you in high school?"

"If you're asking if I always felt this way, the answer's yes."

Barney hadn't intended to be so forward, so maybe that chocolate confession cake has indeed done its work. Every once in a while, a man realizes what he wants more than anything, and that's what's happened to Barney. Maybe the lies that were the foundation of Ethan Ford's marriage have shone a light on Barney's own duplicity in pretending he could be happy with any woman other than Charlotte. At any rate, if he's going to act, he'd better not put it off. Barney Stark stops gazing at stars. He believes Charlotte Kite to be the most beautiful woman he's ever seen, with or without her hair, and that is why at this ridiculous and terrifying point in their lives, he finally tells her so.

As it turns out, Barney is the one who picks up Charlotte Kite and drives her to her first chemotherapy appointment. Once they're inside the hospital in Hamilton, Charlotte turns to him and says, "Thanks for the ride. You can go home now," but Barney acts as though she hasn't spoken. He seems to have the ability to see inside her, and he tells her what she probably already knows—he's not going anywhere. He waits in the hall while she checks in, then accompanies her into the oncology unit, where she's settled into a comfortable chair. Once the IV is slipped into Charlotte's vein, Barney checks to make certain she'll be given the right cocktail of drugs, comparing the label on the IV bags to the medications written down in her chart.

"Husband?" the nurse says to him.

Barney and Charlotte exchange a look.

"I can always tell," the nurse informs them. "You work here long enough, you can figure out what people are to each other."

"No person in their right mind is going to hang around here," Charlotte insists once she's been given her antinausea medicine and the drip is begun in earnest. She has a hollow feeling in the pit of her stomach, a combination of nausea and fear. "Run," she tells Barney. "Run for your life."

But Barney Stark has already pulled up a chair. He has his briefcase with him, which he opens in order to bring forth a magazine.

"What's that supposed to be?" Charlotte's face is chalky, her dark eyes shut against the sheer reality of the room around them. Barney Stark, who has the ability to read almost anyone, can certainly see the terror there. But he acts as though it's not the least bit unusual to be making his intentions clear while poison is filling Charlotte's veins. He acts as though they had all the time in the world.

"I thought I'd read to you."

Charlotte's eyes have been closed tight; when she hears his voice she peers over at what he's brought along. *"Sports Illustrated?"* She laughs, and Barney believes it is the most wonderful sound he's ever heard. Up and down the room, people are hidden behind drawn curtains, each with their own particular illness, their own agony, and here they are falling in love.

The nurse brings ginger ale and crackers, which Charlotte gratefully accepts. She notices the way Barney is watching her. She has no idea what on earth she's done to deserve a man like this, especially at this time in her life, when it is absurd to think such things are possible. Barney smiles at her and in that smile Charlotte sees everything he thinks and feels; Barney's deepest self opens to her, his past and his future and this instant in time. All her life, Charlotte has been chasing after things that were beyond her reach. In spite of everything she's already lost, and everything she has yet to lose, she's here today, in a sunny room, on an August afternoon, sick to her stomach and afraid for her life, but wanting, perhaps for the very first time, to be exactly where she is.

"Go on, then." Charlotte closes her eyes the way a diver might when leaping from the highest ledge. At last she knows how it feels to take a chance when everything in the world is at stake, breathless and heedless and desperate for more. "Read to me," she says.

The Jester

PEOPLE CAME FROM ALL over Massachusetts to see him in that week before he was transferred to Maryland, and when they weren't allowed into the county court building, they settled outside, in the grass and on the road, perching like the warblers traveling south through the Commonwealth at this time of year. It was the last week of the blooming lilies, and the thin, green stems flutter each time a car passes by, the petals falling like leaves. Twice in the past few days, eggs have been thrown at the courthouse, and a bomb threat has been phoned in from a long-distance exchange, but the crowd that has gathered has come to support Ethan Ford, and sitting alone in his cell he can hear people call out his name, and he finds comfort there, where he least would expect to encounter it, in the voices of those who believe in him.

Rosarie Williams is at the top of that list. She has personally sent out thirty thousand fliers, folding paper until her fingers are bleeding, licking stamps until everything she eats tastes like glue. Mark Derry fashioned the task force room right where his dining room used to be, and that's where the faithful congregate, quick to reassure one another that the world they know is not as perilous as some might have them conclude. Good deeds prevail among these people. A fax machine has been donated by the friends of the town council, and the volunteers at the firehouse have presented the task force with a Xerox copier. On most days, Mark has a crew of five or more staff members working away, raising both money and awareness, but Rosarie Williams is his right-hand girl, running back and forth to the jail, making herself useful in the dining room office, donating her time and energy even on Saturday nights, when most girls her age are out looking for a good time.

Mark Derry has grown so fond of Rosarie that he sincerely regrets the fact that she broke up with his son; she might have been a cherished daughter-in-law if circumstances had worked out differently, present at holiday dinners and birthdays. But of course it's clear to Mark that Rosarie is far too mature for a boy like Brendan. She doesn't even glance at him whenever Brendan glumly edges past to go into the kitchen to fix himself a ham-and-cheese sandwich. On evenings when Brendan comes home from his job at the Pizza Barn, with free pizzas for everyone, Rosarie doesn't blink an eye. She's too busy thinking about the way Ethan looked at her when she last went to visit him at the jail, how he'd drawn her close and told her he'd be lost without her, how he would have given up long ago if not for those who had faith in him.

As for Brendan Derry, he pouts at first, tormented by how close Rosarie is, and still, how far away, but soon enough he takes to avoiding his own house. Seeing Rosarie makes him feel wretched deep down inside. He feels the way people do when they start to go bad, a wizening of the spirit, a desire to take fool-hardy chances just for the hell of it. He's stopped showing up for work on most evenings, and he's started driving fast in an aimless loop around town, looking to self-destruct, and tempting fate every time he walks out his front door. He might have done himself in completely, crashing into those big rocks down at the tricky intersection on the way to Lantern Lake, if Barney Stark's Lexus hadn't been broken down by the side of the road one pearly evening.

The blinking lights cause Brendan Derry to slow down, and when he does, he glimpses a scene that causes him to step on his brakes. Kelly Stark and her sisters are inside the car, all of them shaking and pale, afraid they've ruined their father's most prized possession. The three girls are crying about how their father has left them, moved out for no reason to live in his office; they're certain he'll hate them if his beloved Lexus is ruined. But the trouble is only a flat tire, caused by broken glass on the road, easy enough to fix. In fact, Sophie and Josie Stark are given the job of working the jack, which allows Brendan and Kelly to stand together on the side of the road in the dark, listening to the call of the frogs in the lake and finding each other much more interesting than they'd ever imagined they might.

After this encounter, Kelly does her best to avoid Rosarie Williams. She's heard first-hand from Brendan how cruel Rosarie can be, and besides, Kelly has begun to have serious doubts about working for Ethan Ford. According to Brendan, Ethan is nothing but a reprehensible murderer, slithering his way into their lives. Now whenever Rosarie phones, Kelly tells her sisters to say she isn't home. She's repulsed by the way Rosarie has been acting, practically throwing herself at a man in jail. She's begun to think Ethan Ford's wife has a right to know the real story and is tempted to reveal what goes on when Rosarie goes to visit Ethan. There is such intense flirting that the guards are said to be aroused at the mention of Rosarie's name. They grow feverish the minute they see her, drinking so much icy water from the cooler that the bill for spring water at the jail has doubled this month.

Kelly's father is representing Jorie in the sale of her house, and one afternoon Kelly meets up with Jorie in the hall outside his office. Standing there, making polite conversation, Kelly is about to whisper, *Watch out for Rosarie,* but then she makes the mistake of really looking at Jorie. The anguish she observes forces her to take a step backward, so that she lurches into the wall. The idea of causing more harm raises gooseflesh on Kelly's arms, and so she keeps silent, merely watching as Jorie rushes to the realtor with the papers Barney Stark has prepared for her in hand.

When it comes to the sale of the house, Jorie knows she should be thankful that the young couple from Framingham have decided to buy; some people, it's true, won't even look at an address where a criminal has lived. You never knew what you might find when you dug up the garden to put in a swing set. You never could tell what the attic crawl space might yield or what might be hidden in the garage. Luckily, these buyers have no qualms about the house's history, especially in light of the great deal they're getting, thousands less then the asking price of any other house in the neighborhood. It's true, photos of the house had been in both the city papers and the *Monroe Gazette,* but no one pays much attention these days; cars don't drive past slowly anymore, with the occupants' tongues wagging, embellishing and refining an already sad story. Occasionally, a reporter may circle Ruth Solomon's house on Smithfield Road, but Jorie's sister, Anne, has been known to turn the hose on such people, an act of defiance she greatly enjoys. She's on her own family's property, after all, and even Gigi, who is usually such a stick-in-the-mud when it comes to wicked behavior, applauds her mother's efforts to maintain what little privacy they have left.

But most people in town don't need to read the newspapers to get the facts anymore; they've made up their own minds by now, especially when it comes to their opinion of Jorie. Some have made the choice to ignore her completely; she doesn't even exist for such individuals. On the streets and in stores, many people Jorie has known all her life have begun to look the other way when she walks by, as if she'd never set foot in their universe, never sat next to them in school, or shopped at the Hilltop supermarket alongside them, or washed cars at the PTA bazaar, or brought homemade blueberry muffins to the Friends of the Library day. These are the citizens of Monroe who wonder how Jorie has the nerve to show her face, and for the life of them they can't figure out how she's managing to live with herself now that she knows she's been sleeping next to a monster for so many years, dreaming in his arms.

If pressed, some people might admit they haven't recently turned against Jorie; in truth, many held a grudge long before Ethan was brought into custody. They always believed Jorie was too pretty and stuck-up for her own good, and they view her with an indifference that is far from cold. There are quite a number of people in town who always resented the arrogant manner Ethan possessed when he refused an award ceremony back when the McConnell house burned down. Still others have never approved of the way Jorie and Ethan kissed each other in the field during baseball practice, so brazen, right in front of everyone, there for all the children to see.

Sometimes Jorie wears sunglasses when she has to run errands; she ties a scarf around her head and does her best to hide. But there are other times when she stares right back, eye to eye, in defiance of the prying glances sent her way in the drugstore and the bank. Either way, folks who know her can tell she's been crying; her eyes are puffy even on days when she doesn't shed a tear. Her pretty honeyed hair is snarled, her clothes are wrinkled, her face drawn. A few weeks ago, Jorie had been a beautiful woman, but that's over now. She's been avoiding people, spending most of her time inside, behind locked doors. She holds the diary in her hands when she's alone on the sun porch, hiding it beneath her pillow if her sister or mother should happen to approach. She has given up gardening and going for walks with her mother's dog, Mister. Now, whenever she ventures into the sunlight, Jorie finds she breaks out in a rash, sorrowful bumps of grief that rise on her arms and legs and along her chest, in a red line beside her heart.

There are still some neighbors who continue to be concerned, people like Grace Henley, the librarian, and Mrs. Gage, their next-door neighbor for so long, who go out of their way to ask Ruth Solomon if there's anything to do to help out and insist upon bringing over casseroles that sit in the refrigerator untouched. These are the people it's most difficult to see, for Jorie knows they pity her, and their pity makes her even more desperate, it causes her to draw the curtains in the middle of the day and refuse to allow her son to go to the town pool even though the weather is brutal, with temperatures hovering high in the nineties, and cherries ripening too soon, and fledglings dying of thirst in their nests in the tallest of the trees.

Ethan, of course, has his throngs of supporters, those advocates who sprawl on the lawn at the courthouse and have taken up his cause. The family should feel reassured by so many well-wishers, but these good people are the reason Collie gives for not visiting his father—the crowds and the reporters, the traffic and the fuss make him nervous, or so he says. He prefers to stay on the couch with Mister, watching TV. But there's more to Collie's isolation, and Jorie has seen for herself the reason he steers clear of people in town. Just a few days earlier, she'd been driving by the high school during baseball practice and she'd spied two boys throwing balls at Collie as he walked past. She'd thought it was all in fun, until she saw the look on Collie's face. He'd just kept on his way along the sidewalk, ignoring the other boys' taunts and their dares, even though one of the balls had hit him between the shoulder blades, hard.

"Hey, you guys, cut it out," Jorie had heard Barney Stark call. He'd jogged across the field from third base to lecture the offending boys, but the damage had been done. Collie continued on, the sun in his eyes, the late afternoon light turning his hair flaxen, his mouth set in a flinty, uncompromising line, his shoulders hunched to avoid further assault. Jorie knew then that things would never be the same, no matter how she might try to protect him. She found herself thinking of James Morris, a boy like her own, whose life was turned around one ordinary summer morning. She was proud of her son for not giving in to his tormentors. He'd kept on his appointed route despite them; he'd turned them into smoke and ash inside his mind.

When Jorie asks Collie if he wants to go with her to the final rally at the courthouse, she's not surprised to hear him say no. He has plans, he's meeting Kat, and they leave it at that; they don't discuss the fact that Collie doesn't want to get within five hundred feet of the courthouse, not the way he hurts inside, more deeply than he himself knows. It's Charlotte who agrees to accompany Jorie downtown. They drive to the courthouse to get a look at the last rally on this hot August night. Half the town is gathered on King George's Road, and those who are in attendance are in high spirits. Ethan's fellow firemen are there, as are most regulars from the Safehouse, along with the Little League commissioner and several people from the school board. But there are plenty of outsiders congregated as well, and many have hung their towns' banners from the trees: Everett is represented, as is Cambridge, and Newton, and Essex, along with a huge crowd from Hamilton assembled beneath the linden trees. There are women from Boston who have seen Ethan's photograph in the *Herald* and who can tell simply by looking at him that he has repented. There are men from New Hampshire and Maine who have made mistakes in their lives and could use a little forgiveness of their own. Someone has been selling green light sticks and the night is aglow with wands of brilliant jade. Up and down the street, there are several trucks selling ice cream and hot dogs and sizzling fried dough that leaves the air permeated with a sultry, sugared scent.

"Just be prepared when you do go over there," Barney Stark had advised when Jorie came to pick up Charlotte. "There are all sorts of folks getting involved at this point, and probably half of them have their own twisted reasons for coming to this rally. Whatever happens, don't let them get to you."

Barney was still living in his office, but he was spending more and more time at Charlotte's. Jorie, however, felt she had been neglectful; she hadn't been to see Charlotte since she'd decided to shave her head. Charlotte explained that she'd spent so much energy fearing the loss of her hair, she figured it might be best to go ahead and get it over with, slapdash, snip snap. Jorie kissed her friend on the forehead. She had never before noticed how truly beautiful Charlotte was, and when Charlotte grabbed for the hat she'd taken to wearing, Jorie told her not to bother. "You don't have anything to hide," she observed. "You look amazing."

"Amazingly scary." Charlotte had laughed, but she'd left the hat behind.

"You look like you."

"Oh, God. That's even scarier. Let's just say I look like a Martian and leave it at that."

When they had almost reached the street, Charlotte rushed back to the house. At first Jorie thought she'd changed her mind and decided to cover her head, but Charlotte had only returned to say good-bye to Barney, whom she'd forgotten in the doorway.

"See ya, pal." Charlotte stood on tiptoes to kiss him, then, out of breath and happy, she ran back to Jorie, who was holding open the door of the truck. "I don't like to leave without saying good-bye," Charlotte said as they drove away. "You never know when you won't see someone again."

"You'll see him again."

"Actually, I think Barney's here for the duration. You're the one I'm afraid might disappear."

Jorie managed a grin. "I'll let you know if I plan to."

"We'll send each other messages from the great beyond."

Jorie laughed at that notion. And that was fine, as long as she didn't look over at Charlotte and admit that such a loss seemed horribly possible at this point in their lives. "I was thinking more of a change of address."

"I know what we'll do." Charlotte looked so young without her hair. She wore a sweater in spite of the heat, for lately she was always cold. At the hospital, during her treatments she shivered and tried to imagine Florida beaches, a vacation Barney has promised they'll take when she's strong enough to travel. "We have to vow that we'll send each other lilies if we make it over to the other side. If we do that, then we'll know something remains."

"Fine," Jorie agreed. "If I ever leave you, I won't really be gone, and the same better be true for you."

They sealed this promise by hooking pinkies, the way they used to, long ago, when promises didn't hurt as much.

There was so much traffic in town it took nearly half an hour to get to King George's Road, and they had to circle for quite some time before a parking place was found. From their spot on the crowded street, they can at last see the wide lawn of the county offices. People are laughing as they wait for the rally to begin; they're having a good time. Some have brought blankets and picnic dinners; children race back and forth, playing tag in the waning light. Jorie and Charlotte sit in the cab of Ethan's truck with a thermos of milky tea and a box of Kite's doughnuts, jam and cream-filled, between them on the seat, not that either woman can eat. Charlotte's mouth has reacted to chemo with painful little sores that her doctor assures her will disappear before long. Because of this, she's taken to fixing watery oatmeal for nearly every meal; she's actually begun to enjoy the stuff, although Barney continues to refer to it as gruel.

As for Jorie, her stomach is lurching about, a severe case of indigestion brought on by nerves. Watching the crowd that has gathered, she feels the ache of her own aloneness, as might be expected in anyone who was not among the faithful here tonight. Across the darkness, across the lawn, there are Warren Peck and Hannah from the coffee shop; there is Hal Jordan, the Little League commissioner, and near the stage that has been set up by the firemen, Jorie and Charlotte both can spy Rosarie Williams, dressed as though she'd been invited to a party, wearing a pale blue frock she must have borrowed from her mother, for it seems far too adult for a girl of her age. Rosarie's black hair is loose and her skin is shining, illuminated by the diamond-white light streaming from the half-dozen sparklers local boys have set out on the lawn.

"What does the Williams girl have to do with any of this?" Charlotte doesn't like the devout expression on Rosarie's face.

"She's Mark Derry's assistant." Jorie takes a good look at Charlotte and sees that her friend is brimming with suspicion. "It's not what you're thinking. She's helping out."

"Yeah, well, some people are attracted to trouble." Charlotte knows how true this can be from her years of marriage to Jay. "Some people can only fight battles they can't win."

"I see. Because you're in love, you think everyone else is."

"I didn't say anything about love. I just don't trust that girl." Charlotte reaches for a blanket she's brought along. It's a velvet night, warm and lush, but she's chilled to the bone. "Anyway, love is different than I thought it would be."

Everything is different, the way they are sitting in Ethan's truck on a summer's night hoping for the best, fearing the worst; the way their lives have been rattled around, as though they were dice, their futures decided by a throw onto a tabletop.

Mark Derry walks out to the stage, and as soon as he does, the crowd begins to applaud. People around here know Mark from his work on Ethan's behalf, and they respect him; they get fired up when he charges them to show their allegiance, right here and now, so loud and so strong that people all the way down in Maryland will be able to hear. Horns honk along King George's Road and several Roman candles left over from the Fourth of July are set off, filling the sky with bands of scarlet and sapphire light.

Charlotte reaches over and takes Jorie's hand as they watch. Charlotte's hand is small and cold, but she has a firm grip and she holds on tight. As for Jorie, she is thinking of blue skies and fields and of the endings of things. She brings up the image of their old friends Lindsay and Jeannie from high school, two lovely girls who woke one morning without realizing it was to be their last day on earth, who brushed their hair and talked on the phone and walked out their front doors into the inky night, traveling on a road that was slick with pale rain, turned to ice before anyone noticed.

All good men make mistakes, that's what Mark Derry is calling from the podium, and by the time he asks his neighbors for their donations and their pledges, their hands are in pockets, checks are being written. As it turns out, the usually silent plumber is both convincing and reassuring; Trisha Derry, gazing on from the sidelines, with her arms around her little girl, April, has good reason to look as proud as she does. Mark Derry speaks from the heart, he means what he says, but he hasn't been to Maryland, he hasn't walked through the cordgrass or gone through the door into Rachel's room. Rachel's diary is in Jorie's purse, beneath her wallet and a shopping list and a packet of Kleenex, there to remind her of what happened all those miles away. This is a book of hope that has never been finished, a list of dreams left undone. It's therefore no consolation to hear the jubilation that meets Mark Derry's remarks, not for anyone who carries a diary such as this.

Fred Hart's turn at the podium has come, and it's clear the attorney from Boston relishes the attention. He waves his hands in the air, getting people riled up, and when he begins to speak, his voice is just low enough to spur the crowd to lean in close and listen hard. Hart announces that a group of Monroe citizens will be chosen to travel south to assist in the effort during Ethan's trial. No one mentioned this game plan to Jorie; if Fred had bothered to discuss it with her, she would have assured the attorney it was a tactical mistake. She can't help but imagine what the reactions of local people in Holden might be when this group of supporters arrives in town. She suspects the Black Horse Hotel will be unable to accommodate them, as a matter of principle, and that they'll have to stay at the Econo Lodge out on the highway.

But what will people in Duke's Diner say when these strangers come in to order turkey club sandwiches and egg salad on toast? Will folks mention that the graveyard is just up the hill and that the mallows that grow there are carefully tended? Will they say that Rachel Morris came in to Duke's nearly every Saturday to order vanilla Cokes and French fries with vinegar and that she was the prettiest girl in town?

"He wants to have me and Collie go with him," Jorie tells Charlotte.

"To Maryland?" Charlotte is stunned. "And he thinks you would even consider putting Collie through that?"

"Collie could stay with my mother."

"Like you'd ever do that. You're not about to leave Collie behind."

Jorie smiles to think of how well Charlotte knows her, for in fact when she tries to envision sitting on the opposite side of the courtroom, across the aisle from James Morris, she simply cannot see herself. In Holden, she would be an invisible woman, it's true. When she walked across town, she wouldn't leave footsteps. When she opened her mouth, no sound would issue forth.

A wave of excitement has begun to move through the throng on the lawn; it snakes like a current through the grass and the air. People rise to their feet, and from where Jorie and Charlotte are parked they can see that the door to the courthouse has opened. There is a wash of green light across the lawn.

"They wouldn't let him out for this, would they?" Charlotte asks.

But, indeed, they have. Four men have joined the others on stage: Dave Meyers and two of the guards, and with them, Ethan

Ford. The cheering is truly wild; it bursts into the vast night above the courthouse, above the linden trees. Tonight, the rules have been bent to allow for Ethan's presence at the rally, but that's to be expected. This is Monroe, the town that supports Ethan; these are his friends and neighbors, several of whom will travel to Maryland, leaving jobs and families to work on his behalf.

In return for these many favors, Ethan offers the crowd endless gratitude, and people hush each other once he begins to speak, the better to hear. They move in closer, the better to see.

"Do you want to go up there?" Charlotte asks.

To Jorie, Ethan looks strangely small in the distance. Someone has brought him a clean white shirt for this occasion, and he glows the way stars do, so distant that, as it turns out, they're not what they seem to be. Mark Derry stands to Ethan's left, Fred Hart to his right. The men lift their linked arms into the air, victorious and hopeful and so far away they might as well be in another galaxy.

Jorie thinks about the day their life split apart, when Ethan's past was laid out for everyone to see, like an accident on the highway, or a piece of fruit, golden on the outside, gray and coarse within. She thinks of how well she thought she knew him. She would have recognized him anywhere just from his smile. She knew everything—the way he walked, the sound he made low down in his throat when he was displeased, the thumbs-up signal he gave to each and every boy on his team, whether or not the play they made was successful. She knew how he reached for her at night and how she felt when he did so.

"No. I don't want to go up there," she tells Charlotte.

Does she imagine that most things cannot be hidden in the way that Ethan concealed his past? That if she took a single step forward, the diary in her purse would begin to bleed, and once it began, it would continue until the lawn of the courthouse was awash with it, until everyone's shoes were slick and blood coursed down the sidewalk, into the streets?

"Then let's get out of here," Charlotte suggests, and they do exactly that. While the crowed is applauding, while Ethan is thanking those gentle, loyal people who support him, Jorie and Charlotte drive out of town. In any other part of the Commonwealth, this is nothing more than a pleasant August night. They turn the radio up, the way they used to when they were girls. Out of habit, they find themselves on the road to Hamilton; they pull into the parking lot of the Safehouse, but they don't go inside. It's empty in there anyway, with Warren Peck's dad, Raymond, holding down the fort, and only a few customers who are too old or too confused about the issues to attend the rally for Ethan.

"I shouldn't have made you come here with me that night," Charlotte says. "You probably never would have met him if it hadn't been for me."

There is a big moon hanging in the sky, just above the treetops.

"Don't think that way." Jorie closes her eyes, but she still sees the moonlight. "I wouldn't have Collie without that night."

Collie himself is currently wishing that he was miles away from Monroe; anywhere at all would do, as long as it's far from Massachusetts and everything he's ever known. When he walks through the familiar streets he's accustomed to, they feel too small for him, lamplit and shadowy; the linden trees block out the sky, even in the dark they take up too much space. Collie usually waits for Kat on the corner; since moving into his grandmother's house, he can't bring himself to revisit Maple Street. Tonight, Kat rides her bike to meet him, and because Collie's own bike is pretty much ruined, the tires wobbling wildly, the frame bent from the time he slammed into the fence, they ride together on Kat's bike, out to the abandoned house. Collie is behind Kat, his arms around her waist. They are so close, he swears he can feel her heart beating; he can hear his own heart as well.

They come to the old house almost every night; nobody's keeping tabs on them, nobody knows where they are. This place is theirs, at least temporarily. They've found an old couch, which they've set up in the parlor, and they've stored flashlights and cans of soda in the rubble. This house was here before Monroe was a town, only fields and apple trees as far as a man could see, but it won't be standing much longer. Kat and Collie both have the sense

319

that it's crumbling around them. Each time they come here, they're afraid they'll find nothing left, only bricks and slats of wood, all falling to dust. They can feel what little time they have. The summer is fading away, drifting into a green haze. This is what summer will always mean to them, even when they've grown old. The way the crickets called, the way they huddled close together on the old couch that was abandoned here long before either one of them had been born, the way they didn't want to step forward into the future, not yet.

Rosarie was right; it's different between them, and there's not a thing they can do about it. They don't communicate the way they used to, lighthearted and easy with each other. Everything's difficult now. A single word has the potential to break their hearts to pieces. Tonight, they watch the moon through the holes in the roof and they're careful with each other; they don't talk about the rally at the courthouse; they don't talk about anything. When it's late enough for the raccoons to start to take possession of the house, they head back home, but they do so slowly, dragging their feet as they go. This is always the hardest part of the night: coming back to town.

They walk Kat's bike through the dark, quiet streets. It's late and even those people who attended the rally are already in bed, their doors locked, windows latched. The air is aswirl with mosquitoes, so Kat lights up one of the cigarettes she's stolen from Rosarie's dresser drawer; she's intrigued by the way the smoke rises through the dark when she takes a puff. The mosquitoes are chased off, but the smoke causes Kat to cough as well.

"You'd better stop doing that." Collie makes a face. "It's plain stupid."

Kat waves the cigarette around as if she didn't care what Collie thought. A hazy curtain rises between them, and all at once, Kat feels scared. She realizes that this moment will be with them for the rest of their lives. She feels weighed down somehow, as if whatever she says, whatever she does, will be wrong.

"I don't want to be here anymore," Collie says.

It's a terrible thing to hear your best friend say, but Kat doesn't respond. *Oh, please,* she thinks, *don't ever leave me,* but she remains quiet. The odd thing is, she already feels as though he's left her, or maybe she's just telling herself that so she won't feel so bad when he actually does.

Collie is staring upward, searching a sky that is ablaze with stars. White ones, yellow ones, pink ones, ones that have never been seen by anyone else before. Kat looks up, too. She has chills down her arms. She has wreaked havoc and now she is paying the price. She has loved someone completely only twice in her life, and she's paying for that, too.

"I would do anything to make you happy," Kat says. Her voice sounds small, even to herself.

Collie turns away from her, so she can't see what he's feeling for her, but she knows anyway. If they never saw each other again, she isn't sure he'd miss her, not really, not the way she would miss him. Kat throws the cigarette on the sidewalk and steps on glowing embers so that bits of red sparks fly up. She doesn't care how far away he goes; inside, she's never going to give him up.

Above them a star falls from its place in the luminous sky.

"Make a wish!" Kat cries.

It's such a brilliant light, Kat forgets she's made a vow to stop believing in such things. She herself closes her eyes and wishes hard, but when she opens her eyes again and looks at Collie she can tell that it's no longer possible for him to believe. He's done making wishes.

Collie walks her home before he goes on to his grandmother's house on Smithfield Lane. The air is so thick and hot it slows them down; every step takes effort and willpower and courage. The house where he lived before will be painted next week; the buyers want to put their own stamp on the facade, as do any new property owners. Collie stops as soon as they reach the corner. He doesn't dare go farther. They can hear the click-clack of Mrs. Gage's sprinkler. They can hear a dog far away, howling in the night.

That's when Collie leans forward and kisses her. He kisses her with everything he feels, and then he runs off, away toward Smithfield Lane, away from her. Kat jogs the rest of the way home; she cuts across the lawn that is such a mess this summer, filled with brambles and weeds. She's flying over crabgrass and stones, all legs and anguish, her heart throbbing like a beehive, abuzz and already stinging.

Every door is locked, back and front, so Kat climbs in through Rosarie's window, waking her sister as she drops to the floor. Rosarie starts and flips on the light.

"Kat?" Rosarie says when she sees her sister standing there in the dark. Rosarie doesn't expect Kat to throw herself onto the bed any more than she would have envisioned Kat climbing through the window at this hour, but after a moment she understands. Kat is curled up with her legs to her chest, trying to stop everything that she feels.

"You didn't think you were going to get married and live happily ever after, did you? You're not that stupid, Kat." Rosarie runs her hand over her sister's hair. She herself has not believed in love for a ridiculously long time, considering she's only seventeen, but she does believe in going after whatever makes you feel alive.

"Shut up," Kat says to her.

"Make me." Rosarie laughs, then gives her sister a little push.

Kat slips under the covers. She's freezing. Everything keeps ending, and there's nothing she can do about it. "When will it stop hurting?" Kat runs a finger across the burns on her sister's arm. Her skin is so pretty, but the marks won't go away.

"I thought you got it." Rosarie smiles. "Never."

For some reason, the blankets always seem heavier in Rosarie's bed, the pillows deeper. Rosarie reaches to turn out the light. "Go to sleep," she urges. Her voice is dreamy, as though she's already back asleep. "Be quiet."

Moonlight falls in through the window, turning everything silver and blue. A wind has come up, and the bramble bush hits against the house, and Kat listens to the sound carefully. When someone kisses you with everything they feel, you don't stop thinking about it for a very long time.

Collie is thinking about it, too, as he takes the long way back to his grandmother's house, along Front Street, with its darkened storefronts, up Worthington, then through the old lanes overhung with lindens and oaks, past the twisted apple trees that still line the streets. It's dark and late, but Collie doesn't care. He goes past the library and stands looking at the place where the old Westfield Seek-No-Further used to grow. The air smells of sulfur and sweet apples. Collie feels as though he were seeing everything for the very first time, as though he were a stranger in town. Where is he? He doesn't know. Where's he going? He's not certain of that either.

He hears a horn honk, and when he turns he spies his father's truck. For a moment he's afraid he may come face to face with his father, even though he knows this is impossible. Ethan is in jail, and yet Collie's first impulse is to bolt and take off through the parking lot of the library, Instead, he stands his ground. He peers at the driver, and then is relieved. It's only his mother there behind the wheel.

"How about a ride?" Jorie calls through the open window. She's out late, having visited with Charlotte and Barney for an hour or more, drinking Charlotte's favorite green tea that has the unlikely name of Chop Wood Carry Water. It seems as if the rally at the courthouse was a movie they'd seen, a performance they simply couldn't bear to observe.

Collie comes over and gets into the truck. It's long past his curfew, and he expects his mother to question him about where he's been, but she doesn't mention the fact that he should be home in bed at this hour. As they drive, Jorie thinks about what a beautiful baby Collie had been, with his pale fine hair, and what a beautiful boy he'd become. In the past few weeks he's changed, however; he's harder, and quieter, and more withdrawn. He's definitely grown taller. He's staring out at the dark neighborhoods they pass and whistling under his breath. He might as well be a million miles away.

"Are you okay?" Jorie asks, and when Collie looks at her from the corner of his eye, she can feel her love for him in a deep, fierce way, stronger than it's ever been before. She can tell he's about to become a different man than he would have had none of this happened. He'll be moodier and less patient and far more careful in his choice of who he's willing to trust. He's the boy whose father killed someone, that's who he is, the one who refuses to discuss what happened, who walks out of the room when his father's name is mentioned, the one she'll do anything to save.

"What if we moved away from here?" Jorie makes certain to keep her tone light. It's not Maryland she's thinking of, but someplace else entirely. "What if we moved to a town where we could be whoever we wanted to be and do whatever we wanted to do?"

Collie pays close attention. "What would we live on?"

"I could get a job teaching. There's a placement agency that finds jobs in every state. We wouldn't be rich. Anyway, it's just a what-if situation."

"Would it be far away from here?"

"It could be. It wouldn't have to be."

"I'd want it to be." Collie gazes through the window. They are passing the high school, and the dark field beyond. "I don't ever want to see him again."

"You might change your mind. You'll have to wait and see."

She is keeping her voice even. Amazing how she can manage to do that, how close to a lie she feels she's telling by saying nothing at all.

Collie shakes his head. "I know how I feel."

But Jorie is keenly aware of how such things can change. You might feel something one moment—love, for instance—and the next, all you thought you knew and felt could be shaken right out of you, leaving you clear and free to

326

feel something else entirely, something you'd never expected, something brand-new. Throughout the next day, Jorie considers what would be best for Collie. Her house has been emptied, the furniture put in storage, and Anne and Gigi are helping to sort through the belongings that will be kept in Ruth Solomon's basement. They stack mixing bowls and fold sheets; they pepper boxes of blankets with moth-balls and pack the good dishes in bubble wrap to ensure that none will chip.

"This is what happens when you stay in one place for thirteen years," Anne says. "First you own things. Then they own you."

Anne herself moved back to her mother's house with next to nothing. In the past, she would have been jealous of everything her sister owned, but now too many possessions seem like a burden. Gigi, on the other hand, is a collector. She is the proud owner of seventeen pairs of shoes and twenty-six sweaters, and she clearly admires much of what she's packing up.

"When you go away to college, you can take whatever you want," Jorie tells her.

Gigi is amazed. "Don't you want it?"

"She can always buy new things," Anne tells her daughter. When Gigi goes upstairs to get more bubble wrap, Anne turns to her sister. "I didn't want anything when I left, either. Not that I'm saying that's what you should do. I would be the last person to come to for advice, but if I was about to give it, I'd point out the fact that you don't seem to want any-thing that belonged to you and Ethan."

"Maybe I just don't want to be bogged down by belongings."

"Maybe."

"But you don't think so." They never used to talk like this, and Jorie certainly never valued her sister's opinion, but now she's interested. Anne has the ability to cut through pretense and speak her mind, but even Anne can't tell her what to do next.

"The only thing I know for sure," she tells Jorie, "is that I'm late for work and I support you no matter what you decide."

That afternoon, as Jorie helps her mother around the house, she thinks about the way a person's life can change in an instant. She thinks about that ten-year-old boy who raced across the field, tears in his eyes, blood burning his fingers, and her own dear boy, walking through the sunlight, hit in the back by a baseball. She thinks of the moment right before Jeannie Atkins's car hit the fence; how the radio must have been playing, how Jeannie and Lindsay were probably laughing, the way she was laughing that morning before there was a knock on their door.

Sometime after supper, when the sunlight is fading, Jorie takes the phone out to the porch. Funny how she's memorized the number, as though she's been calling it all her life.

The phone rings for a very long time before James Morris answers.

"Hello," he says, distrust in his tone. He's a man who doesn't get many phone calls, nor does he want them.

"It's me."

Jorie has the feeling that he may hang up on her, but instead James says, "Hey, you," as if they were old friends. He's recognized her voice, and what's more, he doesn't seem to mind that she's contacting him.

A dog barks, and Jorie laughs. "Fergus," she says.

"One and the same."

"Is it still as hot down there?" Jorie asks.

"I don't think you're calling to talk about the weather." James Morris has a tang in his voice whenever he thinks someone's being disingenuous, and it's there now. "What is it? Are you okay?"

"Oh, sure." Jorie is sitting there in her mother's sun porch with her house sold, her husband in jail, her life a disaster, but somehow James Morris lifts her up. He makes her consider what people are capable of going through in this world and how much courage it's possible to have. "I think I'll survive."

"I think so, too."

"He wants me to come to Maryland with him."

"That doesn't surprise me."

Jorie can hear a door slam; James is letting the dog out as darkness falls across the fields. He doesn't wish her ill. He wouldn't turn away from her if he saw her in the courtroom; he wouldn't run her off the road if he noticed her driving through town.

"Did you read the diary?" he wants to know.

"How am I supposed to do that? Break it open?"

"I'll bet you anything he's got the key."

Evening is falling, here and in Maryland, a still August night littered with stars.

"And if I read it, what happens then?"

"Then you'll do the right thing," James Morris says.

"Oh, right." Jorie laughs. "Like you know me so well."

"Well enough."

"I thought I knew him well enough."

Jorie can hear the blackbirds, out in the cypress trees. She knows what she wants from James Morris, and he does, too.

"It wasn't your fault," he tells her.

It's a gift he gives to her, and a lasting one at that. She goes to the jail later in the evening, ignoring the threat of a thunderstorm, bringing along supper for Ethan. The sky is shining, the way it always does before a storm, and the roads look as though crushed diamonds have been set in the asphalt. Jorie drives past those banks of daylilies, which haven't much more than another week to bloom. Every time she comes out this way, she finds she has an overwhelming desire to make a U-turn. Words begin to escape her as soon as she turns onto King George's Road, and by the time she reaches the county buildings, she is as cautious as the king rails who hide in the marshes of Maryland, secretive and silent even when danger is near.

Jorie parks behind the jail and walks down the path to the back door, dodging any reporters or well-wishers who might lie in wait. The wind came up last night, and it's still racing through the sky, shaking the leaves on the trees. There are just a few people gathered on the front lawn; die-hard supporters like that pretty Rosarie Williams, along with Warren Peck and Mark Derry, who chat with Dave Meyers as the men gather trash from the previous evening that has been left scattered over the grass. Jorie walks faster and slips through the back door before anyone notices her. Because it's a small town, people at the jail have been considerate for the most part; they've let Jorie visit at whatever times suit her. It's true, there's been some talk about how infrequent her visits have become, just as there have been some whispers about how often Rosarie Williams has come to call. It's gotten so that the men who work at the jail find themselves waiting for Rosarie, and several of them have started to dream about her. Even Dave Meyers, a faithful, honest man, has dreamed that Rosarie asked him to run away with her, although thankfully he woke in his own bed, beside his wife, before he found out whether or not his dream-self decided to take Rosarie up on her offer.

Tonight the two guards on duty, Frankie Links and Roger Lawson, are both disappointed to find it's not Rosarie waiting at the gate, only Jorie. Still, they're polite enough when they let her in. Frankie, who was two years behind Jorie in high school, looks through her purse and the basket of food she's brought with some of Ethan's favorite treats, egg-salad sandwiches, lemon drop cookies, cole slaw fixed with carrots and homemade mayonnaise.

"Crappy weather out there," Frankie says as he leads Jorie down to the holding cells. Frankie is being civil enough, but he's always had a nasty streak, and when they arrive at Ethan's cell he gets a funny smile. "Visitor for you, Mr. Bell," Frankie calls, and he gives Jorie a look from the corner of his eye to see her reaction once he invokes Ethan's real name.

But Jorie doesn't react, and why should she? Everything seems like a dream to her now; the way he'd kissed her, the way she'd loved him. The steel bars that slide open seem real enough, however, as does the echo of Frankie's footsteps in the hall after he shoves the door closed when Jorie enters, so he can return to the guards' office.

"You don't know the way I've missed you," Ethan says to her then.

He comes toward her, but it's as though he were speaking to her from a very great distance away, a place where the fields were green and the dirt was so red it left a film on collars and cuffs, red as the reddest roses. When he's about to embrace her, Jorie turns away. She places the basket of food on the bed, keeping her back to him. Standing there, she thinks for a moment that she hears the ocean, but it's something inside of her, wailing.

"I couldn't bring a thermos in, because of the sharp edges. I guess they think you could smash it and use the pieces to cut your wrists or attack someone, so I just made sandwiches. I probably made too many."

"You haven't been coming to see me, Jorie."
His voice is plaintive, a tone she's never heard
from him before. "It's less and less all the time."

Jorie looks at him. She feels something
racing inside her.

"Mark said he's offered to pick you up and
take you to the rallies, but you won't go. You
don't want to talk about it and you don't
want to see me, and I've been missing you."

Jorie thinks about blackbirds, about the
way it's possible to know someone, yet still be
completely astonished by who they turn out
to be.

"I was at the last rally." She has bitten her
nails down until they are bleeding, little red
half-moons that remind her of how she sits up
nights and frets. "Charlotte and I were there."

"You were there and you didn't come up to
the stage? You didn't come up to be with
me?"

"There was such a crowd." It sounds like
a weak excuse, even to her. It sounds similar
to what Collie's been saying. "You were surrounded by people."

"But none of them were my wife."

Jorie can see how hurt he is, yet she finds
she's unmoved. She thinks of Collie in that old,
abandoned house, crouched down in the dark.
She thinks of the years they've had together
and the promises they've made. If she'd had
to guess where their life would bring them, she
never would have imagined this. But this is
where they are and there's no way out until
they're through.

Ethan sits down on the bed, hands in his lap. He's not angry at Jorie, in fact, he's quite calm. Guilty men are supposed to be anguished, but Ethan has found peace. He's had more than enough time to think this over. Fifteen years, as a matter of fact.

"You want to know how I could lie to you, well, I'll tell you the truth, it was easy. It didn't seem like a lie. For the longest time I couldn't even think about it, and then when I finally could, it was like everything had happened to somebody else. Like it was some story I'd read a long time ago, so far in the past I could hardly remember it anymore. It wasn't like telling lies. I didn't feel I knew the man who did those things, and I still don't. I would never do the things he did."

Jorie has been unpacking his supper, but Ethan takes the basket of food and sets it on the floor, just to stop her from searching through it. He wants her attention. He clearly needs it.

"The man you married? The man you know? That's me. That's who I am."

It's odd the way words echo inside a cell, as though they were coming from so very far away when they're right there in front of you, right in your face.

"Even now, when I force myself to think about it, it's like it never happened."

"I went to Maryland," Jorie says. "And I can tell you, it happened."

Ethan looks at her in a strange way when she says this.

"You went down there? And you didn't tell me?"

Jorie laughs, a harsh sound, even to her own ears. "This is not about what I didn't tell you."

"I don't know where that place is anymore. I couldn't find it if I tried."

"Well, I did." Jorie feels like crying when she thinks about following James Morris through the field. She feels like crying when she recalls the way his dog, Fergus, tagged after him with true devotion, no matter where the path might lead. "It's still there."

Jorie has found herself wishing that Frankie Links would come for her. He would do it out of spite, thinking he was upsetting them if he cut the visit short; he's a mean-spirited individual, but this time Frankie would be doing her a favor.

"Jorie, we can go over the facts again and again, but that's not going to get us anywhere. I didn't have to confess. I wanted to. I needed to. And now I'm asking you for your forgiveness."

Jorie has the terrible feeling that she might choke; she might stop breathing altogether. "That's all? That's all you want?"

Ethan Ford goes down on his knees, there in the cell that has mostly been used for drunk drivers in the past, right on the cement floor. He looks up at her and it's him, the man she married, the one she fell in love with, forever, she said.

"Don't do this." Jorie takes a step back.

"That's all I'm asking for." He has a face like an angel. He has eyes that are so dark you could never look away once you gave in. "I don't care what anybody else thinks, Jorie. I don't even care what they do to me. I just want your forgiveness, baby."

He looks up at her and Jorie realizes that she knows him at least well enough to know what he wants. He wants her to sink to the ground and thread her arms around him; he wants her to kiss him and vow to forgive each and every one of his sins.

"What about Collie? Do you want his forgiveness, too?"

"In time, he'll forgive me," Ethan says.

Standing before him, Jorie thinks of their child, how he'd never hurt a single creature in his life, how he'd went around the house collecting the ant traps she set out every spring. She thinks of the white blossoms floating through town after he'd cut down the apple tree. She thinks about those orange lilies that have always frightened her so, and of her friend Charlotte Kite, with her beautiful red hair shorn. She had loved her husband so deeply she surprised herself, but now she knows the way to Maryland far better than he ever will. She understands that forgiveness isn't so easy to give, and that without it there is only empty space between them, a yard or a hundred miles makes no difference. It's the sort of distance that is impossible to cross.

"I hope you're right about that. I hope he does forgive you someday."

"What about you?"

He has gotten off his knees and is facing her. They can both hear Frankie opening the door into the hallway of the jail. The guard is whistling, a sharp little tune.

"I am who you think I am," Ethan says. "I'm still the same man."

Jorie takes her time when she drives home, passing by the far shore of the lake where she and Charlotte used to go swimming, back before there was a town pool, when they had no choice but to confront snapping turtles if they wanted to cool off in the summertime. Teenagers in town still prefer this place in spite of the turtles and the muck; there's privacy here in the dark water, freedom on the wooded shore. Jorie pulls into the dirt parking lot, and as soon as she gets out, she slips off her shoes, leaving them beside the truck. She takes what used to be her favorite path down to the water, treading carefully because she knows this is a place where wild calla and star grass grow; it's easy enough to trip if you're not careful. On the other side of the lake, she can hear some kids whooping it up. Probably that Rosarie Williams and her gang of friends, sneaking beers, kissing each other with hot, greedy mouths, not caring about the rest of the world, centered only in the intensity of their private moments: the dive off the rock, the embrace in shallow water, the whisper in a pink, curved ear.

The reeds are overgrown around Lantern Lake, and peepers call, a thin, wobbly melody. Jorie and Charlotte used to believe that if a falling star crashed into the lake, the water would turn silver; the glow would light up the whole town. One Halloween, they painted their faces silver; they wrapped themselves in old silver-threaded scarves and came here to dance under the moon. They danced themselves silly, until they collapsed into a silver pile on the shore, and they laughed so loud, their laughter echoed and came back to them across the water, like a gilt-edged cloud.

Jorie walks into the water. It doesn't matter that she's wearing her favorite blouse, or that stones may collect in her pockets and perhaps weigh her down. She likes the feel of mud between her toes, how smooth it is, how slick. Bullfrogs startle as she goes on, and a water lotus drifts near, an elegant yellow variety that glitters in the dark with a soft light, like a watery firefly. The crickets are wild in the heat, they make the night shudder. The thunderstorm that has been threatening has moved on toward the coast and is now passing by with only a few grunts and groans in the crackly air. In between the clouds, Jorie can see stars. The brightest ones are reflected in the lake water, as though that falling star she and Charlotte had waited for had appeared at last.

When she is waist deep, Jorie dives in, grateful for the cool water on her clammy skin. She doesn't think about love and forgiveness as she floats in the dark water. She thinks of apple blossoms and of girls dressed in silver; she thinks how strange it is that she never noticed how beautiful Charlotte was until she lost her hair. Jorie floats until she is shivering. It's a Friday night, and the teenagers on the other side of the lake have lit a bonfire and switched on a boom box. Music falls across the water, and frogs jump in the shallows; the darkness is soft and hot. You could go under here and no one would know it; you'd drift to the bottom, so deep not even the starlight could reach you, so deep you'd never come back again.

Jorie gets out and wrings water from her clothes, then hikes back to the parking lot; she picks up her shoes and gets into the truck. No one who saw her now would have guessed her hair was honey-colored, or that she had once been so pretty other girls had been jealous. They would never have imagined that only a few weeks ago she had been so in love with her husband she'd thought herself the luckiest woman alive. Her clothes have turned a watery gray; her hair falls in strands that are as green as weeds. And yet Jorie feels a sort of light inside her, as though she really had been swimming in water lit by falling stars.

She keeps the windows open as she drives home, in spite of the clouds of mosquitoes, little cyclones buzzing through the night. The funny thing is, when she pulls into the driveway of their house on Maple Street, it just doesn't seem real to her anymore. She understands why Collie refused to come back and pack up his belongings. Jorie's had to empty the house by herself, and in the end she brought most of their clothes down to St. Catherine's over in Hamilton for the end of the season back-to-school jumble sale. Tonight, it doesn't seem as though they ever lived here, but that may change. Years from now, when Jorie and Collie stand on the sidewalk, they may remember things they've forgotten now: how the scent of grass came through the windows in summer, how the snow piled up on the front walkway, how he really did love them, despite what he'd done.

Jorie opens the garage door and goes inside. There are only a few cartons left, Ethan's belongings. On the workbench is his toolbox, along with files from every job he'd taken on during his time in Monroe. Jorie opens the files, one by one. She drips lake water onto the pages and the ink runs, but it doesn't matter, no one will ever bother with these papers again. The new people will set them out on the curb on trash day, and they'll be taken to the dump at the end of Worthington, and that will be that.

Ethan's personal effects have been left in an orderly fashion on the workbench, but then he always was neat and methodical in his habits. On a metal rack, behind glass jars of carefully sorted nails and screws, are the keys to every house he's worked on, each one tagged, in case of emergency. Say a family was away on vacation and the pipes burst, or perhaps raccoons managed to eat through wallboard or if a break-in occurred, Ethan always had the ability to set things right.

Among the keys on the board, there is only one that has no tag. It's silver, smaller than the rest, and when Jorie reaches for it, she knows it's the right one. It's been here all along. The key is attached to a bit of ribbon, frayed blue silk unwinding into strands. Jorie takes the key and goes out to her garden, where for years she has grown the sweetest strawberries, the crispest lettuce, bushels of snap beans so delicious even children begged for a taste. She thinks about the difference between right and wrong; she has already decided that if the key fits she will read Rachel's diary, even if that means she has to leave him.

This key has been in their garage for thirteen years; it's rusted and cheaply made, but it still turns the lock. Inside the diary, Rachel's name is printed carefully; the paper carries the scent of cologne, Jorie guesses lily of the valley, that flowery, young odor, as hopeful as it is sweet. There are pages of pretty, looping handwriting in several shades of ink. Rachel must have had one of those pens that can hold a dozen cartridges, the sort Collie got one year for his birthday, but her last entry is written in blue. That is the entry Jorie turns to, skimming past the pages that record the scant six months Rachel Morris had to live in her fifteenth year. It's the beginning of August, but it's the end of her life. She will brush her hair; she will give her little brother a piggyback ride; she will walk down the road to the store where she works on a day so hot the asphalt melts beneath her sneakers and the sunlight turns her skin the color of apricots, so that for that brief moment, as blackbirds swoop across the distance, she is the most beautiful girl on earth.

The final entry is a hurried, giddy paragraph in which every "i" is dotted with a perfect heart. Jorie can feel her pulse pounding; it's as if someone's life is rising off the page. She can feel Rachel's words in her own mouth, melting there, on her tongue.

I met the handsomest boy in the world today. We went swimming. He kissed me more times than I could count. Kissed at last. Hurray!

After Jorie reads this passage, she goes back to the beginning. She sits in her garden and reads every word. Before long, she knows more about Rachel than she knows about her own sister, and by the time she is through she understands what James Morris meant. She knows exactly what to do. Some other man's wife might agree to go to Maryland, but Jorie has already been there. She knows how the blackbirds sing in the morning and how the roads skirt the brackish water and sweet gum trees. Instead, she'll set off for somewhere she's never been before; she'll pack up everything that's important to her, and she and Collie will drive as far and as long as they want to.

When they're tired at last, they'll stop at a motel where no one knows them, where they can be anyone they want to be, even themselves, if that's what they choose. She won't be thinking of Ethan as she packs up, nor will she dwell on her loss as she cuts down an armful of lilies to leave at Charlotte's door, a small token to assure her friend that there are some things that never change—their friendship, for instance, will go on and on, here and beyond. Ethan may pass through Jorie's mind as she drives down Front Street, a fleeting, sorrowful thought that pains her, but by the time she heads toward the highway, Jorie will be concentrating on the map spread out on the dashboard. She won't care if Collie turns the radio up, and she won't be bothered by the heavy traffic as people return from their summer vacations. Another woman might drive to Maryland, but that's not what Jorie intends to do. Instead, she'll be imagining everything that's out in front of them, road and cloud and sky, all the elements of a future, the sort you have to put together by hand, slowly and carefully, until the world is yours once more.

Good Conscience

I WAITED FOR MY mother on the front porch to make sure she couldn't avoid me. When she came home from work, she wouldn't have any choice but to walk past, and then she'd have to listen when I told her what we had to do. I guess after she pulled into the driveway she could tell it was kind of a trap, because she stayed in her car for a while before she got out. She thought things over, then she came down the path and sat next to me on the porch steps. She shook her car keys until they sounded like bells.

"What is it now?" she said.

My mother smelled good, she smelled like Joy, the scent she always wore, but she looked so tired after working all day that I almost kept my mouth shut. Still, I couldn't ignore my second vow, even though it would have been easier that way. I told her we had some business to clear up, and that we'd better get it settled today.

"Does it have to be today?" My mother sighed and looked wary, as if I were just one of a thousand people who wanted something from her, as if there were a line of needy, demanding daughters that stretched from our house to the highway.

"I want you to take me somewhere," I said.

I expected my mother to argue with me, I thought I'd have to beg and plead to get my way, but she just stood up and went back to the car. She got in behind the wheel and turned the key in the ignition, so I took my place in the passenger seat, and we started driving toward Hamilton. The stonecutter was right at the end of King George's Road, past the Monroe house and the fallen-down stone walls. My mother sat in the car while I went in, but that was fine with me, I knew what I wanted. There were blocks of marble and granite lining the path, every color from pale pink to black, but when I went inside I told the stonecutter I wanted something that looked as if it had been there forever. I wanted gray slate lined with mica, and the only thing I wanted written on it was my father's name.

It was dusty in the stonecutter's office, and the walls were covered with patterns that had previously been used for memorials, messages of heartbreak and love. In the back of the workshop, there was an angel whose wing had cracked in two that the stonecutter was in the process of repairing. There were still bits of granite in the air, floating around like moths, but I didn't care. I closed my eyes and made a wish on that angel; then I went out to the car to get a check from my mother.

"Did we get something expensive?" she asked me.

"We got something he would have liked."

My mother laughed at that. "He would have liked to be here with us."

This was more than we had talked to each other in the past year, and we both sounded funny, like people who'd been lost in the desert, whose throats were bound to hurt every time they spoke. My mother had begun to rifle through her purse to look for her checkbook. She was acting like finding her checkbook was the most important thing in the world. I thought about how I wished I could have seen my father one more time. I thought about how he would always be with me, no matter what.

After I took the check in, the stonecutter wrote out a receipt. He must have thought I was younger than I am, because he patted me on the head.

God bless you, he called when I ran back outside, and for some reason his blessing meant something to me. When I got in the car I didn't wait for my mother to start driving. I threw my arms around her, and she let me hug her. Then we were careful to act as though nothing had happened, but something had. My mother stayed on King George's Road, and she took the turn that leads to Hamilton instead of heading for home, and we went out to the cemetery. We knew exactly where the spot was, the place where the orange lilies were growing, the last blooms looking like sunlight even when they fell onto the grass. I was glad my mother had had that fight with the cemetery owners and that she'd insisted on getting what she'd wanted, at least that one time.

"It looks good," I said to her.

We didn't get out of the car, that would have been too much, we couldn't have taken that just then, but I could tell that the stone I picked would look as though it belonged here. I knew I'd done the right thing. We drove home with the windows open, and for once my mother looked young. We stopped at the Dairy Queen and got banana splits, and my mother laughed when I took huge spoonfuls of ice cream and whipped cream and stuck them in my mouth so that my cheeks puffed out like a hamster's. We had more fun than we'd had in ages, but when we drove home in the dark, I knew my childhood was over. I felt it the way some people can feel the weather changing, deep in their bones.

That night I waited up for Rosarie, who was staying late at a defense fund meeting. I knew what she was planning, but I'd kept my mouth shut.

Where is your sister? my grandmother would ask at suppertime and on Sunday mornings, and I'd just shrug. *She's probably with Kelly,* I'd assure my grandmother, but of course that wasn't the case, since Kelly was no longer speaking to Rosarie.

"I can't believe the way you hurt Brendan! You never think of anyone but yourself," Kelly had said to Rosarie the last time they'd happened to meet at Hannah's Coffee Shoppe. I was there with my sister, and I wanted to say, *Wake up, Kelly. If Rosarie hadn't dumped Brendan, you never would have had him. He'd be right in the palm of her hand, hanging all over her, crazy in love.* But of course I said nothing. I just waved when she huffed off, like I wished her well.

"You have so few friends, you can't afford to lose one," I advised Rosarie as we walked home. "Unless you think the only person you need is Ethan Ford."

My sister looked at me. "For your information, his wife has taken off, and nobody knows where to, but she won't be going to Maryland with him, that's for sure."

I understood then. Somebody had to be

there for Ethan Ford, and Rosarie had decided that someone was going to be her. She was in a spiral, but no one saw it except for me. My mother and my grandmother thought everything was fine because Rosarie wasn't going running around town with one or another of her boyfriends anymore. She was so well behaved that if grades had been given out for all-around conduct, she could probably match Gigi Lyle. If any boys called Rosarie, she refused to come to the phone. She said she had far more important things to think about. She looked so serious these days, with her long hair knotted, and her face washed clean, and her dark eyes burning as though she were on fire. My mother and grandmother didn't see that fire when they looked at her; they didn't notice the suitcase she had stowed under her bed. But I knew Rosarie had withdrawn every cent from her bank account. She'd started confiding in me, so I knew about how she was planning to go to Maryland with Mark Derry and be his assistant so she could stay close to Ethan Ford. I let her talk, I acted as though I was behind her all the way, but the vow I had made to protect her was going to put a stop to her plans. I just didn't know how I'd manage it until I got a letter from Collie.

He wasn't supposed to write to anyone, at least not yet, but he'd written to me. He told me that his mother was trying to get a teaching job in a small town in Michigan, and the funny thing was the countryside was filled with orchards. Even though they had different varieties than we did, Jonathan and Honeygold and Fireside, the air smelled like apples and reminded him of home. It wasn't so bad, not as bad as he'd expected, and the best thing was, he'd gotten a dog. Before they'd bought food or unpacked their belongings, Collie and his mother had driven down to the pound and gotten a puppy, a mixed breed they'd named Toad because it couldn't seem to stay out of mud puddles. He'd send me a picture, he said, and I planned to keep it on my bureau when I got it. I planned to look at it every day.

I was glad that Collie didn't hold what had happened against me. At the very end of the letter he wrote that he knew I'd been the one who made the phone call to the television station. He wrote that he forgave me, and I read that line over and over again. But I couldn't forgive myself until I completed my third task, so I waited for Rosarie on the night before Ethan Ford was being sent away. I closed my eyes for a minute, but I must have fallen asleep, because I didn't hear her come in until she lay down beside me.

"Who said you could be in my room?" she whispered, but I could tell she didn't care. Lately, she liked to have me around. There was something lonely about her now.

"I need you to write a letter to Collie for me." Some lies are easy to tell, and this was one of them. "You have to tell him I don't want anything to do with him anymore. He's gone and I'm here, and I'm not going to wait for him forever."

"Write it yourself," Rosarie told me, but I'd already gone to her bureau for some paper and a pen. "Can't you do anything?" Rosarie complained, but she still got a little charge when it came to breaking someone's heart, so she set to writing the letter.

"Tell him I never really cared about him and that he should just forget about me. Tell him I hate him and that I wish I'd never known him in the first place."

"You're meaner than I thought you were." Rosarie grinned as she wrote to Collie. "Here you go." She handed the letter to me when she was done. "Don't get all sappy about this," she added, "but I've decided that when I'm gone from here you can have my room."

"Gone?" I said, like I didn't know anything about it, when in fact I had been the only one home earlier in the day when Mark Derry stopped by to leave a plane ticket for Rosarie. I promised I'd give it to her, just as I vowed to tell her to meet Mark and the rest of the defense team at the jail at two o'clock the next day, but as soon as he'd gone, I stuck the ticket in my night table drawer. It was round-trip to Baltimore, paid for by the defense fund, and I kept that ticket right where it was, even though I'd wanted Rosarie's room forever. I'd already decided that I wasn't about to tell her where she was supposed to go in order to make that trip to Maryland. "Gone for good?" I sounded so innocent, no one would suspect I had plans of my own.

"You wouldn't understand," Rosarie told me.

But I did. I understood that if she followed Ethan Ford to Maryland she would ruin her life, and it would be my fault, and that's why I had her write that letter that I made certain not to sign with my own name.

That night, I watched the news with my grandmother. There was a good deal of carrying-on down at the jail because on the following afternoon Ethan Ford was going to be transferred to Maryland. People were demonstrating, for and against him. Mostly for, which shouldn't have surprised me, considering how Rosarie had reacted. My mother came in to watch TV with us; she sat on the arm of the couch the way she always told us not to.

"That is one handsome man," my grandmother said when they showed a photograph of Ethan, the very same one I'd first seen at the start of the summer. "Let that be a lesson. You can't tell a book by its cover."

"What do you think it means when someone's reflection doesn't show up in a mirror?" I hoped my question would appear casual, but I saw my mother shoot my grandmother a look.

"It means there's something wrong with the mirror," my grandmother said, but I knew what it really meant was that there was something wrong with the man.

I went out to the garage when I was sure everyone was asleep. I climbed out my bedroom window and crept over to where the roof overhung the yard, then I jumped and circled around to the back of the house. The crickets were calling too fast, the way they always do at the end of August, and the air was humming. I carefully opened the garage door and slipped inside. It was cool and pitch dark. I felt my way along and sat down on the cement floor, where I took out the last two candles and some matches. I thought about my father while I lit the candles. I asked him to watch over Rosarie, even though she had so many bad habits and could be so rude. I begged him to help me protect her and not let her run off with some man who didn't even have a reflection, and I promised if he did this for me, I wouldn't come back to the garage late at night. I'd accept what had happened and what I had lost.

When I woke the next morning, I knew what I had to do. I got my bike and went through town and turned onto King George's Road. It was early and there was no traffic, and I pedaled so fast I was practically flying. I tried not to think too much or be too afraid. I went right into the county building and I told Sheriff Meyers that I had to see Ethan Ford. I said I'd been his neighbor all my life and his son's best friend and that I just wanted to say good-bye before they took him down to Maryland. I got a teary look, and that must have been the thing that convinced the sheriff to let me visit Ethan Ford even though he was getting flown down to Baltimore that afternoon, where he'd be met by a marshal and driven to the Eastern Shore, to the town where the whole thing happened.

"He's got a busy day, little lady, so I can just let you stay a minute or so," Dave Meyers told me, and I smiled like I wasn't scared down to my toes. "Are you ready for seventh grade?" Sheriff Meyers asked, because his son Jesse was in my class, and Jesse was probably excited about a stupid thing like that.

"Oh, yeah," I said to him, like I cared about anything beyond the next few minutes. "I can't wait."

"Weren't you friends with Hillary?" he said, referring to his daughter, who was such a snob she wouldn't speak to me, especially after I wrote what I thought of her on the wall outside the school.

"I don't think that was me," I told him.

The sheriff led me down the hall. He said hello to the guard, Frankie Links, then unlocked the door into the jail. Dave Meyers was cheery and whistling, but that didn't fool me, there was nothing cheerful about what was happening today. Nobody else was incarcerated in the jail, which figured in a town like Monroe, but the emptiness didn't feel like a good thing. The fact that it was clean and had a long line of fluorescent lights switched on didn't hide the darkness inside, and just walking down the hall gave me goose bumps along my arms.

When we got to his cell, Mr. Ford was waiting. He must have heard our footsteps, because you could tell he was expecting company, although he certainly wasn't expecting me. He looked the same as all those boys who came searching for Rosarie and wound up talking to me instead, disappointed and let down, but this time the flicker of disappointment I noticed made me happy. Then, just as fast, I got scared again. Dave Meyers was unlocking the jail cell so I could go inside, which was just about the last thing I wanted to do in my life.

"I can talk to him from here." Even I could hear that my voice was fluttery. "Right through the bars."

"It's fine for you to step inside," Dave Meyers urged. "Go on in."

I had no choice but to do it and be face-to-face with Ethan Ford, even though I knew he had no reflection and that he probably never would. I went up to him like I wasn't nervous, like I'd been to jail each and every day of my life. You wouldn't think I'd be a good liar, but I am. For a second I thought about the fact that Mr. Ford was where he was because of me, but then I closed that idea out of my mind. Too many people's lives have changed because of what I did for me to think about it anymore. So I kept to the subject. I told him Rosarie sent me to see him because she didn't want to let him down in person. She wouldn't be making that trip to Maryland to work for the defense fund and she wouldn't be meeting Mark Derry and the other members of the defense team today, that's what I said, and I used kind of a snippy tone, like our whole family was far too good for him and we knew it. Like he was just some charity work that Rosarie had fooled around with over the summer.

"Wouldn't you know it, but she fell in love," I say.

I see that flicker in his eyes again when I say the thing about love, so I keep on going. I make up a beautiful name, the name of the sort of man who would be honest and true, not that Rosarie deserves that sort of devotion. "Michael Dove," I say with a real sorrowful sound to my voice, like I feel bad for Ethan Ford, like he's missing out on a really good thing by missing out on Rosarie. Michael Dove who's going to law school out in California, and Rosarie's going off with him. She's already a thousand miles away from here, and, anyway, she can't go helping out every man who's in trouble. When it comes right down to it, she's got her whole life ahead of her.

"I guess I'd like to hear Rosarie tell me that for herself," Ethan Ford says, and for some reason I get even braver then. It's hearing him say my sister's name that does it. It's thinking about the look in Collie's eyes when we came out here and the way he rode his bike into the fence, like he couldn't be any more wounded than he already was no matter how he might bleed or what he might break in half.

I hand Ethan Ford the letter, which is a good thing because I can tell he doesn't believe me, at least not yet. You can see doubt in a person's eyes, but that disappears fast when he reads the letter. Rosarie thought what I told her to write was too heartless when she thought it was for Collie, and I guess she was right from the look on Ethan Ford's face. If I didn't know better I'd pity him, but I'm not the pitying kind.

I'd been afraid he'd laugh at me and tell me he was going to write to Rosarie and that he'd manage to get his way somehow; he'd send line after line of sweet words that would lead her down to Maryland eventually. But I guess that letter I had her write was pretty good, and I could tell he recognized Rosarie's handwriting, just like I hoped he would, and I have to say I hope his heart did break, even a little, even though I knew it was impossible with a man like him. The whole time Ethan Ford was begging his wife to come to Maryland, he'd been making plans for Rosarie to be there, too. I bet once he got there he'd find someone else, someone who worked for the court, maybe, some girl who was lonely in some deep way, just like Rosarie. Even I could tell that he was the kind of man who needed a woman to believe in him, and who she was mattered far less than how much faith she had in him.

I thought about Collie on that day when we went inside his house and no one was home. That was heartbreak, pure and simple, the worst kind there was. If I was the cause of that, so be it. Hearts were made for being broken. There's really no way around it if you want to be a human being. That's why on the day Collie left, I didn't go racing over to his grandmother's house. I didn't stand in the street or chase after him. I didn't even cry. Instead,

I stayed in my bedroom and I locked the door, even though I knew he was getting farther and farther away.

"What about Collie?" I said. I had my nerve, I really did, but I just couldn't stop. I didn't even think about the fact that Dave Meyers was down the hall, on the other side of the door, going over some paperwork the court in Maryland had sent up, and that he'd probably never hear me if I screamed. "You're asking about Rosarie, but don't you want to know if I've heard from Collie? I thought you'd be a little more interested in him."

I said it in a rude way, even though the jail door was locked behind me. I really didn't care.

"Have you heard from him?"

I could tell from the way Ethan Ford sounded that even after everything that had happened and everything he'd done, in his heart, Collie was still his son. But that kind of thing never shook me. I knew what my answer should be.

"No," I told him. It was the kind of lie that felt good in my mouth. "Not one word."

I didn't cry when Collie left, or when my father died, but for some strange reason, I started crying right in front of Ethan Ford. I told him I was sorry, and he nodded like he understood, and for a minute I felt like I was ready to believe in him. And worse, like I was willing to forgive him, but that feeling didn't last. It was still so early that the birds in the bushes were waking, and we could hear them even in this jail cell, and listening to their chattering helped me snap out of it. I thought about Jorie Ford crying in her garden, and that's when I saw that Ethan Ford was a whirlwind and that we would all be much better off when he was gone. I thought about my sister being willing to miss out on her senior year of high school because of him, and I didn't feel so bad about turning him in. When one door closes, another one opens, that's what I've found to be true.

I knew that by giving Ethan Ford that letter I was fated to always be envious of Rosarie, but I don't mind. Now that I'd gotten rid of him and the destruction he would have caused, my sister's life will always contain more than mine when it comes to some things, but there are times when I'll know more. I'll know that sometimes those who love you best are the ones who leave you behind.

When the sheriff came to get me out of that jail cell, I couldn't wait to get away. I said good-bye, but Ethan Ford didn't hear me, or maybe he just didn't care to answer. I went to Hannah's and bought myself breakfast. I got my favorite things—pancakes, toast, and a chocolate milk shake, and then a slice of apple pie. Kelly Stark was there with her sisters, Sophie and Josie, and they came over and sat with me even though Kelly wasn't speaking to Rosarie anymore. She was crazy in love with Brendan, and he was taking up most of her time.

"You look like you're celebrating something," Sophie said. She was pretty smart, I had to hand her that.

"Maybe." I didn't have to trust the first person who was nice to me, but I thought if I ever did, it might be Sophie.

"How's Rosarie?" Kelly asked. You could tell in her voice that she was concerned, not that she was going to ruin her life in the name of friendship. Each of the Stark girls was smart, and they had that beautiful long hair, but when you were sitting right there with them, it was difficult to hate them in spite of how lucky they were.

"She's not too good," I said of my sister. "But I think that will change."

That afternoon, while Ethan Ford was being transferred to Maryland, Rosarie didn't know to show up at two o'clock to meet Mark Derry. Instead, she waited by the phone, her suitcase beside her. When darkness fell, she phoned over to the Derrys' to find out what the plan was, but Brendan hung up on her. She had to call again and again, and by the time she finally got through, the plane had already left. Mrs. Derry informed Rosarie that she'd been instructed not to give out Mark's phone number at the hotel where he was staying, the better to avoid reporters and other prying minds, and that Rosarie should probably turn her attention back to school, which started in a little more than a week.

After that, Rosarie stored her suitcase under her bed. Every day she waits for Ethan to contact her, but I guess he's moved on to someone new. Rosarie is still hopeful, even though summer's almost over and the trial has begun. People say Ethan will be put away for a hundred years, that he'll never get out of Maryland again, but my sister continues to wait, even on days when it rains. She has stationed herself outside on the sidewalk, looking for the mailman. Her face is so blotchy from crying that on some days she doesn't even look like herself. People drive past and honk their horns, but she doesn't care. Her hair is dripping wet, as dark as ashes. You can see through her clothes, but she doesn't care about that either. The boys who used to chase after her are afraid of her now, but once she comes to her senses they'll forget how they used to walk right past her, pretending they didn't know her.

Occasionally, Warren Peck's nephew, Kyle, who's so quiet and good-natured Rosarie probably never noticed he was alive, has been thoughtful enough to bring her an umbrella or a cup of water as she stands out in the heat or the rain. I have hopes whenever I see him, even though he's shorter than Rosarie and has a scar over one eye; I always wave and try to encourage him. My sister will need a boy like that, one who'll never notice if she looks out past the horizon, south to the highway and the life she might have led if people here didn't love her, if this wasn't her home.

When it gets dark, my grandmother sends me to bring Rosarie back inside. Lately, we have dinner together, and even my mother sits down at the table.

"Come on," I say. I pull on her arm and

Rosarie follows me, but when she does, I can see how hurt she's been. She's a human being now, with tears that bleed red. She tells me I have no idea of what real love is like. She says love is a pledge that can never be broken, but I know nothing stays the same. I'm well aware that when Collie and I see each other next we'll be different people; we'll have to look beneath the surface to see who we once were and who we've become, and that's not so easy to do. Somebody looking at Rosarie right now, for instance, might see only her pain and her torment. They'd have no idea of how beautiful she is, but I do. My grandmother told me once that when you lose somebody you think you've lost the whole world as well, but that's not the way things turn out in the end. Eventually, you pick yourself up and look out the window, and once you do you see everything that was there before the world ended is out there still. There are the same apple trees and the same songbirds, and over our heads, the very same sky that shines like heaven, so far above us we can never hope to reach such heights.